BROKEN PIECES

Children of Fate Book One

ALEXANDREA LANE

DARKLAKE

Trademark Acknowledgements

Ted Bundy—Nov. 24, 1946-Jan. 24, 1989
Corvette—GM
Miami University, Ohio
Pride and Prejudice—Jane Austen, T. Egerton Whitehall, Jan. 28, 1813, Public Domain
Wayne Manor—DC comics
Girl Scout Cookies—Owned by the Girl Scout Corporation
Kodak
Mustang—Ford
Coke—Coca-Cola Company
Mayberry—*The Andy Griffith Show*, public domain as of 2016
Andy Griffith—June 1, 1926-July 3, 2012
Hogwarts—J.K. Rowling and Warner Bros Entertainment, Harry Potter Franchise
Mary Poppins—P.L. Travers, Disney Corporation

Acknowledgments

Shout out to my person, for listening to my ramblings and letting me brainstorm in chat so I wouldn't lose my ideas. For the hours of Chinese food and plotting. For all the feedback you gave me for all my crazy tangents I took this series on, I can't thank you enough. Vanessa, I love you so much!

My Book Club Bitches for reading as I wrote for continuity. Val, you're the best. Heather, you rock. Thanks, girls.

Gotta take a second to thank our game night friends for answering all my off the wall, oddball, out-of-nowhere questions I came at y'all with. Kenny and Adam, thanks for putting up with my shenanigans.

Next, thanks to my kids Aarynn, Liam, Emilyann, and Kayne. I love you.

Lastly, to my very own Jane Austen man, Josh. You're the best man I have ever known. If I loved you less, I might be able to talk about it more. Thank you for encouraging me and believing in me for all these years. Best Terry Bull I ever met. −Love you most, Tara Bull.

Everybody has a story. A story that makes them...them. It contains heartbreak and broken dreams and hopeless situations which no one can control or fix; but it is how we use our stories that shape us. Do we use them to make ourselves a better person? Do we use them to fuel our hatred and vengeance? I always thought my story empowered me as a woman. But I see now, it hinders me in my pursuit of the goals I set for myself at an early age.

ONE

Samantha

"Want to show your mommy what you learned today?" he whispers.

I giggle and squirm to get down. He is laying face up on the couch in my childhood house, with me on top of him. The skirt of my thin sundress is bunched about my hips.

He ruffles my curly brown hair. "Okay, go stand against the wall and start," he tells me.

I run to face the wall, my back to him. Excited to show all I have learned,   I   start   reciting, "A...B...C...D...E...F...um...G...H...I...J...K...LMNOP...."

SMACK on the back of my legs.

My knees buckle from the pain, but I stay upright, facing the wall.

"No, Samantha, LMNOP is not a letter. Do it again, do it slowly, and say it correctly." He breathes into my ear as he bends closer and kisses my shoulder. His hand caresses my thigh.

I jerk and waken, heart pounding. I roll onto my side and stare across my shadow-filled bedroom. Why bother sleeping?

I glance at the clock on my nightstand to make sure the world didn't end while I napped. 6:27 a.m. Three hours of sleep. Not bad. Maybe today won't suck after all.

I roll out of bed, rake my fingers through my curly brown hair, straighten the blanket on the bed, and consider it made.

My inner voice shakes her head. She's disappointed that, even as an adult, I still think *he* will come out of the shadows and punish me.

Seriously frustrated, I grab my phone and head to the kitchen to make coffee. Yes! I need caffeine. If I were a drinker, I would add a shot of bourbon to hasten the departure of the nightmare. I plug in the coffee maker.

I prefer solitude. Being alone is how I spend my time since escaping my parents' control.

Oh, I had a boyfriend. Until last week, I guess he was my fiancé. I wasn't in love with him. I have never believed in hearts-and-flowers, true love. He had been my closest friend since I was eight. He would have given me space and fulfilled my goal of getting married before I turn twenty-five. I want to be done having kids or adopting before I'm thirty. I know he loved me more than I loved him. He knew it, too, but he still wanted to marry me. Till death do us part.

He should have had time to find a better woman. I wasn't supposed to live a long life, but I guess he was meant to have less time than me. Most girls would have been happy to be engaged and have their whole life ahead of them, but I was melancholy before everything went to shit. The guy who knew me so well and yet knew nothing about my home life was tethering himself to me. Growing up, I never talked to him about the abuse. When we started dating, he had a good idea of what was going on, but, since I never complained about it, he turned a blind eye.

As I pour coffee, I vaguely remember a bubbly, happy girl who strove to please her parents. Then, in a January long since passed, my tolerance for everything that had happened finally imploded. That day, my heart was officially crushed.

"He got in bed with me again last night. That's really fucked up, Mom," I want to yell, but I keep my voice low.

She smiles and shakes her head. "You know he loves you and it's just how he shows it. Stop overreacting, Sammy." She returns to her magazine. "Don't forget to tell your dad goodnight."

I stare in disbelief. Isn't your mother supposed to protect you? Why doesn't she believe me? I close my eyes and absorb the truth. I'm on my own.

I leave the kitchen and wander back to my bedroom. Remembering my mother's instruction, I change my destination. It wouldn't have made a bit of difference if I had told her about the night prior or those other instances. She always tells me I'm overreacting. She's more interested in keeping the peace. By that, I mean, keeping my father happy, even if it means sacrificing her daughter.

I hate the basement—the bar and game room my father built to impress his rich friends. He's sitting on the basement couch, watching TV. I don't want to bother him. If I intrude, he will punish me.

I'm wearing a summer nightgown that reaches my ankles and my hair is still wet from the shower. "Night, Daddy, I'm going to read and go to bed."

Well, technically, he's my stepfather, but he's raised me since I was two or three.

He rises from the basement couch, walks over and hugs me. I try to pull free, to fly up the basement stairs and away from the threat of punishment, but his fingers bite into my sides. He pulls me closer. I push against his chest, but my efforts are futile. He's much bigger than me. He turns me so my back faces him. His hand on my shoulder moves my hair aside and he kisses my neck, while his other hand travels over my nightgown and down the front of my body. I can't stop the tears. I'm angry, I am helpless, and no one cares.

My cellphone's ring startles me from my past. I glance at the number. My blood turns to ice. "Speak of the devil…" I reach for my coffee. It's cold.

I tap the answer button on the phone. "Hi Dad, how is your morning going?"

I hate how fake I have to be when I detest this man. Our

conversation only lasts a few minutes, but in that short time, I visualize ten ways to torture and kill him. I promise to call him back in a few days, which won't happen, thanks in part to my lack of short-term memory retention. I don't mention the engagement or the accident. I know he'll hear it from my would-be future in-laws and he will be insufferable.

I am secretly disappointed that my fiancé, in a lot of ways, was just like my dad. There was no room in Nick's perfect life for anything ugly. Problems needed to be kept from the public eye. I had accepted this life long before I met Nick, so, at least, I didn't have to change my act. Nick never raised a hand to me, but then again, neither did Ryan until a few years into his marriage with my mother.

Of course, anytime I experienced Daddy's ire, it came down to my being too disobedient and him telling me I deserved punishment. Something as simple as hanging a shirt on a hanger wrong could result in a black eye and a busted lip—if I was lucky. If I smarted off to him, I could expect a spanking on a bare bottom with his thick leather work belt...even if I was sixteen. I learned at an early age to fight any punishment he bestowed.

Night was my enemy. It's when my dad decided my company was more desirable than his wife's. Those nights, I got the worst punishments, simply because I existed.

Over the years, I grew angrier. By the time I was sixteen, every touch sent electricity coursing through my blood, ready to defend myself at all costs. I hated men. I hated Ryan for making me fearful of men. They all had hidden agendas. The tricks were learning what they wanted before they could hurt me and staying ahead of their schemes.

Suddenly, I needed to get out of the house. I needed to walk.

'Yeah, like that's really going to help. You need to get out of your head, not out of your house.'

I hate my inner voice. She treats me like a child. I ignore her. I have shit to do and don't have time for self-pity. In lieu of a walk, I take a cold shower. It's good enough. I am more awake by the time I get out and get ready for the day. One glance in the mirror before I leave my house reveals that I look like I took time to dress instead of going through the usual ten-minute routine. Having curly hair and a reasonably nice complexion makes my life just a little easier in the morning. I decide, since I skipped the exercise this morning, I should walk the twenty blocks to work.

The morning is chilly and cloudy, just like the night before.

I moved to this sleepy little town about two months ago. The friendly people are a nice change from the hustle of Los Angeles, California. My decision to walk to work stems a little from our trusty weatherman who said the day would be warm and dry. Well, he was right about the dry part. Thank God for small favors, because I curse myself for not grabbing my hoodie when I left. I locate an audiobook on my phone and listen while I walk to keep my mind occupied.

The college campus I work at is bustling with activity as faculty and administration gear up for the start of a new semester in less than a week. I pull the headphones from my ears as I meander through the crowds toward the administration building. I reach my office fifteen minutes before the start of the workday, sit at my desk, and lean down to open my file cabinet. I search for and retrieve the applications I was working on yesterday. While my fingers dance across the folders, searching for the student's papers I need to follow up on, I hear my assistant's voice get louder as she approaches.

"Good morning, Ms. Harris, how is your morning?"

I look up to see Stacy standing in the doorway. She is a cheerful girl, and I'm happy she works for me, but this morning I have barely enough caffeine in me to play nice. I plant a smile on my face and pretend.

"Fine, how's yours?" my reply is halfhearted, and I suspect she knows it, but she never takes offense. "You know, I prefer you call me Sam. You have no problem outside of work." I chuckle softly. "Why do you insist on being so formal at work?"

"You're my boss. I was taught to show respect." Stacy gifts me with a brilliant smile.

"We are friends, aren't we?" My question seems to catch her off guard. Her smile dims and my heart clenches as I wonder if I asked the wrong thing and ruined the one friendship I have in this town. Times like this, I miss Vanessa so much. Mentally, I push all the emotions aside.

"I'm so happy that you view me as your friend." Stacy looks at me intently, the truth evident in her eyes. Silence fills the office as my mind plummets into dark thoughts yet again. Thankfully, Stacy shrugs, smiles again, and carries herself back to her desk.

Although my day drags, I accomplish a good amount of work. I even get a lunch break, which is totally unheard-of right before the regular school year starts. I guess students don't think about applying for financial aid until classes are days away from starting. While checking my email for the hundredth time, I don't hear Stacy approach the door to my office until she speaks.

"I'm leaving now, Ms. Har- Sam. Do you need anything before I go?"

"No, thanks, Stacy, have a nice night. Be careful getting home."

"You, too." She smiles and leaves.

I glance over my shoulder and out the window. It's dark. Damnit, I hate walking home in the dark. Staying late to try to finish all the applications on my desk was not what I planned. As I stand and prepare to leave, I curse the fact that I didn't check the weather for tonight. Awesome! Hopefully, it's still just mildly chilly, like this morning.

I get four blocks into my walk when the wind picks up, thunder crashes, and rain pelts me in hard, cold, unrelenting drops. With a stream of curses, I start to run. I am soaked in seconds. I spot the small, corner, family-owned diner up ahead and veer toward the building. All that stands between me and the dry warmth of the restaurant is the old steel-and-glass door. The cold metal of the door makes my teeth chatter as I yank it open. I hurry inside, suddenly thankful for the maroon dress-top I wear over my knee-length black skirt. This little diner is either very popular in general or popular because a lot of people walk home from work. I have never eaten here, and I have no clue if people actually walk much in this town. Well, I will find out if it is a good place to eat. It isn't like I have anyone to go home to.

I'm pleasantly surprised that this place has waitresses. I sit at one of the booths along the wall and wait for a waitress to take my order. Despite it being busy, I get waited on in no time. After giving her my order, I look around to see if I know anyone. Not likely. Most of the people I met at work in the past couple months left work at a reasonable hour. I hope by the time I finish my meal, the rain will have let up enough to allow me to head home.

zzzzz zzzzzz zzzzzz zzzzzzz

Ugh, I forgot my phone was on vibrate.

I pull the phone from my wristlet, glance at the caller ID, smile as I roll my eyes, and answer it. "Hi, Nes." I continue to scan the dining area.

"Don't you 'hi, Nes' me," my best friend scolds. "You didn't call me all day. What do you have to say for yourself? I've been bursting to tell you about my day!" She pauses and waits for an answer.

Thankfully, my waitress arrives with my side salad, so I can do something while I'm being chastised.

"Chill, I was at work. I have five days to get these applications finished or these kids don't get into their classes," I tell her without apology. I love Nes, but she can be bossy. She's the only person I allow to get close to me, and even her, I hold at arm's reach.

The conversation launches into the new guy she met today

and how she is having a party this weekend and all our friends are coming. "It won't be the same without you," she says.

Leaving California and moving to Ohio was a hard choice only because I had to leave her. But the job is better and the change was needed.

My turkey sandwich arrives, and I grunt responses until Vanessa finally runs out of steam and tells me to text her later, which won't happen. I'm just not a phone person. I slip the phone back into my wristlet.

As I bite into the last quarter of my sandwich, my attention fixes on three nicely built men sitting in the booth ahead of me. One has blond hair, and the other two have different shades of brown. I don't want to stare, but I'm nosey. I chew slowly and listen to their conversation.

"Did you finish any of your tasks today?" the blond asks.

"The evening's young, I'll get them finished. I always do," the speaker sounds offended.

"How about you, Laine?" the one with his back to me asks the brunette I can see.

Laine has broad shoulders and disheveled, dark brown hair. He has a beard, but it's groomed and cut short. In the dim light, that is all I can make out.

"My assignment's going fine. But I was hungry and wanted some company." He flashes a smile.

"Where are Caleb and John?" Laine asks. Both men are eating and shrug. Laine drops the subject and returns to his food.

I finish my meal, pull out my phone and pretend to check email while I wait for my check. After the check arrives and I've stalled as long as I can, I decide it's time to face the inevitable. Rising, I lay cash on the table to cover my tab along with a nice tip for my overworked waitress. As I make my way to the front of the noisy diner, I am hoping the rain has stopped. No such luck. It is pouring just as hard, if not harder, than when I came in. Great. I pull out my phone to call for a cab.

"Excuse me," says a nearby masculine voice. I jump back from the door I didn't realize I was blocking.

"Looking for a cab?" It is the man they called Laine.

"Yeah, I was just looking for one to call. I'm sorry I was in your way." I continue to search for a number. His voice draws my attention away from my internet search to look at him.

"You're not going to have any luck finding one at this hour," he says with a hint of a smile.

"Then I'll sit and wait out the rain," I say a little too abruptly.

"That could be the rest of the night, and the restaurant is closing. I wouldn't mind giving you a lift."

He doesn't seem threatening, but, then again, neither did Ted Bundy. I could walk the sixteen blocks home, but I really can't afford to get sick. As a new hire at work, I'm still on probation. As I consider my options, he patiently waits for my decision. I am about to decline his offer when a warmth comes over me and my mind clears. Every instinct tells me to go with him. Laine is looking over at the booth where he had been sitting and looks seriously displeased. My brain returns to its usual hum, but I still feel like I should go with him.

"What's your name?" I ask.

"Laine Knightley. I promise I'm not a psychopath and I won't do anything to you." He smiles.

I smile back. "I'm sure a psychopath would say just that. But then again, you don't know if I'm crazy, so it's a pretty even playing field. But I'm going to text my friend and tell her if she doesn't hear from me in twenty minutes to call 911."

"Fair enough."

I text Nes that if she doesn't hear my voice in twenty minutes to call 911. That's not unusual or anything, right? Apparently not, she doesn't text back with anything other than, 'ok.'

Laine pushes open the door and gestures for me to walk ahead.

I leave the diner.

Despite my reputation for being wild and crazy, I never do anything reckless. Don't get me wrong, I love to shock a crowd, but everything I do is carefully thought through. I make sure I come out on top. I only really care about myself, since I am all I have. Self-preservation has always been a huge part of me. So, me leaving with this man I don't know is a mark of temporary insanity. I don't know what it is about him or why he makes me feel safe, but he does.

Laine joins me under the awning and points to a blue truck parked in the side lot. I nod and we make a mad dash to the vehicle. I yank the passenger side door open, leap inside, and slam the door shut behind me. I swipe rainwater off my arms and drip water on the upholstery, then fasten my seat belt while I wait for him to start the truck.

"I feel like I know you from somewhere." Laine is looking at me, the key in the ignition, but he hasn't started his truck yet. "Oh, I know where! You were in the paper last week."

I tense, willing my mind not to flood with images of the accident. All those poor people. I close my eyes and concentrate on my breathing. In. Out. In. Out. I count to five and open my eyes to stare out the windshield. The less I dwell on the loss of one of my few friends and the life I was preparing for, the better. I don't want to talk about Nick's death or speculate on how I walked away unscathed.

"Just get in, Baby," Nick begs. "I want to take you out. Let's have a real celebration for my promotion and our engagement."

I sigh as I climb into the passenger seat of Nick's car. Why bother arguing when I know it's pointless? I pick my battles, and this is not a battle I'm willing to fight.

The wind rushing through the windows of his yellow Corvette whips my hair. I hate when he drives fast, it scares me. No point in voicing my concern since he never listens.

In slow motion, I see the rear tire on the tractor trailer ahead of us blow. The driver swerves across the highway. His back-end skids. Then the truck's rolling. Nick is mid-laugh over something he thinks is hysterical. He sees my wide-eyed terror. He yanks the steering wheel and slams on the brakes, but he's too late to avoid the collision.

Fifty-seven vehicles. Thirteen casualties. I am the only survivor to have nothing more than a scratch or bruise. No one at the scene can believe it. If they hadn't had to cut me out of the car with the Jaws of Life, no one would have believed that I'd been there. They rush me to the hospital convinced I am bleeding internally. They run test after test to make sure I'm fine.

"Ms. Harris, I am sorry to have to tell you that the man you were with didn't make it. There was nothing anyone could do. He was gone when we arrived on the scene." The officer watches me closely, probably to make sure I don't faint.

"Thank you, officer. Could I please get some sleep? It has been a hard day." I'm sure I sound rude and unfeeling about losing my fiancé, but I am beyond tired. The officer nods then wordlessly departs. I lay back in my hospital bed. And for the first time in a long time, I allow myself to cry.

I bring myself back to the here and now. "Yes, I was in the paper, but I would really rather not talk about it." I look at him pointedly, then go back to looking out the window, hoping that shuts him down. No such luck.

"I know why you were unhurt, Samantha."

I whip my head around and stare at the man beside me. My heart pounds as I wait for him to continue, but he doesn't. He stares back. Is he gauging my reaction, or trying to think of what to say? I don't remember telling him my name. I quickly search our last few minutes of conversation trying to remember if I had told him.

He turns the ignition. The truck roars to life. He rests his arm against the back of my seat and checks behind us as he backs out of the space. He seems lost in thought. I am not one for conversation, but I'm curious. I give a heavy sigh.

Laine glances at me, probably to make sure I'm still in the

truck. I'm sure he was lost in thought and forgot I was here. I have that effect on people.

"Okay, I'll bite. Why wasn't I hurt in the accident?" I ask as I try to keep the fear out of my voice. What possessed me to get in this man's truck?

"All in good time," his reply is almost a whisper.

I hadn't realized we had made it to my house until he pulls to the curb and turns off the truck. I don't remember telling him my address or directions. That's weird, but maybe I did and I just forgot.

Laine opens his door, probably to circle the truck and open my door, but before he can reach me, I grab the handle, shove the heavy door open, and hop out. By the time he circles the hood, his cotton T-shirt is plastered to his muscular chest and his hair is dripping wet. I sprint for the covered porch and bound up the stairs. When I turn, Laine stops on the bottom step and looks at me with a mixture of emotions playing across his face—apprehension and curiosity, mainly. Locks of his rain-darkened hair cover his left eye, and I am suddenly aware of his size. He's six feet six and built like he could do damage. Maybe he's a bodyguard. Or a lifeguard, since he hasn't come in out of the rain. I could ask, but when our eyes meet, all thoughts leave my head. It's a welcome moment of silence, one that doesn't happen enough in my life. I close my eyes to relish the peace. The usual hum and buzz of everything that is going on has been assuaged. I open my eyes again and stare at the man who is standing on the bottom step in the rain. The feeling in the space between us isn't quite tension, but it's intense.

zzzzz zzzzzz zzzzzz zzzzzzz

My phone's vibration interrupts the moment.

"Shit." I scramble to get my phone out of my wristlet then glance at the number flashing on the screen before pressing the phone to my ear. "Hey Nes, I'm home, thanks!"

"Is everything okay? What's going on?" she sounds worried, and I feel guilty for making her feel that way.

"I'm fine. I was offered a ride home from a new acquaintance and was just being safe. You know me."

"Are you sure you're all right?" Vanessa's voice is low, like she is trying to gauge my honesty.

"Truly, I'm fine. I'll call you tomorrow. Okay? Love you." I wait for her to respond in the affirmative and then I hang up and go to sit on the porch swing.

Laine climbs the steps to the porch and joins me on the swing. He sits so close that I feel him relax. Shockingly, my fight or flight response doesn't kick in. What is it about this man that puts me at ease? When I sneak a glance at him, he pierces me with his forget-me-not eyes.

"What do you do for a living?" he asks, sounding a little strained.

"I'm a financial aid coordinator for Miami University," my answer is automatic and flat. "What do you do?"

Laine hesitates, but finally says, "I work in human relations for the county." His eyes gleam like he would like to say more.

Why is he still here? His closeness makes me nervous, but not enough to make him leave. Fuck it.

"Why are you still here?" See Samantha, these frank, out-of-thin-air questions are exactly why your family thinks you're insane.

I just like to get right to the point, without games.

"I want to know more about you. There is something about you I can't quite put my finger on."

I shrug. "Fine. Suit yourself, but I have to warn you, I'm an open book. Although, I am not a very interesting book. There are parts you might not want to read." It is the truth. I have a tendency to piss people off with my honesty. People say they want the truth, but they actually don't.

"Where are your parents?" he asks.

A simple enough question, but one I know will invoke the wrong reaction. I am honest, but not when it comes to who my parents are or what they do for a living. It makes my life easier if I don't talk about them.

"Dead." It's so much easier to lie when your parents live hundreds of miles away. My mind flashes to the memo I found on my desk after I got back from lunch today. YOUR MOTHER NEEDS REMINDING. I suppress a shudder. My blood runs cold. I know what that means. It means the perfect life I've managed to create here is about to implode. It means my mother isn't doing as she's told so she needs to be punished. Her punishment typically means I get beaten, or worse, so she straightens up.

His eyes flash. "I won't ask you again. I don't like being lied to."

Fuck my life. I watch him for a long moment. What the hell? "I don't know my real father. My mother and stepfather live in California." There now, he can stop looking at me like that.

"What do they do?" his voice is low and easy, but his eyes don't waiver. His gaze is still intense.

I stand and unclip my keys from my wristlet. I look down and smile at his shocked expression. "Would you like to come in?" I might as well get comfortable if he's going to annoy me with questions.

Why was I inviting him in? Well, when a good-looking guy says he wants to know more about you…. No, that's not it. He intrigues me. His presence is like a balm on my shattered soul.

"Sure," his answer is low and husky.

I can't look away from his gaze.

What am I doing? I don't know him. But part of me wants to. 'What's the harm in a little fun now and then?' My inner voice is lazing on a couch reading *Pride and Prejudice* yet again. 'Really? Again? Stupid girl with your hearts and flowers romances. Whatever am I to do with you?' She looks at me over her book with an arched brow that I know means I should acquiesce on the matter of Laine.

I manage to tear my gaze away from Laine's and unlock the door. He follows me into the house. He shuts the door and flips the lock into place. I turn to stare at him. I don't feel threatened. I should feel at least a little awkward, but it's just not there.

My house is much larger than my childhood house, but so are most apartments. My parents' current house, the one I lived in during my teenage years, is opulent and ostentatious. I'm sure they would not approve of my house. Not that I would invite them or seek their approval, ever. I love my house. It is a little big for one person, but I like having room to move around, to not feel caged.

He walks toward the couch as I enter my open kitchen. "Would you like something to drink, or a snack?" I lean on the counter, watching him from my breakfast bar.

"Something to drink would be nice." He takes a seat on the couch and watches me.

"Soda? Wine? Water? Beer?"

"Wine sounds good." He smiles.

Whoa. He is good-looking.

A man I know nothing about is sitting in my living room. I don't even know how we got to this point. I shake my head to clear it as I turn to pour the wine.

"All right, if you are going to ask me questions, I get to ask some, too. It seems only fair," I say as I cross the kitchen, to the living room couch and hand him a glass of chilled merlot, purchased from the local vineyard. "Do you mind if I change out of my work clothes?" Actually, I don't care if he minds. I head toward my bedroom.

He doesn't answer.

Smart man.

I pull on a tank top and shorts. What can I say? I'm a simple creature. I detour to the washer in the kitchen, toss my clothes in, and start the machine. Saves me from keeping a hamper if I just load the washer until it's full. I strive to be practical.

I decide a mock white Russian is a fantastic idea. I quickly mix one up with my leftover morning coffee and stand at the counter stirring my drink. I know he's watching my every move, but I can't look at him. I need to collect my thoughts. What can I ask that will get the most information out of him? What am I saying? I don't even know what kind of information Laine has.

"Stop thinking so much and come sit down," his voice is low and authoritative, but not harsh.

I look at him to gauge his mood. He doesn't appear irked. I carry my drink into the living room and allow myself to sit on the chair next to the couch. I wait for him to speak. I'm lucky that I don't have long to wait.

"What do they do?"

I look up from my drink. "What? What does who do?"

"Sorry, I forgot you have a memory problem. Your parents, what do they do?" He watches me and waits.

My fight or flight is thinking about kicking in. Really? Now? Of course. While I debate what to do, I'm also trying to figure out how to escape.

"Breathe Samantha, you're fine." He lays a hand over mine, but he hasn't moved closer. I chance looking at him before closing my eyes to concentrate. I haven't had a full-on panic attack in a good while. I don't want to have one right now with a stranger in my house. I will myself back to a sense of calm. I kick my fight or flight into the corner and tell it to chill out while reminding it that it didn't speak up earlier when its advice would have been useful.

It takes all my concentration to calm myself and to stop the walls from closing in. But what seems like an eternity is probably only minutes. I take a quick inventory. Okay, I'm all here and in one piece. I take a deep breath and slowly exhale. Surreptitiously, I check my surroundings to make sure everything stays in place and the walls don't start closing in again. I stop when I get to Laine's eyes. The world pauses and starts to fall away.

"Shit," he whispers. He kneels in front of me and reaches up to hug me. It isn't a romantic gesture, it's reassuring. Contact with his warm body calms me almost instantly. He hugs me tight and breathes with me. The panic passes and I come back into my own head.

"I'm fine. Let me go," I say quietly but firmly. I need him to stop touching me, now, before I punch him, or worse. It's a defense mechanism, and I have little warning on when it will happen. I'm glad he doesn't ask questions and just does what I ask.

"Does that happen often? The panic?" He doesn't ask accusingly; he sounds almost concerned.

"More often than I care to admit."

He stands and resumes his place on the couch. He looks thoughtful and full of questions. I realize it is going to be a long night. Good thing it's Friday and I don't have to worry about working tomorrow.

"How did you know my name?" Let's get this out of the way.

"I read about you in the paper. I have a photographic memory."

Stay on point, Sam. "How did you know I have a memory problem?"

"I actually know a little more about you than that, but it's not what I want to talk about," he says with conviction, like he assumes I won't question him further. I decide to pick my battles and wait to find out more. I don't know why, but I really want to learn more about him. I feel drawn to him, but I have to remain on guard.

My inner voice shakes her head and puts away the images of the accident, then points to our to-do list of life goals. I don't have a ton of time before the first goal is beyond achieving.

"What do you want to know or talk about then, Laine?"

"What is your favorite color?"

"What? How is that more important than answering my questions?" I ask.

He sits silently and waits for an answer.

Feeling exasperated and annoyed, I prop my bent elbow on the armrest, close my eyes, and lean my head on my hand. "Teal."

"Don't lie to me."

He doesn't sound mean, but his tone still gives me a shiver. "Gray. But no one believes me so it's easier to say the next best thing."

He doesn't dwell on my answers. "What happened to your memory, why can't you remember things?"

My brow creases. My first misstep with death cost me most of my childhood memories and damaged my short-term memory. A small price to pay for life, but a serious inconvenience. I open my eyes to look at him. "I have stage 3 COPD and severe asthma. I've had so many bad episodes over the years that the bouts of lack of oxygen to my brain has damaged my short-term memory retention, and most of the long-term memories I did have. It's almost like having a mild form of amnesia for most of my past. Memories come in flashes, or in small snips."

"Will you remember this encounter in the morning?"

That made me laugh. "This isn't some Hollywood movie. Of course, I will remember this encounter. Will I remember all the details or the questions? Probably not. Will I remember you? Maybe. I will remember your name for at least a little while, but if I never see you again, I will probably forget most of you in a week or so. But the general encounter will remain with me."

He smiled when I laughed, but as I kept talking, he looked almost pained.

"What makes you look at me like that?" I don't have time for subtlety.

"I want you to remember me." He doesn't appear to play games, either.

"Why?"

"I've watched you for some time. I've wanted to talk to you for months."

"I've only been here for—"

"Two months," he finishes my sentence. "I've known of you since California."

"You're starting to freak me out."

"Stay calm, stay in your head. Listen to me. Hear me out."

This is seriously weird. Part of me wants to freak out, but another feels like I know this man. How does he know how I think? No one understands that I quickly work a lot out in my head before I act. There is literally close to a thousand ideas, thoughts, and images in my head at one time. I should see someone about it, but when do I have time for someone to tell me I'm insane?

Ugh! Stay on task! Strange guy in your house! Knows a ton more about you than he should....

Part of me is kind of flattered, but a huge part of me feels like I'm in a horror movie and the guy is about to rape and kill me. How did I get so reckless and stupid?

"Hey! I said to stay in your head, not get lost in it! Relax, I'm not moving or going to touch you." He doesn't move. He sits there watching me. Waiting for me to decide what I will do. Yeah, call me stupid, but damn he is good looking and man do I have questions.

"So, where are your parents?" It seems only logical to ask him the same questions he asked me.

"Gone," he says with a finality that lets me know he isn't going to elaborate.

"Oo-kay. I get the feeling you don't want to or aren't going to tell me much, but you expect me to tell you the truth about anything you ask. That hardly seems fair."

"Don't you know? The world isn't fair."

Thank you, Captain Obvious. Why am I even talking to this

man? Why the hell did I let him into my house? I really have lost my mind.

Don't you judge me harshly, I rail at my inner voice before she can say a word. You can't blame me for wanting to make a friend…a very handsome friend.

Damn this man and his deep blue eyes.

TWO

Laine

─────────

SHE'S SEATED IN THE BIG OVERSTUFFED CHAIR NEXT TO THE COUCH, her legs tucked under her, her head resting on her hand. Her curly brown hair falls to her waist and looks so soft I want to run my fingers through it. I don't know why she isn't trying to get away from me. Avoidance is a normal reaction humans have to us, but not her. She looks like she has a list of questions that grows longer the longer she stares at me.

I have so much I want to talk to her about. I know I have shut her down on the couple of questions she has gotten out, but those answers will come later, when I can think clearer, and I don't have to lie to her.

Maybe she isn't repulsed by me because she's been close to death for most of her life. She seems so relaxed around me. Should I take this as a good sign? I can't stop looking at her. She's small even for a human woman. I don't think she's over five feet two on a good day. She's curvy, but it suits her. It's her dark green eyes and her confidence. She knows who she is and she isn't afraid. She has fears, I can read them coming off her in small bursts of emotion, but they aren't directed at me. It comes when I ask about her parents. Her confidence in her mortality is off putting. Most humans aren't aware of their imminent demise, but she is.

I have to be careful how much I tell her before I can get her out of this house. She's very observant. I should have asked for her address or let her give me directions like a normal stranger. But I'm not a stranger. I mean, I know her as well as anyone she knows in her life.

"What are you thinking about?" her question is almost a whisper.

It snaps me back to my task at hand. Samantha is my current task, and I am short on time.

"What are your plans for tomorrow?" I ask, knowing full well she has nothing scheduled.

"I was going into my office to try and finish up the files on my desk. But I haven't made a solid commitment to it. Why?"

"I was wondering if you would like to come to my house. There is so much I would like to show you."

She's watching me. Perhaps waiting on me to add a punch line. Maybe she's evaluating how quickly she can lock herself in her bedroom. I chance a glance at her aura. It's blue with hints of yellow and streaks of green. I remember seeing her for the first time. It's not often you see a human have so much death around them. In my job, sadness is commonplace, so blue is usual. Green is an unusual one. With Samantha, a small part of it is from the yellow mixing with the blue, but these streaks are too dark for that. I will have to reflect on the meaning of the green later. Right now, I need to get her out of this house. She is no longer safe here without our help, and I have been tasked with breaking her perception of her world and teaching her a new life in a very short amount of time. Maybe I should change her will. I really don't want to. It feels so wrong to do that to her.

I am running out of time here.

Fuck it, I will beg for forgiveness later.

I close my eyes and concentrate on her aura. I envision the

aura around Samantha as white. Bright. Happy. Carefree. Trusting. I open my eyes to look at her.

"Will you come with me to my house, please?"

"I heard you the first time. I'm not sure why I would ever do that. I don't know you. You haven't told me much about yourself, and I have no reason to leave." She isn't mad or affronted. She's factual.

I check her aura. It's gone. I don't feel any of her emotions, either. Shit. I'm out of time.

"You said you have COPD and asthma. That must be a hefty medication regimen. What all do you take? Do you take it all at once, or throughout the day?" This is the only distraction card I have to play while I try to figure out a plan.

She appears to debate about answering me. I'm sure no one has ever asked her any of this. "Actually, I have medication I take through the whole day. I have a nebulizer that distributes some of it and pills and inhalers for the rest. Seventeen medications when I am not sick, and over twenty when I am knocking on death's door."

At that exact moment, someone knocks on her door. I can't let her answer it.

"Samantha, you have to trust me for the next twenty minutes or so. I need you to go into your bedroom and gather all the medication you need to survive the next twenty-four hours, at least. I need you to go do it now. Do it as quietly as you can, and without any lights on in your room. Please stay calm and please just do as I ask." I speak very low but I don't take my eyes off the door.

She hesitates only a second before she gets up and leaves the room. Another knock on the door. I check to make sure none of the windows are open and, from where I am sitting, no other point of entry is open. I hear her in her room quietly gathering her things. She reappears in her bedroom doorway, a tattered black backpack gripped tightly in her hand. Her emotions are back. She appears calm, but waves of fear and distress roll off her. She looks weary and lost. I am in front of her in four strides.

"You're doing great. Keep the calm. I'm here. We are going to get out of this house. Where is another door we can leave by?"

"The back door. There's also an exit through the basement."

"Where is your car? I want whichever door is closest to your car or mine." I pull out my phone and call Caleb. He answers before a full ring. "I need you to get here, I'm not sure how many are outside."

I hang up without saying anything else. He knows where I am. I'm sure he isn't too far away. As if he read my thoughts, a car screeches to a stop in front of the house. Smart man! I was almost worried he would pull in and block Samantha's car. Almost. I hear shuffling on the front porch. I hear cursing and muffled talking. I know Samantha is worried, not scared, worried. I will have to figure out what she's worried about later. Right now, we've got to get out of here.

"I am going to pick you up and run to a car. Have your keys in your hand in case yours is the closest. Stay calm. I will not hurt you."

She braces herself as I pick her up. I feel her anxiety. I can almost taste her hatred. She tenses with anger. I don't think it's because of me, but I think it's the only place she can put it right now.

The front door slams open. The lock never stood a chance.

I run with Samantha out the back door as men cautiously enter the small house. No doubt, they know she isn't alone.

Outside, I see my truck is too far away. We have to take her car. I snatch the keys from her hand. Roughly, I toss her in the back and leap behind the steering wheel. I start the car, throw it into reverse, and peel out of the driveway. The men in the house don't realize we are leaving. We got lucky. I'm out on the street and speeding toward the manor with Caleb on my bumper and the men still searching Samantha's house.

Samantha is no longer radiating hatred or anger. Now, I taste fear and sadness. It's sobering. She doesn't realize how much she's lost yet, but when she does, I don't know if I'll be able to handle her emotions.

"Where are you taking me?" She sounds so far away.

Her hands are balled into fists and her eyes are closed. I sense she is on the verge of another anxiety episode, but I am at a loss as to what to do for her.

As if she can read my mind, she says, "Laine, I need you to talk to me. Just mindless chatter that doesn't need any response. I am having a mild panic attack, but if I don't get it reigned in I will throw myself into a major asthma attack. Please talk to me." She sounds like it is taking everything she has to tell me this and to keep a handle on her state of mind.

"I am sorry for frightening you, and for not giving you much of a choice on what to do back there." I struggle with the need to tell her everything, but I am sure it would only facilitate bigger problems. "I want you to know that although you have no reason to trust me, I would never lie to you. Nothing is too small, or too big, for me to not be completely open with you. I wish you didn't have to use so much energy trying to keep yourself together. Is there anything I can do to ease any of it?"

She shakes her head and leans her head against the back seat of her car. After a few seconds she opens her eyes to stare at me through the rearview mirror. Slowly, she takes off the jacket she had tossed on while packing her life into a bag. She is not totally relaxed, or over the ordeal, but she is coming through it now. Her hands are still balled, her breathing uneven, and her eyes, wide, search mine like I am her lifeline. I decide to keep talking, which does seem to help her.

"Caleb is following us to the house, to make sure we aren't followed. It isn't likely, but I want to make sure you're safe."

"Who's Caleb?" she asks in a slow, strained whisper.

"He works with me," I say automatically.

"Do you know who was at my house this late, or what they wanted?" She is loosely in control with minimal effort now. I think she's overcome her attack.

"I have several theories."

"But you aren't going to tell me, are you?"

"I will, but right now, I need to focus on driving, on getting you to my house in one piece." I am shocked when she doesn't freak out again or demand answers. What is it about this girl? I steal glances at her as I drive. She's stunning on so many levels. So disciplined and in control of her whole self. Let's just hope all this works out in the end. I watch as her demeanor goes from regaining control to anger to anguish. I wish I knew how to help her.

I sneak another peek at her through the rear-view mirror. She looks exhausted. "Get out of your head, Samantha." I find myself wondering when she last had a good night's sleep. "You can sleep if you want to. It's a bit of a drive."

"I have a feeling it isn't as far away as you claim and that you don't want me to see where we're going."

I'm glad I didn't try to answer her questions with lies or half-truths. She would have known it in an instant.

I hear her open a bottle. Pills rattle.

"Do you need water or something? We can go through a drive thru."

"No, I'm used to not always having something on hand, but thanks."

"What medication is that?"

"Just my normal regimen. I have to take something every couple of hours. I don't actually get a break, and I can't forget or skip any. My life is set in routine, a very strict routine."

She says it like she has to remind herself. I have a feeling it is her personal mantra. I wonder if this is something she has dealt with her whole life or if her condition got worse as she got older. She told me she's an open book. I have a growing list of things to ask her. Maybe not tonight. I think as soon as we get to the manor she's going to go straight to bed and not wake until tomorrow afternoon. I want to feel sorry for her, but all I feel is protectiveness. I don't want her life to be hard anymore. I want all of this to work out, and for her to be happy. I know she doesn't realize it, but today was her last day as an ordinary human.

I pull up to the manor gate and type in the code to open the gates. It's still a drive to reach the house. Security is a little tighter now that things have escalated, but honestly, we don't expect to be attacked. No one is that crazy.

I pull up to yet another set of gates. This time, I have to press my hand against the pad to gain entry. As the gates open, the manor comes into view. Not all of it, but enough to start to appreciate it. The tree line covers a little over half of it, but again, we prefer our privacy.

"Welcome to my house. Laine Manor."

She laughs at me as I say it. I pull up to the house and step out. I make sure I'm quicker at getting to her door to open it and offer my hand before she can get out herself. Why does she insist on doing everything herself? She ignores my hand and steps out of her car, her backpack hanging off one shoulder. She's admiring the house that moments ago she was laughing at.

I snatch her jacket off the back seat and turn to her. "What do you find so funny, Samantha?"

She laughs again and looks from the house to me. "Laine Manor? Seriously? Couldn't come up with anything more original? Is the manor next door Wayne Manor? Someone needs to name your place something more original."

"Noted, Ms. Harris."

"Laine Lair it is, then." She sounds almost carefree.

I gesture for her to walk ahead of me toward the entrance. Caleb had gone on home. His house is next door, but I'm not telling anyone that he calls it Chateau de Caleb. He's goofy, just like me. What can I say?

The front door opens as we approach. "Welcome home, Sir. Would you like anything before I retire for the evening?"

"Thank you, David, but I think I can handle things from here." I hand him Samantha's jacket.

The older man nods, then retreats down the hallway toward his quarters.

"Would you like a tour, or would you like to see where you will be staying?"

"I prefer to lay down for a little while. Then maybe we can talk some more."

"Absolutely. Follow me. Would you like me carry your bag?"

"No, I think I got it just fine. But thank you for offering."

"Why do you say thank you so often?" I love that she has such good manners, but I am not entirely sure why.

"Because I know how it feels to be unappreciated."

My heart melts as I lead her up the stairs to her room, contemplating what she just said.

"Here is where you will be staying. Please don't wander before I have a chance to acquaint you with the house." I chance looking at her aura again. Still nothing. But feelings still emanate off her. Although not as strong as before, I can still ascertain what they are. It's unnerving not to be able to see a human's aura. It's never happened to me before. I didn't realize until I met Samantha, just how much I relied on that ability.

"Laine, what's wrong?" She tilts her head to one side as she asks the seemingly simple question.

"Nothing, sorry, I got lost in thought for a moment. If you need anything, I'm in the room at the end of the hall. Just knock on my door and I will help you with anything. When you wake up, please come to my room and get me so we can continue our discussion. The servants are in their quarters. I typically give them the weekends off, but they are close should you need them.

Other than the two maids and David, it is just you and me in the manor. Lock your door if it makes you feel safer. I'm the only one with a key to all of the rooms in the house."

Samantha shivers and then exhales as if she has been holding her breath. I start to touch her hand but she steps away from me. Her eyes grow big and fear comes off her in a crippling wave. I still don't feel like the fear is directed at me. This needs to be explored. I step back and turn toward my room.

"I'm sorry. Truly, it's not you, it's all me. My open book has some dark pages. I wasn't lying when I told you I will tell you anything you want to know. Just please be warned, not everything is rainbows and roses, and I don't need or want pity when you do ask. Good night, Laine."

She turns around and enters her room, leaving me in the hallway staring at the closed door. I didn't hear the lock click, which I guess is a small victory, but I'm not sure what battle I'm waging. As I walk down the hall to my room, I hear a faint click and know the earlier silence was a false victory. Tomorrow, I will find out the things I need to, and then I will talk to Samantha about the new life she is beginning.

I open my door and enter the dark room. Not bothering to turn on lights, I close the door and strip down to my boxers and climb into bed. Today was long and draining. I need to recoup energy, even though I won't be given anymore tasks until I get Samantha squared away. She's a priority task.

Before succumbing to the void, I make a mental note to figure out who, or what, was at Samantha's door tonight. I remember how Samantha looked at me, head tilted, as she asked if anything was wrong.

Maybe an hour later, a soft knock on my door wakes me. I stay where I am in case I'm dreaming. The knock comes again, just as soft as the first time. I get out of bed quicker than I would have if I didn't have a beautiful, intriguing woman in my house. I don't bother putting on clothes; she's seen a man in his boxers before. I open the door to the best view I have seen in a long time. Samantha's hair is wild and her eyes just as dark green as yesterday, but brighter. She's wearing the black cotton shorts and teal tank top from the night before.

"I'm sorry to wake you, but you did tell me to come to you when I got up. I don't sleep for very long, even on a good night. I didn't think to warn you about that last night."

She's adorable when she's apologizing for things she can't help. "You don't have to apologize, Samantha. Are you hungry or thirsty? Come in, we can talk for a while. I would like to lay down a little longer, but I also want to talk. So, this is a compromise." I smile as I step out of the way to let her in. I close the door after she enters. I cross to the bed and hear the door lock click before she heads over to sit on the chair that's opposite my king-sized bed. She folds her legs under her as she sits with her head on her hand like she did a few hours ago. She looks as though she has a million questions and is trying to put them into order and context. So many emotions pour off her; too many for so little sleep.

"Do you want to ask your questions first?" she says. "If you hear my answers, you may prefer that I leave."

"Nothing you tell me will ever make me want you to leave." In the months I have watched her, I have grown to really like her. We have a lot in common and, in some ways, we are both lost souls. "But if you prefer, I can ask some of my questions first. I want you to be honest with me and I will be completely honest with you. You're safe here. Why don't you want to tell me about your parents or what they do?"

The air around us gets thick and chilly. I'm sure I'm the only one to notice. I check her aura during her hesitation. I see it. The bright white—the entire thing—is disappearing from my view. She's putting up a wall, hiding her aura! I wonder if she knows she is doing it. I've never seen or heard of a human shielding their auras.

"As I'm sure you remember, I don't know my real father. My mother works as a head nurse at a hospital, or she did when I last was home. And my stepfather is employed with the FBI. He will never retire, it's his one true love."

She is telling the truth, but the explanation feels incomplete. Like crucial details have been overlooked.

"What aren't you telling me, Samantha?"

Her dark gaze holds me in place. She is either deciding what to say, or how to say it. I let her work it out. I have as much time as she needs now that I have her at the manor.

Several minutes pass. She holds a lock of hair with one hand and twirls the fingers of her other hand around her curls. Abruptly, she drops the hair she has been playing with and stands. For a moment, I think she is going to bolt, but to my surprise, she lifts the blanket and climbs into bed with me. Staying as close to the edge on the far side of the bed as she can, she covers herself up, places her head on the pillows, and looks at me. She doesn't speak for what seems like hours. Finally, she says, "You remember how I told you I didn't want your pity? Please remember that for what I am about to tell you.

"I never knew my father growing up. My mother remarried when I was two. It was fine for the first few years. I don't have much memory, but what I do have is enough. Things started to go bad when I was around five or six. I'm going to summarize because I really don't want to talk about my parents.

"My mother has always been an opportunist and a hopeless romantic. She wanted to live comfortably, and to be a renowned member of society. My stepfather gave her both. To her, those things equated to love. As the years went on, my stepfather found cruel and unusual reasons to punish me. When I became immune to the punishments and started fighting back, he decided I had become his personal toy. I don't remember all the details. I don't want to."

"Why didn't you tell someone?" It was all I could think to ask.

"I did. I told my mother countless times. By the time I was sixteen, the punishments had been going on for at least a decade. She kept telling me it's just how he is and to live with it. I even tried running away. My stepfather made my life hell. He brought multiple charges against me, and no one believed me, or cared. He finally offered to drop the charges if I came home, and life would continue as it had before. He threatened to make sure my mother went down, too, if I kept telling people about the things he was doing to me.

"I had spent my life protecting my mother from his wrath, so I agreed and went home. As soon as I turned eighteen, I left and never looked back. I do still talk to them both, but it's only to keep them happy and away from me. 'Keep your friends close and your enemies closer.'"

She seems so weary, like she just drained all her energy answering my question.

She curls into a ball.

I want to comfort her. I want to touch her.

As if she can read my mind, she raises her head to look at me. I know from months of watching her that she has an issue with touch, so I make my intention clear. I lift the blanket and shift toward her. She doesn't move; she is in her head again. I wait for her to come back to the present. She finally does. She shifts closer to me. She reaches a hand toward me. I let her do whatever she wants. Her fingers slide through my hair. She plays with it for a few minutes before pulling her hand back and looking guilty.

"I'm sorry," she whispers more to my chest than to my face.

"I'm not sorry. I like your touch. I really want to touch you, but I saw last night how you react to my touch," I say, sorrow dripping from my tone.

She brings her face closer to mine. Her eyes close as she puts her lips on mine. Her hand comes up to caress my face. I tangle my hands in her hair. She is soft and the sweetest thing I have ever had. I slowly deepen the kiss. I could live my whole life in this moment. The chemistry between us is hot and instant. I feel her desire and passion, but after a few minutes they become reluctance and her wall goes up. I let her pull away and end the contact. She doesn't pull away from me completely. She tucks her head under my chin and burrows against me. She falls fast asleep in minutes, and I'm right there with her.

THREE

Samantha

I wake slowly, evaluating my situation and my actions of hours before. I don't know what I was thinking. I loved how calm he made me feel. Like I didn't have to focus all my energy on appearing normal. The electricity I felt kissing him never dissipated, but the feelings that came were foreign to me. He let me talk and didn't have a look of pity on his face as I described my childhood. Actually, the only emotion that showed above his shock was one I recognize best—anger. I thought for a minute he was angry at me for not leaving and staying gone, but as I kept talking, I realized he was angry at how I was treated, which endeared him to me in those moments. He made me feel safe and, after all that, wanted. I slept the best I ever had next to him.

It doesn't excuse the kiss. I shouldn't have forced that on him. I honestly don't know what possessed me to do such a thing. Tonight has been full of shit I normally would never do. Choices my family would expect of me...

No! I need to stop thinking. I open my eyes and try to remember how I got here. Luckily, I've only slept a couple of hours so I have a pretty good handle on what has happened thus far. Laine is sleeping soundly, turned toward me. I lay next to him and consider this man. He looks so comfortable and content. His thick dark hair is an unruly mess and his beard is a little longer.

I roll onto my back and stare at the ceiling. Why do I keep doing things without thinking ahead? What is wrong with me? What were those feelings I had when I kissed Laine? I drape my arm over my eyes and try to forget my bad choices.

"Get out of your head." It's a gruff, whispered command.

I lift my arm enough to turn my head to stare at Laine.

"Why do you keep saying that?"

"Because you get quiet and go a million miles away from me. I know it's you getting lost in your thoughts. I say it to bring you back to the present."

Part of me hates that he seems to know me, but a bigger part of me really likes having someone who understands me. I turn my head back and reposition my arm over my eyes. Maybe it will save me from having to answer more questions. Wait! I have questions!

"Why did we have to leave my house?" I ask without moving my arm.

"It wasn't safe there."

"Who was at the door?"

"It appeared to be a group of people. I honestly don't know for sure, but I knew they weren't selling Girl Scout Cookies." He lifts my arm and peers at me.

I feel exposed.

He releases my arm and I put it above my head. "What do you want with me?"

He looks at me in thoughtful silence. My fight or flight must still be asleep. Figures. It hasn't been in commission since this man introduced himself. My inner voice is scowling. She seriously needs to get laid. I throw a random smut book at her. She rolls her eyes and settles on her chaise lounge to read. At least, it's easy to appease her this morning.

"What are you thinking?" he murmurs.

I raise my eyes to Laine's. I momentarily forgot he is here. He looks almost tortured as he waits for my answer.

"I'm arguing with myself." I smile as I say it, but hold my breath to see if he writes me off as totally insane.

"About what?"

"My deplorable actions over the last few hours. Actually, since I met you. I just feel so torn over everything that's happened."

"Torn about what, exactly?"

It is an innocent question. How do I answer? With the truth, obviously, but what is the truth? I take a second to gather my thoughts. I need to compartmentalize all of this. Okay, I need to figure out when I can go home. I also need to figure out why my head feels so empty when he's near me. And what exactly those feelings were when I kissed him. I also need to go back to my room and take a shower and get dressed. Shit. Did I even bring clothes with me?

"Samantha, talk to me, please."

I lift my head off the pillow so suddenly that Laine appears shocked, but he doesn't remove his head from his hand. I tilt my head and gaze at him, unsure of what I actually want to do next. I feel so drawn to this man, this stranger. What is wrong with me? I stare down at the comforter. Movement catches my attention and brings me back. Laine has lifted his free hand off the bed and holds it in front of me, like he is waiting to touch me. Why has he stopped? I'm grateful that he hasn't tried to make contact, but it's off-putting to have someone anticipate that I need to be warned, at the very least. He's non-demanding. His fingers trail from my shoulder to my hand before he withdraws his touch. I think he is gauging my tolerance or reaction. I'm not sure which one, maybe both, who knows. He watches me as he repeats the trail in reverse, but instead of withdrawing his hand, he traces a line from my shoulder to my ear. He shifts closer and buries his hand in my hair. His breathing is shallow as his lips move to cover mine. His is a light, gentle kiss, almost like he's using a good amount of restraint. Is this what I want? I feel like I have only seconds to decide what to do. He starts to pull away and I make my decision. I slide my hand into his hair and pull him closer. I like how he feels kissing me. I marvel that I don't feel a need to run and I don't feel guilty. The lack of anxiety is a novelty. I pull him with me as I lay back down against the pillows. My other hand joins the one in his hair. Laine licks my bottom lip and I let him deepen the kiss. My head is totally empty except for us. I love it. It's been decades since I have had silence inside my head for this long. I am not ready to go back.

He removes one hand from my hair and places it on the mattress next to my chest. His finger grazes my clothed breast. I think he's asking if he can have more. How does he just get it?

I break away from the kiss long enough to give him a cautionary look and place his hand where he wants to go. He groans and reclaims my mouth as he caresses me through my shirt. I move one hand from his hair to his boxers. I like knowing I affect him. I grab him through his boxers and start moving my hand. He moves his lips to my neck as his other hand starts playing with my other breast. Stopping my assault on his manhood long enough to pull his boxers down, he springs free into my hand and I continue. Turning my head, I get him off my neck and back to my lips.

Laine slips his hand under my shirt to touch me skin-to-skin. I tense and almost stop working him, but my mind is quiet. He reaches his goal and stops kissing me to look at me, probably because I tensed up. His eyes are scorching, his lust evident. He watches me as I realize that the panic is not coming, the anger is not there. He kneads me and rolls my nipple between his fingers. It's not gentle or subtle, it's wanted. I arch off the bed, giving him more of me as I double my efforts on him. He bends his head to me, takes my shirt in his teeth and pulls it down to expose my breast. His mouth is on me almost faster than I can register the action. He pulls my nipple into his mouth and sucks hard, his teeth grazing me.

Thinking a little clearer, I shove him off and onto his back. His shock and worry are evident. Is he worried he's upset me or worried he isn't getting any more? I could tease him, but what good would that do either of us? I trail my fingers down his stomach and grab him again. He closes his eyes and leans into the pillows. I bend down to lick him where my hand was seconds ago. I rest my hands on his thighs as I ease him all the way into my mouth. His eyes fly open and he raises onto his elbows to watch. I swirl my tongue around him as I suck hard. I keep up the rhythm I had set earlier and in minutes I have him near the brink.

"Samantha! I'm gonna come!"

I roll my eyes. Duh. That's the point. I take him all the way in my mouth and bare my teeth. It's his undoing. It's fantastic to watch him come apart, to know that I made him do that.

I sit up and smile shyly as he lands back on Earth. He takes a hot second and then sits up and reaches for my back and my hair as he invades my mouth again. Laine pulls me down with him as he lays back. Hmmmm, I don't think he's finished.

I check with my mind to see how I feel about all of this. Harlot. She's nodding emphatically at me to keep going. She gestures around to show there is nothing else pressing to think about or do. Mmmmmm, a quiet mind. Laine rolls me so I am under him. He pulls the straps of my tank top down and pushes the shirt down to the waistband of my shorts. I'm bare chested and I'm almost okay with that. He hooks his thumbs into my bunched-up shirt and pulls it and my shorts down and off my body. I am completely naked before this man and am mildly aware that I normally would be in the middle of a freak out.

He kisses a line from my ankle to my knee. He reaches back, grabs the comforter and brings it with him to cover us as he kisses his way to my breast. I tangle my hands in his hair, concentrating on what he's doing. Willing myself to stay calm.

"It's okay, Samantha, I'm here. Stay calm. I got you." Laine's eyes bore into mine.

He goes back to work on my breasts. His hand travels down my body, stopping at the apex of my legs. He strokes me once and stops, letting me choose if I want that. I shift my leg to grant him access. He strokes me again with more purpose, and slowly inserts a finger. His lips graze mine.

"Mmmmm, I want you Samantha, but if you don't want to, that's fine. Just let me know what you want." Laine watches me.

Whoa! The chemistry is bubbling. I am astonished that I haven't hit him or screamed. I haven't been scared or felt anything except unadulterated lust. Laine moves his finger inside me and adds another. Oh my! He speeds up a little and adds pressure. I move my leg back to where it was, forcing him to withdraw his fingers.

"Please," I whisper against his mouth and kiss him.

Laine slides his body over mine and makes room for himself between my legs. Without breaking our lip contact, he lifts my knee up to his hip and holds it there. He pulls away from the kiss to stare at me as he lowers himself into me, slowly, as if savoring the experience. When he is all the way in, he leans onto his forearms, which bracket my head, and starts a slow, tantalizing rhythm. I wrap my legs around his waist and move with him. The pressure builds slowly, and I grab his arms to steady myself. He kisses my neck and murmurs things I'm too lost in the moment to hear. Finally, he reclaims my lips. He licks my lip and bites it, sending me spiraling over the edge, screaming his name. He's right behind me.

"Samantha!" He strains over me. After a few minutes, Laine nuzzles my neck and strokes my hair. He doesn't get up. I don't want him to go anywhere. I glance around the room.

"What are you looking for?" Laine runs his nose down my throat.

"I am looking for the time. I have to take a couple of meds soon."

Laine lifts his head and glances behind me. "It's 3:47."

"Yikes, I'm cutting it kind of close."

Laine rolls aside, grabs my clothes, and hands them to me. Our fingers brush as I reach for them. That touch sends a shiver down my body. For the first time in my life, it isn't a shiver of repulsion and hatred. That realization freezes me mid-motion. I look at Laine in shock.

Laine must see my shock, but he slowly lowers his lips to reclaim mine. The kiss is a reassurance, not a demand, as if he's saying that he's not going anywhere. But that's crazy. He doesn't know me.

I break our connection and get up to pull on my clothes. How stupid can I be? I have known this guy all of three hours and I sleep with him? I assume he is watching me dress. It isn't until I get my shorts on that I realize he isn't in the bed. I look around a little alarmed. I don't like not knowing where people are if they are in my vicinity. He walks out of an attached room with a pair of boxers and a T-shirt in hand. He purposefully walks over to me and holds them out. Oh. He's giving me fresh clothes to wear. Well now, isn't that sweet? I tentatively take them and turn to leave the room.

As soon as I enter the hallway, the mental quiet leaves with a thunderous roar of static. So many thoughts run through my mind, the assault almost brings me to my knees. I stagger to my room, almost fall in, and all but run to my bed to catch my breath. The panic is coming and I hope I can win this round. Remember that game I play with death? This is another round. I brace myself for the first blow.

Sitting on the edge of the bed and holding onto the mattress with my eyes squeezed shut, I vaguely hear Laine knock on the door and call my name. I want to yell for him to help me, but my power of speech is gone. All my willpower is needed to cling to my mortal coil.

My blood is turning to ice. I know by now my lips are blue. I frantically look around for my bag of medications. Maybe if I get to it, I can see exactly where my oxygen level is and stop the panic attack, then work on getting the COPD episode under control. But I can't get up from this spot without using too much energy and most of my limited oxygen. I close my eyes again to focus on staying conscious.

"Samantha! Look at me!"

Despite the desperation in Laine's voice, I can't look at him. I need to focus. His arms encircle me and he pulls my back to his chest. I hear him on the phone with someone.

No! I don't want to go to the hospital, I don't want to get hooked up to life support again. It wasn't long ago when I was last in this same spot. It isn't fair!

Stupid girl, life isn't fair.

I begin to slip away. Death can't have this round! I strain to sit up. I start clawing at the bed and at Laine, trying to stay, trying to keep above water.

"Stop, Samantha. Relax. Breathe with me. I got you. I won't let you go. Trust me. Breathe with me."

I try to mimic Laine's breathing. I take three breaths to every one of his, but I keep at it. Suddenly, the light to my room comes on. I start clawing at Laine again. This time, I'm not sure if it's because I still can't breathe and I'm scared, or whether the arrival of strangers while I'm weak, frail, and vulnerable is causing me to panic more. My eyes are wide as I search Laine's face for answers and comfort. I am quickly exhausting myself. I don't have much time before I pass out and leave my fate up to EMTs and doctors.

Someone is kneeling in front of me while Laine holds onto me. A woman with flawless cocoa skin and bright gray eyes that study me with concern. Her raven black hair falls in soft waves to her shoulders. She's stunning. She puts a gentle hand on my cheek, but I flinch as if she has burned me, and I let out an ear-splitting scream as darkness overtakes me.

I HEAR RUSTLING AND MURMURS. DOCTORS? AM I IN THE hospital? I'm still fighting to breathe, but I don't experience the panic that normally accompanies that struggle. My eyes won't open, but that's nothing new. After a blackout, it takes me a few hours to recover.

"I've never seen a human physically fight against the pull. It's fascinating," says a woman.

"Do you see how much death is on her? She shouldn't physically be here. Her time was up long ago, how is she still alive?" says another woman.

"Her aura shines green to me," Laine whispers.

"I see it, too," a man says.

"What does that mean? That's not possible." Laine sounds upset, almost territorial.

"It would appear, if she makes it through this, that the choice is hers. It also probably means she will have some sort of connection to both of you," says one of the women.

Are these people talking about me? It makes no sense. I need to get up and take my meds. That would greatly help my current situation. It takes a few minutes, but I finally gain some control over my breathing. I concentrate on opening my eyes.

"We're leaving now."

"Call us if you need anything."

A door opens and closes. Quiet follows.

Panic is returning, and I don't have any fight left in me. I still can't open my eyes or move.

The bed dips next to me. "I'm right here, Samantha. I'm not going anywhere." Laine takes my hand. "Can you open your eyes?"

I try. I don't have much hope for success. Typically, a bad spell like this requires hours of recovery, but this episode was different. I was more present. I heard conversations.

To my surprise, I can open my eyes, but the light hurts. I quickly shut them again. Laine releases my hand, and the mattress rises as he stands. There's a faint snap of a light switch. The door lock clicks into place. A lamp switch snaps near my head. He settles back onto the mattress and retakes my hand. I relax almost completely.

"Try to open your eyes again. I turned out the light."

I do as he asks and look at him. He caresses my hand with his thumb. I'm exhausted from the lack of oxygen and the struggle to not pass out completely. I'm still trying to breathe, and I know if I don't start getting some medication in me, I won't be able to continue this battle.

"Where are your medications?"

I try to talk but can't form sound. I point to the other side of the bed. Before I can figure out how to tell him which ones I need and how to prepare them, he is off the bed and back with my bag. He opens it and starts lining the contents up in front of me. He hands me my pulse oximeter and goes to plug in my nebulizer. I have never taken my medication in front of anyone who wasn't part of my medical team. My inhaler, maybe, but not all my medications. Massive prescription drug use isn't a great indication of a healthy human. My family hid this large flaw of mine as best they could. I should feel self-conscious, but I don't. I pick up the bottles of medications I know I need now and look around for a clock to see if I need any more coming up.

"It's 5:17 a.m."

I scan the room and find Laine standing against the wall, watching me. Our eyes lock for a second before I return to my task. I select two more bottles and pull out what I need. Then I check my oxygen level. Ninety-one. Okay, it's above the 80s. So far, so good. I tilt my head to glance at Laine again. He hasn't freaked out, but it looks like it's taking all his self-control to stand against the wall. I look down at the pills I've arranged on the nightstand. I sit up, gather them in my hand, and attempt to collect enough spit to take them all.

"Here." Laine offers a bottle of water. I reach for it with my other hand and he twists off the cap before I take it. Two good swallows and I am ready for my machine. I remove a vial from my bag and turn toward the nebulizer. He's there, holding out the cup for me. I empty the vial into the cup. He twists on the cover and hands it to me as he switches on the machine. He seems hard-focused, holding himself in. I grab his hand as I breathe in the medicine. He steps closer, lifts his other hand, and buries his fingers in my curls. He stands like that for the entire treatment. We just watch each other. Nothing is said. Nothing needs to be said. I've won this battle. Fifteen long minutes pass before I can hand Laine back my mask. While keeping my hand in his, he puts the mask back then flips the machine's off switch.

"Thank you," I whisper.

"You don't have to thank me."

"Of course, I do. You didn't have to help me. You don't know me." Releasing his hand, I start putting away the bottles of medicine.

When I finish, Laine places my bag on the floor. After it's off the bed, he resumes his seat beside me. "I will always help you. I want to know everything about you. You never have to thank me for anything."

I meet his gaze.

"I think you really should nap. You're probably drained."

I touch his cheek. His neatly trimmed beard is surprisingly soft. He leans his head into my hand and closes his eyes for a second. He's beautiful. I caress his skin with my thumb. He opens his eyes and removes my hand from his face, stands, and backs away from the bed. "I don't know how much more self-control I have left, so it's probably best if we don't touch."

"Sorry," I mumble, drop my hand, and look down at the comforter. I fight my own battles; I don't need support. Why am I acting like a scared little girl? This is not a new song and dance.

What does he mean, self-control? My subconscious is still sleeping. Lucky bitch. I'm not as tired as I normally would have been. Maybe because I wasn't out for long?

"Talk to me. What are you thinking?" his voice is strained.

"I'm trying to decide what my next course of action is."

"You need to sleep."

"No, I need you," comes out as a whisper.

Where did that come from? I don't know him! But I can't deny that he makes me feel safe. Need him? For what? To guard me? As a cuddle buddy? For sex? Love? I inwardly roll my eyes at myself. Don't be stupid. You've known the guy for a second and you're ready to reverse your philosophy on life? Moron. You're just freaked out by all the recent crazy shit. Three panic attacks and a full-blown COPD episode while staying in a stranger's house will play tricks on your head.

FOUR

Laine
____

"WHAT DID YOU SAY?" I NEED CLARIFICATION ON WHAT I THOUGHT I heard her say. I want her to need me. I want this woman's world to begin and end with me. But before I can think about getting her on that page or near that book, I have to tell her everything.

Samantha looks me in the eyes. "I said, I need you. I don't know why, but right now you are what I need, and I am not about to fight it. You make me feel safe. The noise in my head goes away when you're near. I need you."

My heart beats faster, like it's about to burst from my chest and take flight. I am a little disappointed that she doesn't seem interested in more than a physical relationship, but I will take anything she gives me. And, right now, she has decided she needs me.

She has shown interest in learning more about me, I remind myself. That thought gives me hope.

I am a little shocked when she reaches a hand to me. I want to hold her and touch her so badly, but I refrain. I don't want to scare her. Plus, she's still breathing hard. Her aura is a bright yellow beacon, but the outline closest to her body is emerald green. I'm so captivated by the colors that I don't realize

Samantha is now standing and touching me. Her fingers slide up my arm and make their way to my shoulder. Looking down at her brings so many feelings front and center. I need to protect her. I need to make sure she gets better.

"Samantha, you need to rest. You're still having a hard time. Give the meds time to work." I reach to touch her face, but she flinches. I drop my hand immediately.

Her fingers reach my hair. She pulls herself to me. We're nose to nose. She's searching my eyes and face. I want to touch her. To kiss her.

I need to wait until I tell her everything.

Her lips touch mine.

I shouldn't touch her until she isn't struggling to breathe. My arms ache to hold her. I want to be as close to her as possible. I don't want to hurt her after the ordeal she just went through.

"Get out of your head, Laine. I need you. Now. Please."

Her polite sweetness crumbles my resolve. I groan and lean into her hand.

"Touch me."

Instantly, I thread a hand into her hair to hold her close. With my other hand, I remove her tank top. She still hasn't put on the clothes I gave her.

Frantically, she shoves my boxers off and touches me. I lean down to kiss her neck and get her shorts off. In seconds, we are both naked. She licks my bottom lip before removing her hand from my shaft and taking me in her mouth. For ten seconds, my dick is in her mouth, then she's straddling me, priming me at her core. She gets me right where I need to be and stops. She's watching me, her teeth worrying her bottom lip. It's one of the ways I know she is trying to work out things in her head. I wait for an indication of what. She's radiating white, with yellow on the fringe. It's enough clarification for me. I put my arms around her back and roll her so she's under me. I kiss her thoroughly. Nondemanding, nonthreatening. I lift her leg to the side of my hip and kiss her neck while I position my tip at her entrance. I stop kissing her so I can watch her face as I enter her. "Open your eyes, Samantha."

She complies. "Please, Laine."

My restraint is shattered. I plunge into her. I don't need to see her aura, it is blinding. She's all emerald, nothing else. She's mine. Her hands find my back and her nails rake my skin as she matches my rhythm. This isn't going to take long. It's what she needs, and I am not going to argue. I move quickly, watching her approach release. I reach down and stroke her and she detonates, taking me with her.

I lay on top of her and nuzzle her neck, waiting for her to speak. I can feel the wheels turning in that pretty little head. "What are you thinking?" My lips brush her skin.

"I have been reckless and stupid. I don't know what exactly I feel, and I know nothing about you. I should be angry at myself, but since my head is so quiet, I can't think about that right now." She plays with my hair. "What are you thinking about?"

"I'm thinking about all the things we need to talk about so that maybe you won't feel so conflicted about us." I kiss her cheek. "I won't hold anything back. I'll tell you everything you could ever want to know about me."

"What things do we need to talk about?" She shifts until she's laying against the pillows. She looks exhausted. I pull her close. She tenses for a fraction of a second but relaxes as I situate us. She falls asleep almost instantly and I wish I could join her.

I reach over to the nightstand to retrieve my cellphone. I should update everyone on the situation. Noting the time, I realize that most of my colleagues are heading to the first meeting of the day, which takes place in a little over an hour. I push my phone under my pillow and replace my arm around Samantha, letting sleep claim me.

FIVE

Samantha

It's so quiet. Where am I? I'm really hot.

I open my eyes to a vaguely familiar room. Laine is asleep beside me. Is this deja vu? I realize I'm naked. I leap out of bed, spy the boxers and shirt Laine gave me earlier, and grab them on my way to the bathroom.

"You okay?" Laine asks through the closed bathroom door.

What do I say to him? I hate that I have to ask him to hand me my bra. I know I will not be able to be near others without freaking out if I don't have my bra on. I'm glad I had the fore-thought to bring a couple of basics with me when he made me pack. "Could you please hand me my bag and my bra?"

I open the door just enough for the items to pass through. He doesn't say anything as I close the door. Maybe he's still half asleep. I should offer to make coffee or something. I rummage through my bag for my hairbrush and toothbrush. "Laine, what time is it?"

"7:39, Samantha." I love how he says my name. It's almost like a quiet prayer.

"Thank you."

I line my clothes out on the counter so when I leave the

shower, I'm naked only as long as absolutely necessary. The water's as hot as I can tolerate. I step in and scrub myself with more vigor than necessary. Is this normal? I should probably ask Nes the next time I talk to her.

My body is sore. Why was I so reckless?

"If I could have had you without marrying your mother, I would have. I only married her to have you. All I have ever wanted is you. You're mine. Don't ever forget that."

I rush out of the shower in time to vomit in the toilet. Was that a dream or a memory? It feels like a memory. Luckily, I don't have anything in my stomach. I wrap a towel around me to cover as much of myself as I can.

Snap out of it! Go make some coffee. You're fine.

I slip on Laine's boxers. They're a little big, but they aren't falling off. Next comes my bra and Laine's shirt. His scent fills my head and feels like coming home. I instantly feel better. When I open the bathroom door, Laine's sitting on the foot of the bed.

"Morning."

"Good morning. How did you sleep?" I'm worried he's going to be mad and exhausted over all the trouble I caused.

"I had the perfect nap." He smiles. "Would you like some breakfast or coffee?"

Having just vomited, I don't think food is a good idea. "I'll grab some water in a few. Thank you."

"I'm going to jump in the shower. I'll be quick."

He turns on the shower as I set up my machine. Minutes later, he walks back into the room with a towel tied around his hips right as I get done with my meds.

"I'm going to get dressed. You good for a few?"

"Yeah, I'm fine. I'll wait here."

A couple of minutes later, he knocks at my door. I appreciate that he cares about my privacy. I open the door to find him wearing dark blue jeans, a gray polo shirt, a black belt, and black work boots. His forget-me-not eyes are piercing. Good lord, he is hot.

"Would you join me for coffee?"

"Please. That sounds good right now."

Laine takes my hand and leads me down the stairs to his kitchen. I take a seat at the bar and watch him set up the coffee machine.

"What's your favorite food?" he asks.

"Chicken and dumplings. What's your favorite food?" He appears shocked and I laugh. Is he surprised that I want to know about him? Why?

"My favorite food? Chili cheese dogs. Do you miss your fiancé?"

It's my turn to be shocked. "If I'm totally honest? No. I never loved Nick like that. He was my best friend, so part of me will mourn the loss of his friendship, but no, I don't miss him being my future husband."

"Why were you marrying him if you didn't love him?" He pops bread into the toaster.

"I have goals I want to achieve before I die. Getting married by twenty-five and having kids before I'm thirty are two of them. He would have fulfilled those goals."

"Would he have filled them completely?" His back is to me as he retrieves jam and butter from the fridge.

"I don't believe in romantic love." I watch his every move.

"Why do you think death is coming sooner rather than later?" He places coffee cups on the counter.

"I've been sick my whole life. The doctors have already told me I won't live to be fifty. Battling death is the only thing I'm good at." I grab one of the black mugs and hold it, waiting for the next question.

"Why do you have an issue with me touching you?" He pours coffee in my cup and in his.

"Laine, it's hard for me to let anyone touch me. You're the

only person to touch me since I was eighteen. Making sure no one got close enough to touch me worked until I met you. I'm sorry if it's a learning curve for me. I have lived without intimacy for almost seven years now. I don't have all the pieces to tell you why I am the way I am, but the pieces I do have make being me hard. I randomly have flashbacks and some of them make me physically ill. Remember my stepfather? For over a decade, he was the only thing I knew about sex."

"Then why aren't you afraid of me?" He places a plate of toast between us, grabs a slice, and proceeds to coat it with butter and strawberry jam.

"Should I be afraid of you? I feel safe when you're near me. I put your shirt on, and your smell feels like home to me. I don't understand everything I feel right now, but I do know I have never had any of these feelings ever. They scare me and they confuse me but I'm not willing to fight them right now."

He finishes preparing the toast and offers me one. Gingerly I take a slice, careful not to get any of the greasy, sticky mess on my fingers.

"I love how straightforward you are. You don't mince words or play games." He takes exactly four bites to finish his slice of toast.

"I don't have time for games. If I say the truth and you decide that you're not interested, then we can move on and no one has to be hurt. No pretending, no mixed signals. I strive to be honest. I want you to always be honest with me."

"Then I'll be more upfront. What kind of birth control do you use?"

The world stops. The last bite of toast I was about to take is frozen in my hand halfway to my mouth. I have been ridiculously reckless. My body can't handle a baby right now. Pregnancy is a variable I am not prepared for. Laine is waiting. I need to concentrate on what he's saying.

"Samantha."

"Sorry. I don't have birth control. With all the antibiotics I take, it's ineffective. Why didn't I think? I'm so stupid."

He circles the bar, and pulls me into his arms, hugging me tight. "You're not stupid. It's unlikely you'll get pregnant right now. I thought since you were engaged that you were on something. It's fine. You're okay. I won't let anything happen to you."

He gives me a few minutes to collect my thoughts. I relax a little because, to be honest, there is nothing I can do about it now. It's out of my hands.

"A few people are coming over for lunch that I would love for you to meet. Are you up for that, or would you prefer that we meet in a different room of the house?"

I don't do well with crowds. "How many people?"

"Six, if they all come."

"I would love to meet them." I hesitate after I answer.

He notices. "Just say what you're thinking."

"How are you introducing me?"

"I know you won't understand this, but I am going to tell my closest friends that you are mine. If you don't want me to, tell me now."

"What do you mean yours? Like your girlfriend?"

"Dating isn't a thing we do. Claiming a mate is what we do. As you said, there's no reason to play around. Makes things easier."

"Being yours means you are claiming me… What if we learn things about each other that makes it impossible to be together?"

"You were about to marry someone you weren't attracted to."

He had a point there. I can't deny the chemistry we have. What if he finds out everything about me and my past? What if he can't handle all that or can't get over all my issues?

Laine grabs both my hands and leans his forehead against mine.

His eyes are cerulean. I could get lost searching for Atlantis in them.

"Come back to me, Samantha. I will protect you always, I will do anything to make you happy and I swear nothing you ever tell me will make me want to abandon you. Agree to be mine."

"Is that some weird proposal?"

"In your world, I guess it is."

"Because I might be pregnant?"

"No. That's a minor detail that may or may not be."

"What do you mean *in my world?*"

"In the world you grew up in. So, what will it be? Am I telling them you're mine now, or should I tell them at a later date?"

I should be in shock. I should be upset. But in reality, I was willing to marry a man I had no chemistry and no love for. There is chemistry here. Could there be love? Maybe we could grow to truly love each other. My subconscious is all in favor. She's tapping her watch. Why? Because he wants my answer now, or because my first life goal is coming up fast? She throws her hands up. Ugh, she annoys me. His words echo in my head, 'the world you grew up in.'

'Pull yourself together, Samantha,' Ryan says. 'Stop the tears. Crying will never solve anything. This entire event took almost a year to plan and you're going to play your part or so help me, Samantha, tonight I might actually kill you.' He steps back and looks me up and down to ascertain if I am presentable. It is the first time I can ever remember going to my beach, finding my happy place—a place where no one can hurt me and I don't have to feel. His voice brings me partially back to the realm of hell I live in, 'If you don't play your part correctly the entire time I will lock you in your special room, it has been awhile since we have played in there.' His smile makes my stomach sink. Nodding, I straighten up and return to my beach. It was best to remain silent and look pretty, like Ryan expected.

My real world was desolate, but full of demons, people who only wanted to hurt me. Hurt me by ignoring or by touching me. Either way, my world was pure hell.

A gentle shake on my shoulder brings me back to the present. I tell Laine what he wants to hear, "You can tell them now." My answer is hesitant, but he doesn't appear to notice. I was about to do far worse by marrying Nick. He would have kept me in my hell. He was a social climber just like my mother. I want someone to care about me; Laine seems like a good idea.

The look on Laine's face is almost comical. He turns my hands and kisses my palms, then claims my mouth. He doesn't have a chance to take things further because the front door opens and in walks his friends. We stop kissing, but he doesn't step away from me. His smile is infectious. I smile back as he yells for the group to come into the kitchen.

"Show time," he says with a wink.

A slightly familiar voice I can't quite place is calling to Laine as they walk toward the kitchen. Her voice is light and airy. "Glad you finally decided to host a meeting, Laine. I really am sick of the diner every single day." It's the woman from earlier. The beautiful black woman. I'm envious of her flawless skin and lithe body. She smiles at me and holds out a hand. I try to suppress my flinch. Laine holds me a little closer. I relax against him. I take her hand and shake it. Three men halt in the doorway behind her.

"Samantha, this is Elvia."

I refocus on Laine.

"Elvia, this is Samantha. She's mine."

She releases my hand and steps closer. "Samantha, may I hug you?"

"Y-yes, that would be welcomed."

I step away from Laine as she opens her arms and embraces me. I'm not used to hugs. I feel awkward putting my arms around this woman I don't know, but the discomfort is short-lived. She squeezes me and makes me feel normal and loved. It's nice. Women don't make me as anxious as men do.

As Elvia and I disengage, she reaches for a slice of toast and jam. One of the men standing in the doorway I recognize from the diner the night before, but the other two I have never set eyes on. I wait, anticipating Laine's introduction. It doesn't come. I turn to look behind me and discover he is nowhere in sight. A shiver runs down my back and my throat constricts. I turn back to where the men had halted inside the doorway of the spacious kitchen. Only one stands there now. I back toward the wall. I don't take my eyes off the man. I'm cursing myself for not keeping track of all three of them when I had the chance. A hand grips my arm right and tugs me sideways with a hard jerk. Found the one of the other guys. He is burly, harsh looking. His eyes are liquid gold. I realize I must have been holding my breath when my vision starts to go hazy. I try to twist out of the hold, but his grip tightens on my arm.

"You don't belong here." The man's voice, barely a whisper, is hot and harsh in my ear.

My world falls away as I collapse to the floor. It's the quickest, quietest attack I have ever had. Death is learning new tactics. My world is black, but I hear snippets of conversation.

"Damn it. Quick, go find Laine," Elvia says.

There is a shuffling and then silence. My body is lifted and placed on a soft surface. Seconds later, Laine is yelling, "I go take a call and find I can't leave you alone for a minute?" He is furious. Is he angry at me? "I'm here, Sam. I am bringing in someone to look at you."

I don't know how much time passes, but eventually someone comes. I welcome the quiet that follows the piercing burn of a needle in my arm.

SIX

Laine

———

"Laine," Jacob keeps his voice low, his gaze fixed on the couch where John laid Samantha, "it's up to you if the others stay, although I think they can lend you information and support if they do."

"Fine. Now tell me why this keeps happening. I watched her for over four months and she never had this many spells in one twenty-four-hour period." I pull up a chair next to the couch and take Samantha's hand while I wait for Jacob to make sense of the repeated attacks.

"Samantha has been through a lot in her short time on this earth. It appears her number was up long ago. I know Samantha very well. I was assigned to evaluate her every time she took a bad turn, up until she moved down here to Ohio. She had a handful of bad spells before she was six, but nothing like what you have seen today. As she got older, new close calls, which had nothing to do with her medical conditions, brought more than just me to her side. Being that she is one of us, or at least half, The Sisters were summoned by her blood on the darkest night of Samantha's life. She had been tied up and beaten, used for sexual gratification, and starved for almost a week. She was left without medications, except for one inhaler. The Sisters altered fate just enough for Samantha to scream for help when her parents went out to some social event."

"Who heard her? Who did that to her?" Rage coursed through my body. I could barely speak.

"Fortunately, her grandmother happened by for a visit. She found Samantha. She called a life squad. Samantha was on life support for over a month. When she finally got well enough to be taken off, the damage to her memory had already been done. She can't stand to be touched. She craves solitude. To answer your other question, Laine, her stepfather did that to her. He had been doing that to Samantha, not to that extreme, since Samantha was about six.

"While she was on life support, the doctors found that she was pregnant. She wasn't physically able to carry the baby and her body tried to self-abort. Her body couldn't carry through and the fetus turned toxic. Add that to the conditions they found her in, and she shouldn't have made it out of that house with a pulse. Since she had no memory, and with her stepfather being a member of the FBI, they accepted his claims. Her mother collaborated everything her stepfather said, and the investigator concluded that Samantha must have had a try-and-fail at a BDSM relationship. They informed Samantha's parents that due to this she would likely never be able to have children. When her parents took Samantha home from the hospital, the incidents of abuse increased because the threat of pregnancy was gone, though I don't think they ever told her that she might never have children. Samantha ran away from home shortly after and tried to report her stepfather, only to have charges brought against her. He threatened to harm her mother. It was the only leverage he had. Samantha was not concerned with her own wellbeing, but the threat against her mother was enough to bring her home and keep her mouth shut. The abuse escalated. She was beaten and raped a few times a week.

"She's a fighter. He has many scars from her. His are physical, whereas hers are almost all mental.

"We have never had a half human make it to adulthood and be tapped for the job. I don't know what will happen with her mental state, if her disease will improve, or if she will live as long as we do. I can only remain close for anything you all might need.

"I have a theory on why she keeps having these attacks. She's close to her transition, she's living near us, and if I am not mistaken, she has been claimed. If that is the case, and she is claimed, you need to be on the watch for changes due to that." He looks pointedly at me.

"I'm not apologizing. It's not wrong to claim her as my mate. We will be a family. I won't let anyone hurt her." I turn toward Kevin. "What did you do before she blacked out?" I try and fail at hiding my disdain.

"I grabbed her arm and asked her why she was here. I knew you were tasked to watch her—not claim her or fall for her—just watch her. I didn't think she should be here. Why is she here, Laine?"

"Her house was raided, and she's too close to her transition to let her stay there. I had to bring her here sooner than I wanted, but it'll work out in the end."

"We'll start the meeting in the dining room so you both can rest." Jacob nods to the others as he opens the door to usher them out. Before following the others, Jacob offers me a blue folder with Samantha's name on the tab.

"She might not remember any of this, but this is the file on her, which includes every event I was tasked to look into. I warn you, Laine, it is in no way easy to read. I need it back, but you need to understand her better and I know she has no way of communicating all of this since she just doesn't remember. I advise you not to discuss this with her unless she were to ask you."

I watch in stunned silence as Jacob leaves the room. The file is huge. I notice most of the pages are hospital notes. I thumb through and land on a random entry:

Samantha, Age 7. Patient is a 7-year-old female with a history of severe COPD with asthma. Patient was referred for evaluation of possible panic disorder. After talking with patient, I have concluded child does suffer from a panic disorder. Possible PTSD and an anxiety when she has a COPD episode or asthma attack. I am referring child's file to local CPS for investigation into her home life.

I thumb to another page.

Samantha is a 9-year-old female with a history of severe COPD and asthma. She also has a short-term memory retention disorder as well as anxiety. Parents are very protective and appear to provide stability. Patient's parents claim patient collapsed without warning and stopped breathing. CPR was performed until paramedics arrived. She was brought to the ER, and at that time had improved enough to not require intubation.

Again, I thumb to another page.

Samantha is a 10-year-old female who was brought to the ER after suffering a fall down the steps in her house. Parents claim patient had tripped at the top of the steps or miscalculated where the steps were. She has bruising on her spine and on her hips that are not consistent with a fall. When asked, patient claims she is clumsy.

I leaf through more pages and stop on the next random entry.

Samantha is an 11-year-old female who has been in respiratory failure and is intubated. She was brought to the ER on 1/13 where she developed progressive hypoxemic respiratory failure. She was intubated when her room saturation levels reached 69/100, now on a 100% rebreather. Conclusion: no definite pneumonia identified. 26 days on ventilator with minimal change. Parents have been informed of the complications associated with extended intubation.

I skip a few pages.

Samantha is an 11-year-old female who was intubated for 39 days total. All tests performed came back negative. CT scan showed both lungs had inverted upon total collapse with no prior provoca-tion. Patient presented with typical asthma attack in the ER that ultimately escalated rapidly. Her stats have been consistent for us to send her home with steroids and follow up with her doctor.

So far, I am not reading anything that I wouldn't expect to see in her chart given her medical conditions. I find a new page to read.

Samantha is a 13-year-old female who has been intubated several times in years prior. Extended history of COPD and asthma. Was brought into the ER for an asthma attack. With her history, we are admitting her. Upon initial exam, patient has bruising on her wrists, thighs, and hips. When asked about them, she presented with sever panic attack and needed sedation. Parents deny knowledge. SANE nurse findings: female appears sexually active, parents confirm she does have boyfriends. Pregnancy test via blood analysis is negative. She is negative for STDs and drugs.

Thirteen? I reread the first sentence, then skip ahead.

Samantha is a 14-year-old female presenting with severe asthma attack coupled with an anxiety attack. Sedation was administered. Exam shows bruising on wrists, hips, shoulder, and throat. Parents acknowledge daughter is sexually active. Blood tests show elevated hCG, parents sign for a D&C and have been told the risks involved. Parents also request patient not be told about the pregnancy.

I might be sick. I watch Samantha sleep for a moment or two before finding another entry:

Samantha is a 16-year-old female who has been intubated many times in the past. She has a history of ectopic pregnancies, COPD, severe asthma, and anxiety. She presents to ER with severe stomach pain. Upon exam patient has a healing black-eye, healing busted lip, bruising on her wrists, hips, ankles, thighs, and throat. Patient collapsed upon standing up in the ER room. Parents not on site. Patient became hypoxic and was intubated on site. Patient positive for pregnancy, but levels are not consistent. Ultrasound showed fetus has no heartbeat. Conclusion: Patient's body could not regulate to self-abort and became toxic and hypersensitive. D&C performed, patient is stable.

A paper toward the end of this massive file catches my eye. It is a yellow copy of something. It is a carbon copy of a police report…or a part of one.

Samantha Harris. Age 17. White Female. Came into my office to report multiple rapes. She claims they have been going on as long as she can remember. She is accusing Ryan Harris. Ryan is employed with the federal government, in the FBI. Findings concluded Samantha is an unruly teen upset at her stepfather over domestic issues. Mother, brother, aunt, and grandmother who live in the same household as both Samantha and Ryan collaborated Mr. Harris' statements. CASE CLOSED.

I don't know how long I sit there in shock after reading those reports. I have no interest in ever reading more. My sudden need to be sick is drowned out by overwhelming rage.

I move my chair back to its previous location so I can sit on the floor in front of the couch where Samantha sleeps and lay my head on her hand. My mind races. I need to keep control of my temper. Why did no one help her? Why did she stay? I close my eyes and drift into a dreamless sleep, holding my mate's hand.

SEVEN

Samantha

———————

I'M ALONE AND CLIMBING A STONE, SPIRAL STAIRCASE. THE SILENCE in my head is pronounced. I'm barefoot and wear a long white nightgown that sweeps my ankles as I climb. The stones are cold beneath my feet, but my body seems unaffected. I need to reach the top of the tower.

Why? What is up there? Why am I so compelled to find out?

Finally, the stairs end and I face a heavy, solid, opulent door. There is nowhere else to go. I either open the door or go back down the stairs. Fuck it. I already journeyed this far. I give the door a hefty shove and it opens. I release the breath I didn't realize I had been holding. The room is circular. A woman tends a fire that burns in the fireplace. The fire and a couple candles placed on various tables about the room are the only light sources. As I study the scene, my eyes adjust to the dim light.

Three women occupy the room. All three are about my height, also barefooted, and each wears a gown similar to mine, but of different colors. One woman sits alone at a small stone table. I can't make out what she's doing, but she is concentrating hard on whatever task she is working on. She is old and appears frail. Her long, curly, gray hair hangs past her shoulders, and her thin white skin appears luminous. Another woman has a dark complexion and looks a little older than me. Her hair falls to her waist in soft curls, like mine. An impressive hair comb adorned with huge blue sapphires holds her hair away from her face. Her gown is cerulean blue. Her eyes are limitless as she looks up and holds my gaze. I could get lost in those eyes. She smiles wide and welcoming but doesn't speak, just holds out her hand to me. I take a step toward her before I hesitate. There is now too much noise in my head. What could she want with me?

My hesitation causes the third woman to turn away from the fire and approach. She is about my mother's age. Her short blonde hair curls toward her chin. The dress she wears is the red of a polished apple. On her ring finger glitters a brilliant, faceted ruby. Her eyes are the same color as mine, the dark green of emeralds. She holds out her hand in welcome. She's closer now. I don't know what to do. They don't appear threatening, but I stand frozen, trying, through the static in my head, to ascertain how I feel about this situation.

"Come here, my child," the blonde says, still holding out her hand. "We will not hurt you. You have been through so much already for one so young. Come, let us talk. My name is Morta." She points to the dark woman. "This is my sister Lachesis, but she prefers to be called 'Lotti.'"

The dark woman inclines her head, her smile unwavering.

"And over there is our eldest sister, Nona." Morta gestures to the woman sitting the farthest away from us.

If not for her white gown, the same shade as mine, Nona would practically disappear into the shadows. A walking stick leans against the wall beside her, its top adorned with a huge white stone. She doesn't look up or acknowledge any of us.

"Please, won't you sit and share tea with us? We have so much to discuss."

Morta pulls out a chair at the large, round, wooden table in the middle of the room. She waves a hand and the room illuminates with candles that had not been lit a second ago.

Neat trick.

"You are not easily rattled. That is a good sign. Tell me child, what do you seek here?" Morta pours tea into four floral china teacups as I sit down.

"I'm not sure I understand. I found myself climbing stairs. I don't know how I came to be here, or for what reason.".

"Curious. Samantha, do you know where you are, or who we are?" Lotti asks as she sits opposite me at the table.

"I'm sorry, but I don't. Should I know?" I feel like an intruder and am trying to think of a polite way out.

"You are here because this is your purpose," Nona answers from her secluded table. "You are exactly where you are supposed to be, exactly at the time you were meant to be here. Do not fear us. We are your mother. We brought you into being."

I stare at them dumbfounded, trying hard not to burst into laughter. All three of them? My mother? Not possible. I know my mother. She's far from perfect, but I know who she is and where I came from. So, all I can think to say is, "This dream isn't making sense. I want to wake up."

The women at my table share a grimace between them.

"Samantha," Nona's voice is clear and sounds much closer than she is, "this dream is the only way we can communicate with you right now." For such a frail person, Nona's voice is strong.

"I'm sorry, I don't follow. I'm confused. I'm dreaming? So, this isn't real?"

"There is no easy way to tell you this, but you are not completely human." Lotti pauses, her eyes wary as she waits for me to speak. "Samantha! Breathe! Deep breaths. Talk to me, child," her voice is soft, concern lacing every word.

"You don't have long, Sister. She can't stay much longer," Nona says.

"Samantha, you are in Laine's house right now?"

I slowly nod.

"I think he means to claim her," Lotti whispers, still keeping her eyes on me.

"Does he? It's about time he found someone and settled down. Has he talked to Nona yet?" They talk without taking their eyes off me. It's alarming. I feel like my entire world has stopped and the rest of my life is being decided in this moment.

"No. I paid him a visit months ago to discuss this assignment and to give my blessing should he find someone," Nona speaks lovingly to her sisters. "You know, I know everything about everybody."

"Samantha." Morta takes my hands in hers. Her skin is warm and soft against mine. I realize I am freezing. I should have thought to put on slippers. I typically run a low-grade fever, but not here. "You need to listen to anything Laine tells you."

"We can't burden him with explaining all of this!" Lotti's whisper is sharp.

Lotti takes my face in her hands as she says, "Samantha, we are the sisters of Life and Death. We decide when people live, when they die, and the important points in their lives. We decided thousands of years ago to propagate so that our descendants could help us do our jobs. Humans had become too many for the three of us to handle alone. So, we created the leathoes. They help us release spirits and prepare humans for their deaths and afterlives."

"Do you have questions?" Morta asks as she squeezes my hands. "You are only half leathoes. We do not know exactly who your father is; Nona doesn't tell us everything she knows. Half humans have never lived past their adolescence. You are unique. We don't know too much about what to expect of you, and Nona can't see, either. Your leathoes blood makes your future invisible to us. Leathoes are not prone to disease and rarely succumb to death. They typically have one child, maybe two, in their entire lives as we wanted to limit the population of our children. Being mated is not to be taken lightly. Mating is for the rest of your life. Your lifeline and your mate's get tethered together and cannot be undone. One cannot live without the other. Thus, leathoes are very protective of their mates. You, being half human, we do not know exactly what that will mean for your mate, should you wish to have one, after learning all of this. We have no way of knowing if you will live as long as a full-blooded leathoes or if you will be able to help release souls. When your transition comes, it will be hard on you. We do not know all the details, but your human body will have to die for your leathoes genes to activate. I wish we knew more to tell you. I am so sorry, my child, that we don't have more to share with you." Lotti drops her hands from my face and gathers me in her arms for a hard hug. Morta lets go of my hands so I can hug Lotti back. I feel more arms around me. I lift my head from Lotti's shoulder and see Morta has her arms around us, too.

"It is time," Nona calls out.

"Remember," Morta whispers against my hair, "that Laine is there to guide you. You can depend on him. He is a worthy male."

"Laine is an excellent choice for a mate," Nona says.

"Nona does know everything. Best to listen to her, my child." Lotti kisses my forehead.

My body is freezing. I can no longer open my eyes. Only my hand feels like it is held over an open flame. I can't move.

"Samantha, deep breaths. Remember what we told you. Do not forget. You will be able to move again in a few minutes. Calm down. We love you. If you ever need us again, your heart knows how to find us."

Lotti's voice fades from my head.

"Samantha? Can you hear me? I'm right here. I got you." Laine is close.

I try moving my fingers. I find I can squeeze whatever is in my hand. It's liquid fire. I'm still freezing.

"I'm going to move you. You are cold as ice."

Laine picks me up and carries me. A few minutes later, he places me on a soft surface. I think there's a pillow under my head. He draws a blanket over my body. "Samantha, can you open your eyes?"

I mentally prepare myself and do as I am asked. He brought me back into his room. A lamp provides dim light. Laine's blue eyes are so lost and worried. I am sure he has never seen such a sick woman. Why is this strong, healthy, good-looking man still dealing with me? I just want to disappear. I roll onto my side and shrink into a ball.

Laine kneels next to the bed and studies my face. "Why are you so sad?"

"What makes you think I'm sad?" I whisper.

"The blue is all over you. It's radiating off you in tsunami waves."

"Blue? You see blue? Maybe you need a doctor." Closing my eyes, I assume our conversation is over.

"You aren't always blue. Over the past few months, you have been red. Your red aura has sparks in it when you are really mad. When you moved and had to leave your friend, you were light blue. When your fiancé died, you showed gray. You were so lonely. Last night, after we had sex, you were the most beautiful: almost completely white. You stayed blindingly bright until a few hours ago."

"You thought I was beautiful? What happened a few hours ago?"

"You are the most beautiful woman I have ever seen. A few hours ago, I thought I was losing you. You were really sick. But your aura, since we first had sex, has been a rich, dark green. That is the most beautiful color on you."

"Hmmm. I never thought green was ever my color."

"Colors all mean different things to us. Red is anger. Blue is sadness. Light blue is loss. Green is the color of our mates.

Humans typically have many colors around them, they are fickle, emotional creatures. But our mates have almost an outline around them, so we can always find them. Like a beacon."

I open my eyes. Laine is waiting for my reaction. What am I supposed to say? I have known him for like twelve hours and, all of a sudden, I am supposed to tether myself to him? In a rush, Nona's words come back to me. *Laine is an excellent choice in a mate.*

Laine's fingers brush the side of my face. His touch makes my skin burn. Instead of flinching, I lean into his hand.

He rests his hand on my face and whispers, "We really need to talk."

"About us, or about what is expected of me as a leathoes?" No use playing coy. According to my dream, I'm running out of time. I might as well see if what I dreamt held any truth.

He is shocked into silence. His eyes search mine as if seeking answers. That must be what I look like during most conversations. It's fascinating.

"Where did you hear that term?"

"Lotti. Lotti told me. She and Morta told me as much as they could. Since I'm only part leathoes, they don't have much to go on."

"You've met The Sisters? When? How? What did they tell you?" His hand leaves my face as he stands and looks down at me, his expression a combination of worry and shock. He starts to pace alongside the bed as I sit up.

I'm fascinated by his body language and energy. "While I was passed out on the couch, I dreamt of walking up stone steps in a tower. I met Lotti, Morta, and their sister Nona. We talked about what I am, and why they created the leathoes. They told me they didn't know who my father was. They said that because I am the only half-leathoes they have ever seen make it to adulthood, they have no idea what to expect from me. They don't know how I will transition, or how long I'll live. Nona cannot see my life after my transition because my blood is not human.

"Honestly, I was hoping I'd say 'leathoes' and you would look at me like I was insane. I wanted you not have a clue what I was talking about so that I could chalk it up to a strange dream."

EIGHT

Laine
____

I can no longer see her aura. "How does all this information make you feel?"

"Doesn't the color tell you how I'm feeling?" She tilts her head, sending a few lone curls to spill over her left eye and cheek.

"I don't know if it is because you are part leathoes, or if you have some unique ability to block me, but I can't always see your aura." I rejoin her and push the hair off her face, leaving my hand in her hair as I sit on the edge of the bed.

"I hope your ability doesn't change when I change," her voice is soft but determined.

"Leathoes can't see each other's auras. The only color we see is green if we encounter our mate. The Sisters hated watching unhappy humans live with mates they didn't love. They wanted to make sure their children didn't suffer in that way. We always thought auras were just a human's soul giving off lights based on feelings, but now I'm not so sure."

"I want *you* to always see me. Even when I try to hide, I want you to see me exactly how I am." Her emerald eyes flash with fierce emotion. I don't need to concentrate to see her aura. It's emerald, like her eyes. Nothing else shows through, not even the yellow. Her intensity takes my breath away.

"Samantha, you might not totally understand it yet, but I am serious about wanting to be your mate. You don't have to decide now. I just want you to know before you meet everyone else and all the other unattached, attractive guys start trying to claim you." If nothing else, I know she will appreciate my directness.

"Why in the world would you ever want such a broken person as a mate? No one even knows what I will be like if I make it through the transition. You don't need to anchor yourself to a sinking ship; you deserve so much more than I can ever give you." She scoots toward the other side of the bed. Her emerald aura changes to brown anguish. I rush toward the far side of the bed.

Her hand comes up, palm outward. "Please, don't touch me. I need to gather my thoughts." She leaves the bed, enters my bathroom, and locks the door behind her.

"Laine"—her voice is muffled by the closed door—"if leathoes free souls upon a human's death, how many times has one of you come to release mine?".

"Someone has been near you anytime you were close to dying."

"So how many people know about my past? Everyone?"

I note a tremor in her voice. "Up until today, only one of us knew your entire past, because they were called to you anytime you were fighting for your life. As of a few hours ago, he was the only one. After your attack, he handed me your file and I skimmed through a few pages. Would you like to read it?" I keep my voice low, but I know she hears me.

The lock clicks and the door opens enough for her hand to extend, fingers spread wide. I retrieve the file from the nightstand and hand it to her. The door closes once more, but the lock doesn't engage. I hear her shuffling pages. I stand at the door, eyes closed, listening as hard as I can, taking what I'm hearing and creating an image in my head of what she is doing. I hear page after page turn as she devours the information written on those pages. I hear her retch and the toilet flush. More pages, more retching, and a couple more flushes. Just when I think she is done reading, I hear what I was waiting for—her soft crying. I open the door and the sight brings me to my knees.

Pages, separated into piles, encircle her and she is kneeling, crying into her hands.

I stand and go to pick her up.

"Please don't touch me. It's wrong for you to want anything to do with me after reading this. I'm too broken, Laine. I don't know how to give anyone the kind of things a woman should be able to give a boyfriend or husband. I never had good examples of love or respect growing up, and my introduction to sex, as you have read, was not love or passion. I don't know how to do any of that. As much as I love the idea of romance, and want real love, when I read about them, the concepts scare the hell out of me. My brand of crazy eventually scares everyone away, and if it doesn't, my stepfather will."

"You still talk to him?" the shock in my voice is unmistakable.

"Laine, the last time I didn't talk to him, he had me jailed over a holiday weekend. He put out an APB that I had stolen a car and I should be considered armed and dangerous. When I moved across the country to get as far away from him as I could, I didn't take his calls for a week. He had cops come by for wellness checks every couple of hours. It makes my life a little easier not having to deal with that shit all the time. My last boyfriend, before Nick, disappeared completely. He is still a missing person in my hometown. Ryan didn't have to worry about Nick. He approved of him."

"Why did he approve of him?"

"Because Nick and I had known each other for decades, and Nick knew to look the other way when Ryan came over. By that time, I had accepted my fate. It had been all I knew for over twenty-five years. Better the devil you know than the one you don't."

I stoop down and pick her up out of her circle of hell on paper. She tenses, and I feel waves of apprehension rolling off her. "Do you want to lay in my bed, or would you prefer to go to your room?"

Her body relaxes a little as she lays her head on my shoulder. Her lips find the point under my chin that makes my blood race.

Before she can answer, a catchy pop song fills the space. Her muscles tense and she jumps out of my arms to find her phone. She slides to answer it, her eyes pleading as she holds a finger up to her lips to silence me.

"Hi Dad, how's work? No, I had a meeting for work. How's Mom? No, I was going to tell you. Hardly matters now, since he's dead… Dad, it has been a long day already, I really don't need this right now. Okay, yeah, I can do that. Can we make it 2 p.m.? It would be better for me. Thanks, Dad." She powers the phone off before tossing it on the floor. She looks exhausted as she goes to lay across the bed.

I check the clock on my nightstand, 11:41. She is going to meet the Devil at 2. I am trying to process all of this and decide what I should do or can do when a voice fills my head.

You need to let her figure this out. You can't fix this for her, Laine. Let her take the lead. My son, protect her, but don't interfere. Trust in your mothers.

My thoughts return to me as if I have just had an out-of-body experience.

I hate when they contact me that way. Thankfully, they don't do it often. I should feel comforted knowing my mothers are watching over me, but I don't.

"I'm sorry, Laine." Samantha lays with her face turned away, pain in her voice.

"Why didn't you use an excuse to get out of seeing him? He can't come across country often. Why are you doing this?"

"I told you already, I'm broken. I do it to preserve my world, and to make sure he doesn't hurt my mother."

"Your mother sold her daughter to maintain a comfortable lifestyle!"

Samantha's whole body flinches. "You have no idea how many times I have said that exact same thing. My mother is crueler than he ever was. She turned her back on me time and time again. She never came to my rescue, even when the abuse happened right in front of her. Do you know how many times I dream of killing them? That might not fix my issues, but it would make me infinitely happier." Anger and sadness roll through her.

"Laine, this is the only life I have ever known. I know she's my greatest enemy, but I still can't help wanting my mother. A daughter will always want her mother. I can't explain it."

NINE

Samantha

"Laine, I'm serious when I said you don't want me. I won't
hold you to your earlier promise and request."

I leave the bed and return to the bathroom. The lock clicking
into place is like a tomb closing.

I hate crying. I rarely cry. I'm getting soft.

I look at the piles of papers on the floor. I bend down, gather
them, and replace them in the folder. I turn the shower on as hot
as it will go and step in. The pain is welcome. It numbs my mind
and my body.

Showering is my routine to prepare myself. I know I will be
doing this again as soon as I get back from meeting with Ryan.

When I finish scrubbing, I wrap a towel around my body and
another around my hair like a turban. I undo the lock and open
the door. The bedroom is empty. A stab of pain runs through my
heart as I leave his room to go to mine to look for something to
wear.

My room is empty, too. I rush to toss on shorts and a tank
top, cursing myself for not bringing my jeans and a big T-shirt. I
hate going near Ryan in anything that shows skin. Maybe I can
ask Laine if I can borrow one of his shirts. My attention falls on

the floor, where one of his shirts lays. Vaguely, I remember him lending me boxers and a shirt. I toss his shirt over my tank top and tie the side of it to make it fit a little better. Definitely not something I would wear, but in a pinch, it works. I love that it smells like Laine.

I take my meds then brush the wet tangles from my hair.

"Let me help you with that." Laine's husky voice is close to my ear. His fingers close on the brush in my hand. Without thinking, I whirl around to land a punch. He catches my hand before I strike his face.

Horror and embarrassment wash over me. "Oh my god, I am so sorry. I didn't mean to do that."

"Never apologize for being you. I had a bad lapse in judgment. I apologize." His smile looks strained, like he's smiling because he thinks I want him to.

I hand him my brush and sit on the corner of my bed. "Care to share what's on your mind?"

He starts brushing where I stopped. "Do you want me to go with you?"

"That would make things worse." Ryan is ruthless, godless, and above any laws he swore to uphold.

"Okay." He finishes and places the brush on the dresser. "When you get back, we need to start working on your training." With that, he leaves the room, closing the door behind him.

I will mourn the loss of Laine later. Right now, I have to get moving. I gather the inhalers and the meds I will need for the next few hours. I slide on my black slip-on shoes. I learned long ago that you can't run in flip flops, and tennis shoes make Ryan angry. They show I have a hidden agenda to run from him.

At least, he wanted to meet somewhere public. I walk to Laine's room to get my phone from the floor. His door is open and he is not around. I grab it off the floor and turn it on. As I start down the stairs, Laine's doorbell rings. I hear David, presumably Laine's butler, open the door. I hear *him* before I see him. A small sense of relief runs through me. I knew he would find me and look into who owned the place I was occupying. He is still just as predictable as always. I made the only logical choice when I agreed to meet him, knowing full well this meeting would be painful. There is always someone I must protect from Ryan. Now, on top of my mother, there is Laine to protect. The life I want with him needs safeguarding from the evil that shadows my every step.

"I am looking for my daughter, Samantha Harris. Could you tell her I am here to pick her up?"

My blood turns to ice. My mouth goes dry. I shake. He's mad. He's fucking irate. I take a deep breath and command my body to calm, to prepare it to go numb. I finish walking down the stairs only to see Laine headed toward the man I call Dad.

"Hello. Welcome to my home. I'm—"

Ryan cuts him off, "Laine Knightley. Yes, I know who you are. I have come to pick up Samantha. I know she is here."

The threat and malice are unmistakable. I dig my nails into my palms.

"Hey Dad. I was just about to leave to meet you. You are so thoughtful to pick me up. Thanks. You know me, I get lost walking in my own house." I smile, trying to deflect the tension and soften the blow that is about to land.

"Come, Samantha. We have much to discuss." He holds out his hand.

I give Laine a cautionary look and take the Devil's hand.

TEN

Laine

———————

THE COLORS OF REPULSION, APPREHENSION, PAIN, LOSS, ANGUISH, and sadness swirl around her, completely eclipsing the dark green. I had decided to follow her, but I hadn't anticipated her tormentor coming to my house, or even knowing where I live. The guy has stones, that's for sure.

I knew it was a bad idea to turn off all security during the day. That practice will change as of today. I know Sam didn't tell him where she was. How did he know?

Realization dawns. She turned off her phone after their talk. She must have known he would look for her. He probably knew where she was long before she answered his call.

My mind is racing.

They are getting into his car. I have no time. I grab my keys and run to the garage. On the way, I make a mental note to have Caleb help me retrieve my truck from Sam's house.

I back my Mustang out and creep down my drive. Before I reach the main road, I put on sunglasses. The tint on the car windows will help conceal me. I follow Ryan's supped up blue Corvette through traffic and across the bridge to the restaurant closest to the police station. At least he chose a public location.

I call Caleb to join me for lunch and give him an overview of the situation. He reaches the parking lot and joins me in my car. We sit in silence and watch the blue Corvette.

Why aren't they getting out of the car? Maybe they're waiting for someone.

ELEVEN

Samantha

———————

RYAN GRIPS THE STEERING WHEEL, HIS KNUCKLES WHITENING. "Who is he, Sammy?"

"A friend. I had a scare last night. Some people came to my house in the middle of the night, and I didn't know anyone else around here." That was the truth.

"That isn't all of it, is it, Sammy? We both know he isn't just a friend."

"Excuse me? When have I ever lied to you? I'm not a masochist."

His hand strikes my face quicker than I can prepare for the blow. He grabs my hair and forces my face close to his.

"Do you think I'm a stupid man, Samantha? Do you think I wouldn't notice his shirt on your body?"

"I told you, I ran from my house last night. I didn't have time to take much with me. He lent me a shirt so I would have something clean to wear to lunch with you." Okay, not totally a lie.

His lips crush mine. I brace myself and try to leave my body. He tongue tries to find a way into my mouth. I clench my jaw. He pulls my hair harder, but I'm already numb. His other hand pulls my hand into his lap. He's used to having to do all the work when it comes to that. He can't force my hand to do what he wants. I'm not prepared when he twists my hair and jerks my face to his dick. He should know better. I don't break easily, no matter how mad he is. The hand that holds my hand on his dick grabs my pinky and bends it toward my wrist. He pulls his penis out as I open my mouth to scream and shoves it into my mouth.

"If you think about biting me, I will kill your mother. Be a good daughter. The faster we get done the faster we can go eat." He shoves my head down to take all of him. Tears threaten, but I won't give him what he wants—to see me broken. I don't move. I am not participating. I will myself to go elsewhere. My beach is empty. The cool sand presses between my toes. It's sunset. The waves caress my feet.

A tsunami wave crashes over me, forcing salt water into my mouth. I'm thrown back into the present, choking on his cum. I retch and spit it out, not caring where it goes as long as it isn't on me.

"Such a good daughter. See, that wasn't so bad. There are napkins in the glove box. Clean up this mess so we can go in."

The small restaurant is mostly empty, except for maybe ten people. That includes the staff. A waitress takes our order and leaves.

To normal people, I expect we look weird sitting next to each other in the booth, as opposed to sitting across from each other. Ryan likes to sit next to me so he can touch me. I hate that I didn't have jeans to wear. I need to get my clothes ASAP.

"You are mine to do what I want with. You need to stop fighting this, Sam. No one will ever want you or love you like I do. Besides, you know I don't share. Remember Tommy Hetrich? Because of you, Sam, he's missing and will never be found. His parents will never get closure, all because you are a slut."

I flinch as if he has slapped me again. I keep my head down, wishing this farce would end, or I would die. No such luck. Ryan's hand is heavy on my thigh.

"You know why I love this place so much, Sam? The staff is paid to not notice anything. So, screaming or struggling won't help you. But go for it, Sam. I love to hear you scream. Seeing you cry, and in pain. It's heaven." His hand travels up my thigh, caressing it. He's positioned us on purpose, me seated against the wall, trapped. Why didn't I anticipate his manipulation of our seating? The rage in me is consuming. Any second now, I'm going to snap.

"Do you want to fight me, Sammy? Do you want to hurt me? I'll give you the first shot. Just remember, it's a federal offence to hit me. And trust me, you and your mother will suffer. She might not live. You know how fragile she is. I would never kill you though, Sam. Beat you within an inch of your life, like I've done a time or two, or twelve, but I love you too much to kill."

Thankfully, the food arrives at that moment. His hand leaves my thigh and he starts eating. I had only ordered a drink. I knew I wouldn't be able to keep down anything solid. I take a quick sip of my soda, hoping it will stay down. At least he hasn't tried to fuck me, and he hasn't beaten me, so maybe this little meeting will be over and done with soon, and I can escape with minimal damage.

"I booked us at the Marriott, under a pseudonym, of course."

My heart sinks. So much for a reprieve.

"What am I supposed to tell Laine? Isn't Mom going to wonder where you are?" Logical questions, right?

I am rewarded with a hard slap to my cheek, which jerks my head sideways.

"Stop thinking about that asshole. You're never going to see him again. What, Samantha? Did you think one day you would meet someone who would sweep you off your feet and take you far away from me?"

"I wasn't going anywhere. Nick and I were committed to being here. You allowed me to move here!"

"Yes, Nick knew what was going on and turned the other way.

I told him the same thing I am telling you. I. Don't. Share. No one takes from me and lives."

I snap my head up to glare at him. "I'm not yours!"

The malicious smile creeping over his face is the scariest thing I have ever seen in my life. My eyes widen as the truth descends on me. "You had him killed! You killed Nick! No! That's impossible, it was an accident. Lots of people died."

"Oh Sam, your old man has his ways. Now do you understand? You should just come home with me, forget all this. You know you could have just as nice a life as your mother. I would make sure you were happy. Why won't you heel?"

"I'm not a pet! I'm not my mother! You want something, you should be going to her."

"You know I only married her to have you."

My nightmares are living and breathing right in front of me.

"I need to use the restroom, please."

Ryan moves to let me out of the booth. He stays standing as I make my way to the bathroom.

I flush and open the stall door to find Ryan on the other side. The blood drains from my face. He has locked us in. He yanks me from the stall and shoves me to the floor. He struggles to get my shorts off. I kick wildly and scratch at anything I can reach. The first punch lands in my stomach. As I struggle to compartmentalize the pain of that blow, he gets my shorts off. I slam my knees together and try to thrust the bottom of my palm into his nose. He's too big and he is trained to fight.

He slams my head against the floor. Maybe death has come to rescue me, I think, as darkness consumes me.

TWELVE

Laine

─────────

LAINE! GO! NOW! SAVE YOUR MATE! DO NOT TAKE HIS LIFE, IT IS NOT his time. My mother is screaming!

Caleb and I race from the car to the restaurant. Inside, it takes seconds to figure out she's in the bathroom. We charge the door and shatter it. The scene is worse than anything I have seen in my 203 years. Samantha is lying unconscious on the dirty bathroom floor, naked from the waist down. Blood from her mouth smears the floor beside her head. The Devil thrusts into her. Blood runs down his arms and face. She put up a hell of a fight. Caleb tackles him. His yells and threats echo off the walls until Caleb slams his head against the wall, silencing him by knocking his ass out.

I locate Sam's shorts and put them on her, noting blood trickling down her legs. I reach for her neck and search for a pulse. She's cold, but her pulse is steady. I pick her up and carry her out to my car. Caleb has Ryan slung over his shoulder and deposits him into the back seat of his car.

I'm texting furiously when Caleb slams his car door shut and calls out, "I'll take him back to my place and secure him there. Mother says we can't kill him. She said she'll talk to us when we get home. You should call Jacob to meet us there to look over Samantha."

"I already shot him a text. Meet you back at my house, Brother." I jump behind the wheel.

The drive to my place is quick. I am anxious for Jacob to look at Sam, and I want to see the mothers. I finally reach the front door, leave the car running, and gingerly lift Sam out of the passenger seat. Jacob is waiting on my porch, front door wide open, and follows us up to my room. I pace at the foot of the bed while he examines her.

"Laine, are you sure you want to be here?"

"Yes, and I want to know every cut and bruise she has so I know everything I need to do to him," my growl is low. I mean every word.

With a slight nod, he turns back to my mate. He removes her clothes as quickly and painlessly as he can. Sam winces twice but doesn't wake.

"She has a good-sized cut on her head. She has hair missing." He pulls a spool of thread from the small bag next to him, and later reports that it took six stitches to close the wound.

Jacob shines a thin pen light into her mouth and then checks her eyes. "Her mouth is bruised, mostly on the inside. Her throat is bruised both inside and out. Her lip is split. She has the beginning of a black eye and she has suffered a blow to her stomach, hence the bleeding. The blow assures she isn't pregnant, if she was. I will keep an eye on the bleeding, but I suspect it will ease in a few days.

"Her pinky is broken in two places, by the looks of it." He makes quick work of taping her fingers. "In a few hours or tomorrow, she'll look much worse. The bruising will be more pronounced. I'm so sorry, Laine. She's a fighter. She's made it this far. We know she isn't scheduled to die so we will count that as a win. The mothers are coming, we should get ready for them." He quits the room, leaving Samantha and I alone.

I text Caleb: *Jacob on his way. Meeting in my bedroom, I'm not leaving her side. Thanks for having my back.*

No problem, Brother. I will always have your back. Be over after Jacob leaves. Will bring report.

True to his word, he arrives within thirty minutes. "Want the details?"

"Always."

"He has bruising and is missing skin from his arms and face, but that's about it. Fucker is massive. He will have a hard time explaining those scratches away, though."

"I should have gone in sooner. This is my fault."

"It might have been worse if he saw us there. We need to deal with the now, not the 'what ifs.'"

"Caleb is right," Lotti says from the doorway. "It does no good to dwell on the past."

We watch the mothers enter my room. Morta halts beside Caleb, Lotti joins me at Sam's side. Nona settles into the bedside chair opposite us. The worry on their faces is mirrored in both of ours.

"The fact that you let him live and did not disobey our instruction, prides us, my son," Lotti says.

"In all honesty, Mothers, my only focus was to get Sam away from that monster." Shame falls over me for not avenging her right then.

"He is not yours to release, my son. He is her destiny. She deserves that peace. Don't feel shame for letting your mate find her purpose," Nona says, the only time I have ever heard her speak.

"Laine, her transition is upon us. You need to show her, to prepare her." Morta watches me.

"I know, Mother. I won't fail her or you." I watch Sam's face and trail my fingers over her palm.

Lotti smiles. "It is wonderful to see you in love, my son. We are very happy for you both. She is an excellent choice."

"With her being half human, can she be mated the same as the rest of us? Others see her as green, too. I won't lie, that bothers me." I glance at my mothers before returning my attention to Sam.

"I wish we could give you more reassurance, my son, but we just don't know. Has her character given you the idea that she would stray or leave you?" Morta's brow furrows.

"Mother, we have only known each other for a day."

"Jacob has known her twenty-four years. You have observed her for the last few months. Did she ever stray from her intended? Loveless union as it was, she was steadfast in her commitment." Lotti presses my arm. "Have faith, my son."

"The question is, Son, can you see beyond all of her past and the dysfunction around her and love her despite it?" Morta asks so softly I must concentrate to hear. "She has been dealt bad cards. Her burdens are heavy. Eventually, the humans who harmed her will pass, sooner than you think, but her suffering will affect her for many years to come. Are you prepared to help her deal with the anger, the sorrow, the guilt, the rage, and the loss of faith in humanity? Can you be her rock to crash on, and her beacon to bring her back when all feels lost?"

"I love her. I would do anything for her."

"Do you want to be mated before her transition, or after?" Nona stands and places her hand on Sam's forehead.

Before I can answer, Samantha's eyes open.

"I am sorry you have suffered, my child," Nona says soothingly. "I am sorry you must suffer more before this is through. But I offer you the gift of dreamless, painless slumber until you are healed. You are free to accept it or decline."

Samantha shakes her head.

"You are wise beyond your years, my daughter. The sooner your transition comes, the better everything will be for you." Nona gives Sam a brittle smile before she returns to the chair.

Lotti studies me. "Don't look so confused, Son. Sam declined because this is pain she is familiar with. She doesn't want to waste a gift from us on something that she views as trivial." Lotti's eyes are bright with affection for her daughter.

THIRTEEN

Samantha

———————

The mothers leave shortly after making me the offer of sleep. My throat hurts too much to speak. Thankfully, I don't have to use my voice to speak to The Sisters. I am not sure if everyone else can communicate with them through thoughts, but it sure makes things easier on me.

"Do you want anything, my love?" Laine reaches for the chair Nona had used. He pulls it close enough to the bed to be able to sit and hold my hand. He knows enough about my injuries to avoid my pinky, and he seems to understand my voice isn't working.

I point to the clock. That's all I have to do. He hurries from the room and returns in seconds with all of my meds and a bottle of water. As soon as I am done with all the meds, he asks, "Would you like me to run you a bath?"

A bath is probably best since I am not sure I can stand, but I am bleeding, which would ruin a bath. Ugh. How do I explain that? I want to scrub *him* off my skin. I feel disgusting.

"A shower would be better wouldn't it?"

I nod, but then shake my head no.

"Would you consider a *yes* if I help you in the shower?"

I nod but purse my lips.

"I just want to take care of you. I won't do anything until you want to."

He enters the bathroom and starts the shower. He returns naked. He scoops me up and takes me into the bathroom, locking the door before setting me on the tub ledge. While he helps me out of my clothes, his phone, lying on the counter, vibrates but he ignores it. He enters the spray, pulls me into the tub and shields me from the water until I can acclimate. I reach down and change the temperature to the hottest setting. Leaning against the shower wall, I start scrubbing off the first layer or two of skin.

I have fingerprint-sized bruises on my hips and thighs. I'm sure my throat does, too. My stomach is dark purple, almost black. My eye and lip are definitely swollen. God, I must look like a hot mess. I should have fought harder.

Laine doesn't say a word, and there's no pity in his eyes. His arm around my waist, which keeps me on my feet, is the only body part touching me. Finally, I turn off the water and wait for him to help me out. I sit on the edge of the tub while he leaves to find a shirt and pair of boxers I can sleep in.

A flash memory of Ryan's cock in my throat makes me race to the toilet. That's where Laine finds me, defeated, broken and crying into my towel. He drops the clothes, scoops me off the floor, sets me on the chair next to the bed, and helps me dress. Afterward, he strips the bed and puts on a fresh mattress pad, sheets, and pillows. In minutes, the bed is remade. He helps me onto the bed, then sits brushing my hair until I am close to falling asleep sitting up.

"Lay down, Love. No one will hurt you here."

He always knows what to say. He leans over and brushes his lips over mine, then circles the bed and gets in on his side. I lay against the pillows and scoot as close to Laine as I can get. He wraps his strong arms around me, and I know I am home. I tilt my head up and kiss him under his chin.

"Don't. You're hurt. You need time to heal. We have a lot to do tomorrow. I love you." He sounds exhausted.

I feel like I have been hit by a bus, but I needed him to know. "I love you, Laine," I whisper as I tuck my head under his chin.

His arms squeeze me for a second, and he drops a kiss on the top of my head.

"I want to be mated to you before my transition."

"What did you say?"

"I want to get married before I die, and since The Sisters said my human part has to die as part of my transition, I want to achieve at least one goal. If you still want me. It is a lot to ask, I know." The remorse can't be helped.

Laine pulls away to look at me. "I will always love you. I will always protect you. I will always want you. We can be mated this second if you wish it, my love."

"I did horrible things today, Laine. I really want to forget today ever happened, but I don't want to forget it, because I want to hold onto the rage. That isn't normal."

"It is normal, Sam. Rage is healthy in this situation. I have so much rage over what he did to you, not just today but since forever. I want to kill him. I want to torture him. The only thing stopping me from doing it is the mothers asking me not to."

"Why would they tell you not to?"

"It isn't his time. We aren't killers, Sam, we are extricators.

"Can the mothers talk to anyone anytime they want?"

"The mothers only talk to their children. It's a curse sometimes. Your mother will always be able to talk to you, my mother can talk to Caleb and me, and, of course, Lotti can talk to Nessa. Elite also project the gifts that are indicative of their mothers. I'm not sure what Vanessa will be able to do, but her mother decides how long humans live. Since my mother decides how people die, if I am close to the person, I can alter the how, either when they are extricated or when they are about to die. It takes a lot of energy to change the will of my mother, so I typically don't use my gift. Caleb can warn people how they will die by making them fear the thing that will kill them."

"Oh? Like a phobia?"

"Phobia? What's that?" The word feels wrong on my tongue.

"A phobia is an irrational fear humans can develop over situations or everyday items. Please tell me more about what you do."

"What do you want to know?"

"What if I don't want to extricate souls? Do I have a choice?"

"No. If you don't do it, you will eventually be caught and killed. And when we are mated, if you die, I die."

"What!"

"That's how it works. If a leathoes ever loses their mate, their heart stops, too."

"How long do leathoes live?"

"In theory, we are immortal, with an asterisk." He chuckles.

"Explain, please."

"Well, we can die if our mate dies, and if we are killed by a vengeful soul. If we don't exonerate a soul, it gets trapped in this world and relives its final days for eternity. If you get too close to a soul that was not released, it can and will possess you and stop your heart."

"So, if I don't get to a soul to free it, it becomes what? A ghost? Then I just have to avoid that area for the rest of eternity. That doesn't sound too hard."

"Until you are called to release a soul near the one you left, like a century later."

"Then I would ask someone else to do it so I wouldn't get near the one I missed."

"Nope, your assignments are your own. No one else can do them."

"Okay, so I would just never do any more releases in that area.

High concentration of ghosts, paranormal chasers would flock there." I laugh out loud.

"Any soul trapped is never forgotten. The leathoes that missed that soul would forever feel their pain. They experience that human's death, and relive it on the human's death day, for the entire day." He looks pained.

"Have you ever missed a release?"

"No, but Caleb has. To see him in pain hurts me to my bones."

"Why did he miss it?"

"Sam, what we do isn't always easy. It isn't always a little old lady, warm in her bed, who has lived a long, full life. More often than not, it is something painfully tragic, and not up to us. Caleb was new to the job. One of the first humans he had to release was a single mother of a young child. He agonized over it the whole day and just couldn't bring himself to release her. What you need to remember, Sam, is they die either way. When their time is up, it's up. Caleb got very lucky. He has to feel her death every death day, but she isn't a trapped soul. When she finally passed on, the mothers granted her guardianship. She got to watch over her daughter."

"How long does guardianship last?"

"If the mothers decide you earned it, you can become a guardian; and as long as someone on Earth thinks of you, you are summoned back to guard. So, thinking of the deceased once brings them back to you until your last breath."

"Do other things need to be released?"

"Oh yeah! If it can die, it has a soul. But animals don't need release the same way humans do. Humans need release so they can go on to be judged. Humans are not guaranteed reincarnation. Some don't need to come back to get it right. Some were too horrible to be allowed back on Earth, and some suffered so much in this life they were granted reprieve in the beyond."

"You don't know what happens to a soul after it leaves a body?"

"Not a clue."

"How do you know if you are successful in releasing a soul?"

"The light or spark in their eyes fades, and they either get goosebumps or the hair on their neck stands up."

I lay still for a few minutes thinking about what he's told me. How many times have I gotten goosebumps right before passing out? Too many to count. I know the sequence my body goes through on its way to losing consciousness. First, I feel the warmth and color drain from my face, then my blood turns to ice, which causes my skin to prickle, and lastly, if I don't manage to let out one last scream, my world is hurled into darkness.

My thoughts snap back to the present. Laine has fallen asleep. I glance at the clock and laugh. Who goes to bed at 8 p.m.? Seriously.

It has been a really long day and a half. Hopefully, when we wake, things will be much better. I snuggle closer and drift toward sleep.

FOURTEEN

Laine

___

"Sam. We gotta get up. We have a meeting at nine every morning. Come on, Love." I nudge my mate. I am learning fast she is not a morning person. I'm not sure I can get her up.

"What time is it?"

"Eight twenty-seven."

That does the trick. She leaps out of bed and runs straight for her meds.

"I slept through four alarms for meds. How could I be so stupid? How am I not dead yet? Ugh! Stupid, stupid girl!"

"Calm down, Love. You take those and I will get you a water." I cross to the small fridge in my room and toss her a bottle of water.

She finishes her routine and heads for the bathroom. I listen to the patter of water. Eventually, she comes out already dressed for the day.

"Laine, I need to go back to my place and get more clothes."

"We will get you some clothes. You aren't going back to that house."

She cocks her head.

I dare to check her aura: pink and green with her usual bursts of bright yellow. She's beautiful. I let the colors fade. I close the distance between us, cup her face in my hands, and kiss her, mindful of her lip. I start to pull away, but she pulls me close and deepens the kiss. I roll at her pace.

"Laine, I need you. Please." Her fingers tangle in my hair and pull.

"You're still hurt, Love. We should wait."

"I want you to help me forget. Please, Laine. I love you. Please?"

I groan at my defeat. She pulls me onto the bed, removes my shirt, and starts working on my belt and pants. I get her shorts and tank top off and kiss from her neck to her breast. She arches, hooking her legs around my waist.

"This isn't going to be as slow and gentle as I wanted it to be after you got better," my voice is husky against her breast.

"Please, Laine. I don't need slow and gentle right now, I just need to feel you." She reaches between us and positions me at her opening. She starts to sheathe me, but I beat her to it. One thrust and I am in. Our joining steals her breath for a second. Her nails dig into my shoulders. She starts to move against me as I move quickly against her. As I get close, I reach between us and apply pressure to her clit. She explodes at the same time I do, with my name on her lips before she starts coming back to Earth.

"Welcome back, my love."

"Where is this meeting?"

"Luckily, it's in my dining room today." I kiss her forehead as I pull out of her and notice her wince as I do so. We have a bit more clean-up than normal because she isn't fully healed. I feel horrible that I didn't go easier on her.

In the bathroom, she hands me a washcloth and runs her fingers through my hair. "Get out of your head, Laine, it was perfect."

"Can you read minds now?" I grin as I start cleaning myself.

"I can read you." She kisses my forehead and then strips the bed. She's already dressed and has the bed in order by the time I finish dressing. She's quick and efficient.

"Ready to go, Love?" I offer my arm.

She takes it and we leave to face the world together.

We make it to the meeting with minutes to spare. David has outdone himself on the breakfast bar. No one will complain today.

"Glad you finally decided to show your face in your own house!" Caleb smacks me on the shoulder.

"You know, only you are allowed to make fun of me, Brother." I laugh loudly and smack him on the back as I go in for a hug.

I glance at Sam. She smiles as she watches our exchange, but her aura is pulsating shades of blue and gray. What a puzzling combination. Sadness, loss, and loneliness. In a room full of people, she feels alone. How is that possible?

"Do you have other siblings?" she directs her question to both of us.

"We have a sister," Caleb answers, and he watches me as he speaks, "but she hasn't been tapped yet for the job. She loves humans, so she's out being crazy. For now."

"What's her name?"

Neither of us answer. We look at each other, an unspoken communication going on right in front of her.

"Okay, what is going on? Aren't you allowed to talk about family?"

"It isn't that easy," I say.

"Actually, she is supposed to be here today. She's supposed to train with you, Sam," Caleb says more buoyantly than I feel.

"Where are your parents?"

Caleb looks at her like she is insane, and I know my expression mirrors his.

"What?"

"The mothers are our parents."

"No, not who created you. I mean, who birthed you?"

I know we must look like we think she has two heads, but how is she not getting what we explained earlier?

"Okay, the sisters told me leathoes can have children. They are the mothers of this race. So, who birthed you?"

"We literally came directly from the mothers. We were not birthed by a common leathoes. Caleb and I are fraternal twins. Our direct mother is Morta. Our sister is a little younger. She is Lotti's daughter directly."

"Who is Nona's child?"

I glance at my brother at the same time he glances at me. Caleb licks his lips. "You're Nona's child, Samantha."

She lifts a hand to silence us. Her brain is working; it is fascinating to witness. I will never tire of watching. Finally, she says, "I have questions. Please let me get them all out before you answer. The sisters told me they had no idea who my father was. Why would they say that? How can we be mated or married or whatever if we are directly related? How am I half human? Why was I left to live like I did? Why didn't my mother help me? I'm so confused."

I take her into my arms. "I don't have answers, Love. Call for the mothers if you need to ease your heart." I kiss the top of her head.

"I hear, my daughter. Come, let us talk. Bring your mate." Nona holds out her hand to Sam. Sam eyes it with apprehension. Her eyes shine with hurt and unshed tears. I grab her hand and squeeze. She squeezes back and takes Nona's hand. Nona leads us into the living room. "Now, ask your questions, my child." Nona sits on the couch and waits.

"Who is my father?"

"At one time, more than six hundred years ago, I fell in love with a human who was fated to die in battle. I took a piece of him and held onto it, trying to decide what to do with it. I decided that I loved him enough to honor him with the gift of a child to carry on his blood. But my ability to make life had long since passed, and it will be many centuries before I am able to do so again.

"My sisters were making their direct children at about that time, so I decided to use a leathoes host. She died many years after your birth. For centuries, I kept you with us in our tower, but I knew, eventually, I had to let you have a chance at being human. I also knew that half-leathoes children did not survive to adulthood, but I hoped that your time with us had given you the extra edge to live through to your transition.

"When I sent you into the mortal world, your father was granted guardianship. He sent for me many times. We shouldn't alter fate, my child, but on one occasion, I did. You were dying. It wasn't until your blood sang that I was able to do anything. I sent your grandmother to check on you, and to alert the authorities.

"In essence, you were adopted, since not a drop of my blood runs in your veins, but I love you more than anyone. And because I made you, I am your direct mother in every way, even though I did not get to carry you.

"Laine and you can mate if you wish it, when you wish it. Your heritage makes you one of four elite. Laine, Vanessa, Caleb, and you make up the elite of the leathoes. It also means you will endure more burdens. Laine's mother is Morta; therefore, Laine has the unique ability to change how someone is fated to die. Typically, he allows fate to run on auto pilot, if you will, and doesn't utilize his talent. Caleb has the ability to warn humans of how they will die. If someone has an irrational fear of water, that's because Caleb has warned them that is how they will perish. Now Vanessa hasn't been tapped to become an extricator, but when she is, her ability will be knowing how long a person has left to live. And I am sure you are wondering about yourself. Being as you are half human and my adopted child, you will need a talisman in order to utilize your talent." Nona stops talking and hands Samantha a small silver ring with a star sapphire surrounded by diamonds. "Put it on, daughter."

Samantha slides the ring on her right index finger. The light catches the stones and sets them sparkling.

"When you wear this ring, you will know if a human or leathoes is with child, and how far along they are. Because you are elite and half human, you have the burden and ability to help strengthen our population."

Samantha finally says, "My body will never let me carry a baby to term. I am sorry to disappoint you, Mother."

Her sadness grips my heart. I pull her in for a hug.

"Never despair, my child. I spin the thread of life. I know what I am talking about."

Samantha looks at her mother in shock. I'm not sure if she's shocked because she was just informed that she can have children, or that her mother knows everything.

"That's your job? To spin lifelines? What are your sisters' jobs?"

Nona laughs softly. "Always inquisitive. Morta decides how someone will die and how fortunate they are in their life. Lachesis decides how long people are to live. It is my job to spin their life. I decide when someone is born, and any major life events they will experience. That is all there is to it, my child. Now, come hug your mother, and get on with your meeting. Eat something so you can heal, my love."

"How long ago did you say I was made? How is it my human mother doesn't mention adopting me?" Samantha asks as she goes to hug her true mother.

"I fixed her thread to include you in her memory. Very tedious. But you were worth every second of work. I made you over two centuries ago. I kept you in the tower with me until Morta and Lotti convinced me to let you make your own way. Time works differently in the tower. If a human ever entered our tower, their lives would be completed within an hour. I am sorry you had such a hard life, Samantha. We can't play favorites when we make lives, even those of our own children. You drew the short stick this round, daughter. But your life only improves from here. Soon, you will leave humans behind and know the love of your true family." Nona vanishes as quickly as she arrived.

"How are you, Sam?" I try to gauge her feelings, but her expression is blank and her wall is in place.

"Let's get to our meeting." She starts to leave the room.

"Where is Sammy?" I hear in the other room. "Why isn't she here with you guys?"

Sam stops short. "Nes?" she breathes.

"Oh my god! Eeeeeeeeeeeeek! Sam! I missed you soooooooo much!" My sister runs at my mate full charge and jumps on her. Sam staggers, and Nessa gains her footing still hugging Sam. "Sam! I missed you so much! I'm so glad you can finally know everything about me!"

A spark of realization hits Samantha's eyes. "Nes! Oh, I've missed you!" Sam wraps our sister in a hug, tears shining in her eyes. Sam clears her throat.

Vanessa disengages from the hug. "I heard what happened yesterday. Are you okay?" She looks Sam and I over from head to toe.

"I'm healing." Sam holds her arm against her stomach.

"Oh, I'm so sorry, Sammy. I wasn't thinking. Can I get you something?" Vanessa reaches toward the arm that Sam's positioned as armor against another assault.

Sam takes a step back, a smile still on her face.

My sister gestures toward the kitchen. "Let's go sit down."

We follow her into the kitchen. Sam gingerly sits at the bar.

Caleb looks at Sam. "So, Sis, did you get all the answers you were looking for?"

"Sister?" Nessa looks at Caleb like he is insane.

"Vanessa, meet the direct daughter of Nona. And Laine's mate," Caleb's voice is pure mischievousness, and complete joy lights his face at Vanessa's shocked expression. The way he announced Sam as my mate, however, sounded off, strained.

"Sam! You're elite! We're true sisters!" Nes seems to be over the moon. "Wait. Laine's mate. Like, my brother, Laine? Laine will never take a mate. He'll die first. The man doesn't know what to do with women. Are you sure you want Laine?" Vanessa looks in my direction and cringes. "No offence, Brother!" She turns back to Sam with a pleading look. "I mean, you just got here, shouldn't you look around at the other prospects?"

"You know me, Nes, once I make up my mind, that's it." Sam beams at me.

I keep an eye on her as she helps herself to small servings of food.

"And that is it, I guess," Jacob finishes the meeting as we finally stop talking. "Anyone have anything to add? Laine, are you taking Sam out to train?"

"That was my plan. Did you have something else in mind?"

"No, that's fine. I have to go check on our captive, then I can head out with you, if you don't mind a tag along."

"Captive?" Sam asks the room at large.

"You still have him at your house?" I thunder. I can't help it, I am fucking mad.

Sam's fork drops to her plate with a sharp clank.

"Until the mothers tell me otherwise, yes," Caleb hedges.

"You have my dad in your house?" Sam whispers to Caleb.

He nods.

She turns on her heel and leaves the room.

I war with myself on whether I should follow her or give her space. I have nothing to offer to make any of this better.

FIFTEEN

Samantha

———————

My tormentor is next door.

My blood is ice, my head is buzzing. I need to get out of here. Ryan is too close. He can come get me at any time.

I fly up the stairs to my room, engage the lock, and begin throwing my few belongings into my bag. Someone knocks on my door.

"Sam, can I come in, please?" Laine sounds worried and weary.

For the first time since I got here, I ignore him. There's too much going on in my head to add whatever he brings to the mix. As I finish packing, I notice him standing in the doorway watching me. I know I locked that door. Panic grips me.

He is in front of me before I can blink. His hands cup my face and the panic vanishes, my head stops buzzing, but my heart goes into overdrive. My blood is on fire. I close my eyes and lean into his touch. His lips find mine—my reassurance that he cares for me.

"I won't let anything happen to you. You are safe here. Sam, look at me, please," his voice is soft. He waits for me to comply.

I open my eyes.

"Sam, he could be in the same room as you and he'll never have a chance to touch you. I will never fail you. I love you. Your enemies are my enemies, your family is my family. The fact that they are one in the same doesn't matter to me. I will always keep you safe. Even if you decide you don't want me."

The last sentence pierces my heart. "Why would you ever think I don't want you? Have I given you reason to doubt me?"

"I just don't want you to feel like you have to do anything out of obligation or your twisted life goals." He drops his hands and steps back.

"Laine, I want you to listen to me and actually hear me. I love that you get me. No one has ever interpreted the things I need before I need them. You save me from my thoughts and silence my head with just your touch. You have seen me at rock bottom and never once did I see pity in your eyes. You will never know how appreciated that is. You rescued me when I was being attacked. You're strong and powerful, you're beautiful. I haven't noticed anyone else who comes here, I only have eyes for you. You accept that, sometimes, I just can't or don't want to be touched. Not many men can handle that. I need you to understand that I may never be able to give you the things you need and deserve emotionally. I am trying. I know I love you—a foreign feeling to me—but I'm positive that's what it is. All I can promise is to try to show you more, and to feel more. I never want you to feel less than you are, or to feel unwanted." I wrap my arms around him, lay my head on his chest, and listen to his heartbeat.

He wraps his arms around me and rests his head on top of mine. We stand like that for a while.

"You feel like home," I say. In a world I never felt I belonged to, in a family that never saw me as anything but an item to be traded, I feel safe, wanted, and loved right here with this man.

"Why are you packing then?" His breath tickles my ear.

"Lapse in judgment."

"We have much to do today. We should get going. I'm sure my sister is waiting." He pulls away, but his hand finds mine.

He leads me to his car. I get in just as Vanessa and Jacob leave the house, heading toward us. They stop beside the driver's side door. "What is the plan today?" Jacob asks.

"I was going to trail Caleb. Vanessa knows how most of this works, she just needs a better understanding of the process. And Sam can see from start to finish how it all happens."

"Excellent idea. Laine, we need to discuss a few things when you have a moment." Jacob flashes a quick smile then heads to his car, calling over his shoulder, "Nes, you wanna ride with me?"

Nes throws me a curious glance…looking for my approval? I smile at her and wave.

She follows Jacob while Laine climbs in and starts the engine. He grabs my hand and kisses my knuckles before heading out toward our destination. Scenery flies by me as he expertly weaves through traffic to wherever Caleb works. He pulls over in a run-down neighborhood.

"Sam, I need you to observe and not interrupt, please." Laine runs his fingers through my hair and brings his hand to rest on my shoulder. I nod. He goes to step out of the car and I follow his lead.

It's clear Caleb isn't alone. Nes and Jacob pull in and park behind Laine's car. They are out and at our side in seconds. As we approach Caleb's car, Laine grabs my non-injured hand, squeezes my fingers tight, and I look at him in surprise. He puts a finger to his lips; I extend to him the same courtesy he showed me during my call with Ryan.

I hear soft moaning and see a woman in the car with Caleb working his cock with her mouth as if she were a pro. She is a thin little thing with short black hair and sun-kissed skin. She might be a pro, but she is top of the line and well taken care of. Caleb's head is back, teeth clenched, trying to prolong his release as long as possible. She takes note of us standing close. "It's gonna cost you more to have people watch, Daddy." Her gaze lands on Laine. "Unless he wants some too. I can deal a two-for-one, for him."

I tense, trying to stop myself from beating this woman to death. Laine shakes his head at her while Jacob steps forward and slides a bill to her. She goes back to work on Caleb.

I look at Laine with a million questions running through my head. I open my mouth to ask, but I'm cut off by Caleb's final moan. She sits up and opens the door to spit, and starts making herself presentable before exiting the car. "You come back anytime, Daddy. I'll make you feel good every time." Caleb reaches over and touches her arm as she turns and walks away.

Caleb joins us. "I love my job. At least, on assignments like today."

"What the fuck?" I can't help exclaiming.

"We have to touch the human who is marked to die. Since she's a pro, I decided to have some fun before her demise." He shrugs, without remorse.

"When will she die?" I ask the group at large.

"Her pimp will beat her to death tonight while on a high," Laine answers in a factual tone.

"No! No more violence! Laine, please. Please don't make her suffer," I plead for the life of the woman on the corner trying to solicit another man in a car.

He looks at me, searching my eyes. For what, I don't know. I hope he finds whatever will get him to comply with my request. He closes his eyes and his whole body tenses for a second.

A commotion begins down the street. I turn and see people surrounding the woman who was just blowing Caleb.

"What's going on?" Caleb cocks his head and narrows his eyes at Laine.

"I changed how she will die. Now she ends in a warm hospital bed with minimal discomfort." He pulls me into a hug. "Does that make you happier, my love?"

"Thank you. I'm sorry I asked you," I keep my voice low so only he can hear, "but I just couldn't stand more beatings."

"I understand, Love. Please realize, I can't be here to fix every person's death, but if I'm near someone who's about to suffer anything you've suffered, I will make the effort to alter their death." He squeezes me and lets me go.

"I don't think I have ever seen you use your gift, Brother. How will she pass when her time comes?" Caleb sounds both impressed and curious.

"Brain aneurysm. It was all I could think of off-hand. She's literally a ticking time bomb."

"Ha! He blew her mind! Get it?" Caleb laughs and the others join in. I don't. I wrap my arms around my body and hold on for dear life. What am I getting myself into?

"You can't change who you are, Sam. People were coming for you. I couldn't let you stay there." Laine slips an arm around my shoulders.

"I actually have more information on the raid at Sam's house, Laine," Jacob says a bit hesitantly.

"Can we discuss it after training?" Laine asks.

Jacob nods.

"My next assignment is on the other side of town," Caleb says. "You guys want to carpool or follow me there?"

SIXTEEN

Laine

———————

"WE CAN FOLLOW YOU," JACOB ANSWERS FOR ALL OF US.

I am glad to get away from my twin. I don't like that my mate got a good look at him while he got his dick wet. I know it makes no sense. I think he appalled her more than anything, but since I couldn't see her aura, I just don't know. Her wall went up as soon as she figured out what was going on in his car.

"Where are we going?" Sam whispers without shifting her gaze from the window. Her chin resting on her hand. She seems sad, or maybe drained. Maybe humans aren't able to handle the type of training or information I have to share.

"No idea. Each of us has our own assignments. I can't do any Caleb is supposed to do, and vice versa." Her silence is making me uneasy. "What are you thinking?"

"What if I can't do this? What if I'm asked to extricate someone I know? What if I'm told to release a child or baby? How can I live with myself?"

The pain in her voice crushes me.

"Do you want to see what happens if we don't complete our assignments? Would that help you understand?"

"Maybe. I feel like a traitor to my race."

I pull my car over to the shoulder and fire off a text to Jacob and Caleb. Both cars pull over in preparation to turn around to follow me.

Ten minutes later, we stop in front of a playground, vacant except for a single child on a swing. None of us gets out of the car. There is no reason. I know Sam sees him. Her breath is slow and shallow, her body on edge as she watches him.

"How old is that child?" I barely hear her.

"How old is he now or how old was he?"

"What?"

"That child is proof of what happens when we don't help humans move on. Watch him, Samantha."

Her attention never leaves the child. He swings higher and higher. He jumps off mid upswing. He lands on his feet and runs to the monkey bars. He is all over them. Then he reaches the top and begins to walk across them. I watch Samantha. I already know how this ends. His foot slips. His leg falls through the bars. Half his body slips through and his head makes a hard crunch. His body stays suspended on the bars for minutes until he vanishes and the swing start swinging again. "He is doomed to repeat this for the rest of eternity, never getting to move on. Never getting back to his family. He's been here for over forty years. He was four when he was to be extricated, but that never happened. Too painful for the leathoes who was supposed to do it."

She is out of the car and running to the child before I can react. He might not be able to kill her, but he is a danger to all of us. I open my door to yell for her when she reaches him. He is on the monkey bars now. He is about to slip.

Sam flies up the monkey bars, catches him, and cradles him. She smooths his hair and speaks softly. He doesn't fight her. She leans down, kisses his forehead, and he vanishes from her arms.

I am frozen in shock. The others are also out of their cars holding on to their doors for support, the look on their faces mirroring the shock I feel. The swings don't move. The child doesn't reappear. Samantha climbs down off the bars and walks back to the car.

"Why are you all looking at me like that? Did I do something wrong?"

"Sam, no one has ever freed a spirit without giving their life. What made you do that? What did you do?"

"I don't know. I just know when I was little, I always wanted my mother if I was hurt. I didn't want him to hurt anymore. I did what I thought I would do if that were my child. He wanted his mother, she came and got him." She looked at each of us in turn, gauging our reactions.

"Are you hurt?" Vanessa runs to Sam and starts checking her over.

"Why on Earth would I be hurt?" Sam sounds as shocked as we look.

"That is the only way we can die, Sam," Jacob says in a mix of anger and awe. "If we miss an extrication, the soul can possess us and stop our hearts. Our life in exchange for their freedom from this purgatory. It only happens if we get too close to their area, but after a few hundred years, it's easy to forget where a missed spirit is. Souls can hurt us even if we aren't the leathoes who missed their assignment. Some are powerful enough to kill any leathoes that gets too close to them. You literally just went willingly to the one thing that could kill you."

"That isn't true. I'm mortal. I'm human. Anything could kill me right now." She looks at me as if daring me to challenge her. "You've told me about missed assignments before, haven't you?"

"It's okay, Sam, I will remind you as often as I need to, on anything you need. Every morning when you wake up, if I need to, I'll remind you of the vengeful spirits that can kill us, and that I love you. We'll revisit this after Caleb completes his assignments. Let's get back to work." I get back into the car.

Sam joins me.

The last few minutes weigh front and center on my mind as I drive.

"I'm never going back to the human world am I? My house. My job. Any friends I had. I forfeit all of it when I change?" Sam's question is more to the universe than at me.

I answer anyway, "If you don't want to live at the manor, we can find another home. Your only job will be to extricate. Of course, you can still see your friends. As you age, you can alter how they see you by bending their will."

Sam is silent for a few minutes then pulls out her phone. She types for several minutes, takes a deep breath, then touches her phone once more before putting if back in her pocket. Her gaze returns to her window.

"You okay?" I ask tentatively.

"I just emailed my resignation to my boss. I won't be able to work at the college and do this. There is just no way." She stares out the windshield until we reach the hospital Caleb is stopped at. "I love the manor. I've never been picky on where I live. I just know wherever you are is where I want to be."

I park in the hospital lot, lean over, and kiss her before we get back to work.

SEVENTEEN

Samantha

———————

Finally, the day winds down. We have been all over Ohio, it seems, in every kind of place. The hospital, the grocery store, the mall, and a nursing home. I learn how leathoes get into places they have no business being. Apparently, humans are easy to convince. Leathoes not only read how humans feel but can change a human's will for short periods of time. They have the gift of a silver tongue. Caleb had no problem getting into the rooms he needed to access, and no one batted an eye at him at the nursing home. The hardest one for me was the teen at the mall. She couldn't have been older than fourteen, but Caleb did what he was supposed to. I have to keep reminding myself we don't kill them, we make a way for them to escape.

When Laine goes to Caleb's to check on Ryan, I settle on the living room couch and my thoughts turn inward. 'Mother, can you hear me?' I concentrate hard to see if I can reach her.

'I'm here, my daughter. Do you have questions?'

I see Nona in my mind as I replay the events of the day. 'Laine is really upset. I don't know what I did. I didn't know, Mother. I'm sorry. I couldn't just sit there and not try to help. He was so little, so alone.' Sadness and remorse wash over me.

'My daughter, I am so proud of you. Apparently, you are destined to have more gifts than I gave you. Perhaps this is a much greater talent than seeing life within life. I'm sure I will have Morta to thank for this. Take care, daughter. If your heart tells you there is danger, then take heed. Souls are not always small children. Not all of them will let you near them without trying to hurt or kill you.'

A shiver goes down my spine.

'Samantha, I must ask. Are you sure about being mated to Laine?'

I answer without hesitation, 'Of course! I love him so much. I'm not used to these feelings. I am worried I will push him away with how closed off I can be. I told him I would try harder. I will. I am just so broken.'

She nods and gives a brilliant smile. 'I advise you to wait until after your transition for the mark ceremony.'

'Why?'

'At the mark ceremony, you will be bound one to the other. He will bear your mark and you his. If something happens to you and you don't make it through the transition, he will die. I prefer that you wait, but you need to talk to him. This has to be a decision for the two of you.' She bows her head as her image leaves my mind.

"What were you doing?" Laine asks as he enters the living room.

"Talking to my mother about things that happened today and about being your mate." I remember what she said, and I shake my head.

"Nona was here?"

"No. My mother talks to me in my head sometimes. She said today is a result of my gift being altered by Morta, apparently. She said if my heart tells me to stay away from a soul, then I should take heed. I agree completely. Then she told me to talk with you about our…um…oh, what did she call it? Some kind of ceremony." I lose my train of thought trying to recall what she said. Cursing my memory, I close my eyes and rest my hand against my forehead.

EIGHTEEN

Laine

————————

"The mark ceremony." I breathe. I wasn't prepared to talk about this after the amount of information she received today.

She brightens and flashes a smile that stills my breath. "Yes! The mark ceremony. Ugh, that makes my mind quiet a little. Thank you. Yes. So, we need to talk about when we want to do that."

"Honestly, we can do whatever you want. It's just formalities, at this point, Love."

"I talked it over with Nona. I agree with her that we should wait until after my transition. Please. I never want to be the reason your life ends."

"Then we will wait." I pull her to her feet, hold her close, and sway to silent music neither of us can hear.

Without stopping the peaceful slow dance with my mate, I bury my nose in her hair and relax.

"Sam, I'm sorry, I'm sure you have had information overload today, but Caleb and Jacob are wanting to talk to us." I stop our dance and pull her toward my study where both men wait.

Caleb looks up when we enter and raises a brow. I give a slight nod.

"Hi, Sam," Caleb says. "I know you are new to this world and you haven't had much time to process what you've learned, but we just don't have time for you to learn everything at a slow pace. With that being said, I need to know what you know about the mothers so I know what I need to catch you up on." He doesn't sound as impatient as his body language indicates.

"I know my mother is Nona, I know she spins the thread of human lives. I know that Lotti is Vanessa's mother. She decides how long a human lives. Morta is both your and Laine's mother, and she decides how long humans live and when they die. They are always aware of us and talk to us whenever we need them," Sam's tone is matter-of-fact.

"Do you know any more?"

"I'm sorry, that's all I know." Sam looks at each of us as if to gauge the adequacy of her answers.

"The mothers are actually four sisters. Their sister Loviatar, or Veda, as she prefers to be called, had a falling out with them hundreds of years ago. She absolutely hates humans and searches for ways to cause as much damage and chaos as she can. If you hear of war breaking out, a volcano erupting, forest fires—those are caused by her. Both natural and unnatural events that cause a large number of human deaths are typically her doing. She doesn't always work alone. Most of the time, when it comes to humans killing each other, she has inside help. You've heard of humans bartering for favors with their souls?"

"Sure, like selling your soul to the devil for talent or a new car."

I fidget, hoping Sam will remain enthusiastic about the family after hearing what Caleb has to say.

Caleb smiles broadly. "Exactly. Well, she is what you would consider the devil. Humans can sell their souls to her to gain something in return. The price isn't just their soul. When they die, Veda can do what she pleases with their souls. She uses these traded souls to possess other humans and have them do horrible things. Terrible things that create a high body count."

"What happens to those souls after the possessed human passes on?"

Clever girl. I'm proud at how quickly she processes information.

"Well, after we extricate the possessed human and they die, their soul goes on to be judged, or whatever actually happens to them. But the soul that Veda owned is cast into the Great River of Longing, where they are trapped forever, never to find peace or return to this world." Caleb watches Sam to make sure she's following.

"Okay, why are you telling me this? What does this have to do with me?" she sounds exasperated. I know she's been given a lot to process today.

I take her hand and bite the bullet. "Sam, Ryan bartered with Veda. Your mother's life—for her to die—and for you to be his again."

NINETEEN

Samantha

FOR THE MILLIONTH TIME IN THE PAST COUPLE OF DAYS, MY WORLD stops. "What does that mean?" I can't help the panic that threatens my sanity. Even Laine's hand holding mine does not quiet the rage that fills every fiber of my being but, surprisingly, I have complete control over my mind. The panic has been contained, though I don't know for how long. Why doesn't Ryan just leave me alone? It's not fair!

'Life isn't fair, stupid girl.'

Thanks for the reminder; look who's finally awake. I pull myself out of the battle with my subconscious. I can't deal with her right now.

"Sam?" someone is calling my name but I'm not paying attention.

I realize I'm being shaken. I look up and see Laine standing over me, worry all over his beautiful face. I hate that all I seem to do is cause him worry and stress. A sear of pain in my hand shifts my attention. I'm bleeding. When did that happen? I open my fist and see the imprint of my nails in my palm. My rage is slowly receding.

"I'm sorry. I don't know why I did that." I search Laine's face for answers I know he doesn't have.

"It means, Sam," Caleb says, "that when he dies, he is still a danger. It also means you and your mother are in danger. We suspect the people who came to your house the other day were sent by Veda to take you to Ryan. Have you spoken to your mother since you left your house?"

I know he is trying to show compassion, which I'm sure is difficult since he sees humans as part of a job and not as family or part of his home life.

"I text her a few times a week, but there isn't a reason to talk to her every day. We don't have that sort of relationship." My voice sounds forced even to me. I am almost afraid to ask, "So, now what do we do?"

"I think it is best that you arrange to get your mother here," Jacob says. "Maybe invite her to visit so we can assure her safety."

I had forgotten he was in the room, he is so quiet.

"Okay. I know she will want to stay in a hotel. She hates my house and where I live in general—not grand enough for what she is used to." I am rambling. "Do you want me to text her now?"

"Might as well. No time like the present," Jacob says.

"Did you have anything to add, Laine?" I can't hide my weariness. I have reached my limit of things that I can handle today. My mind is warring with itself. Why now? Why is Ryan going to this extreme? The fewer answers my brain can supply, the more agitated I feel. With no one to take my frustration out on, I'm lashing out at the one person who cares. It isn't fair to him. I am completely irrational, but I'm cornered. My temper won't stop.

I whirl and rush up the stairs to the solitude of my room. I slide the lock into place and then gather all my meds and anything I will need before, during, or after my shower. I storm into the bathroom and turn the shower on as cold as it will go. I begin my ritual of laying out everything in order of use. Standing naked in front of the mirror, seeing all my things laid out before me, I swipe my arm across them and then climb into the shower. My body is numb long before I step into that freezing water. The cold comes from deep within me.

"Sam!"

He sounds so close, so worried. Why do I keep hurting him?

I'm not ready to talk to anyone. I just want time to process.

I'm quickly done with my shower, but I don't want to get out yet. I sit in the tub with the water pelting my back. I bring my knees up to rest my head on. Listening to the water, I can drown out Laine's knocking and calling. He doesn't need the craziness I bring into his life. No one should have to settle for all the baggage that comes with me. I'm a danger to anyone who gets near me. If I had gone back home with Ryan, my mother wouldn't be in danger.

Why am I so compelled to help her?

'Because she is your mother; you will always want your mother.'

But that's not true. I have a mother and siblings. I have a whole new family. I could have a husband and children. But what happens when Ryan shows up again and demands to see me or my children? What if Laine goes missing like Tommy did? Ryan might not be able to kill him, but I am sure he can find a way to hurt him. Bury him in an unmarked location so no one will ever find him. That sounds like something Ryan would do.

I can't let my past keep hurting my present and future. I'm going to do what I do best.

I turn off the water and step out. I know Laine is on the other side of the door. "Laine, could you please just give me some space to process everything I have been through? Please," my voice is no louder than a whisper, but I know he can hear me. "Right this moment, I just need space."

"I will be downstairs when or if you need me, Love." The door to my bedroom opens and closes.

I don't have much time. I throw on the shorts that I packed on the fly when we fled my house, and one of Laine's shirts. I take the meds I need and put the rest into my bag. I grab my keys and head out of my room. I sweep down the stairs, make sure no one is around, and walk straight out the front door. My car is easy to reach and getting out of the estate is simple since Laine turned off the security for today's meeting. I reach the highway in no time. I check my rearview mirror to make sure I'm not being followed. Now I just have to figure out where I am going and what I am going to do. I check that my inhaler is close and my ID and bank card are within reach. I relax a little. I love driving. It takes some of the buzz out of my head because of the concentration demanded.

My heart hurts. Physically. Like it's being ripped from my body the farther away I drive.

'Samantha, what are you doing, my child?'

I swerve, startled by my mother's voice.

'You need to get back to the house. It isn't safe out here.' Nona sounds desperate. Like my fate is in jeopardy.

'I am a danger to anyone who gets near me. Ryan is never going to stop. Laine deserves better. I can't live always looking over my shoulder.' I am beyond sad, I'm numb and resolved to my decision.

'You can't go through this transition alone, my daughter. You need someone with you. Someone who is bonded to you would be ideal. You have that. Please go back.' Nona's voice grows distant, like she is walking away. Or am I walking away?

Running is what I do best. I will keep running. Ryan can't stay locked at Caleb's forever. And when he is released, I won't be anywhere near him.

Run. Run away, and never look back.

TWENTY

Laine

———————

I WAIT DOWNSTAIRS FOR WHAT SEEMS LIKE AGES. I AM ON EDGE. I hate that Samantha is hurt and upset and won't let me close. Finally, I'm done waiting. I rush the stairs and stop at her door. I take a deep breath to calm myself. I knock. Nothing. I knock louder. Still nothing. What if she is having another attack?

I turn the handle. The door's unlocked. Progress?

I run into her room expecting to see her in the throes of another episode. She's not there. Her bathroom door is open and the light is off. I check there, too. Nothing. Her bed is made and her cell phone is on the nightstand, but something is off. I search the room trying to put my finger on it. Her bag, her medications, all of her clothes are gone. I fall to my knees as the truth crashes into me. My heart calls out to my mother.

'I hear you, my son. This is unusual for you to call upon me. What is the matter? Your heart is heavy.'

'Samantha is gone. Missing. I don't know what to do.'

'She is not missing. She is where she wants to be. It is not where she needs to be, I agree. You have ways of tracking her, I suggest you start there. I warn you, you do not have long.'

Her voice fades as fast as it came. I can't track her cell, she didn't take it with her. *Think, Laine, think!* The light bulb pops on in my head. She's my assignment. Until my assignment is complete, I will always be able to track her. I close my eyes and concentrate on my breathing. I focus on Samantha. I see her emerald eyes and her secret smile. Like a pip on a radar screen, I see her.

I run to my car and tear out of the drive. I keep visualizing Sam. She's moving at a steady pace. She must be driving. I don't remember seeing her car in the driveway. She has a good head start on me.

Traffic is not my friend today; too many slow drivers and a couple minor accidents causing jams. If I wasn't so determined to keep track of her, I would be more annoyed. I finally reach the open highway and gun my Mustang. Wherever she is headed isn't a good idea.

'A word of caution, Laine.'

The voice isn't my mother's. It doesn't faze me that my mother talks to me in my head. After a century or so, I've gotten used to her interrupting my thoughts. But neither of the other mothers has ever contacted me this way…or in any way.

'My daughter thinks she is a burden and a curse. She might always feel that way, we don't know. Her choice to leave was her idea of protecting those she loves, to keep you safe. When it comes to her family, her inclination is to run. She's beyond terrified, but the rage coursing through her right now is dangerous. I fear for her and anyone who might happen upon her. Take heed, Laine. She needs you now more than ever, but she is lost not only in the world, but in her head. Please, be careful.'

I shake my head to clear my mind and go back to tracking my mate. She's stopped. She still has over an hour's jump on me. If luck is on my side, maybe she is stopping for food or rest. My foot presses harder on the gas pedal, and I hope I can reach her sooner rather than later, when it might be too late.

TWENTY-ONE

Samantha

———————————

UGH! LEAVE IT TO ME TO GET LOST DRIVING ON AN INTERSTATE! Of course, in my haste to leave the manor, I didn't grab my phone. Okay, think Samantha. What did people do before cell phones? Map. I need a map. I get off the next exit I see and head toward the first place that serves food. Might as well kill two birds with one stone.

I walk in and grab a seat toward the back of the diner so I can watch the door. I'm not taking any chances. A middle-aged woman takes my order. After ordering, I ask if they have maps for sale. She says they might have a few at the counter and goes to check for me. Luck is on my side; they have one. I open up the paper and figure out where I am.

I consider my options. Where do I want to go? Disappearing is out of the question. I doubt that changing my identity would do me any good. The pain in my heart is trying to break to the surface of my desensitized self. I double my efforts to suppress the feeling. I can't afford to think of Laine right now. The rage that fueled me earlier, I lock away, deep inside, to be unleashed later. I inhale whatever food is placed before me. I ask my waitress for a to-go coffee and a large soda. I like having options. She brings them to me along with my check. I fold the map to show where I am right now and a general idea of where I want to go.

As I pay my bill at the counter, my attention returns to the booth full of men near the door. I had noticed them while I was eating, but they didn't feel threatening. Being close now, I can almost feel the danger coming off them. My skin is crawling, and I want to run from here as fast as I can. Taking a calming breath, I walk to the door and sprint to my car. I get in and lock the doors. I rest my head against the headrest and let out a sigh as a hand goes over my mouth.

My rage rears her ugly head. I don't bother to see who grabbed me. I dig my nails into the wrist of the hand over my mouth. My embedded nails don't get me what I want so I take a page out of Ryan's book and bend my assailant's pinky toward his wrist.

I'm free. I yank open my glove box and grab the wrench I keep there for emergencies. One rage-fueled whack and he is down for the count. It takes all my self-control to not kill him with the damn thing.

I start my car and drive a few miles before pulling over. He's still out. I open my trunk and pull out the zip ties I keep in the emergency pack I carry. I bind his wrists and ankles with the ties and haul him out of the backseat to the shoulder of the road. I slam the back door, get into the driver seat, and take off, leaving him in a cloud of dust. I check my rage back into the temporary cage I have for her and sneak a glance at my map.

After that last encounter, I know for sure I am doing the right thing. I couldn't live with myself knowing I might cause one of Laine's friends or family members to get hurt or perish.

I shake my head to clear it and tighten the knot on my emotions.

TWENTY-TWO

Laine

———

I ENTER THE DINER AND DESCRIBE HER TO THE WOMAN BEHIND THE counter. I tell her my fiancée is getting cold feet and I am desperate to find her, which is true, even if Samantha is more to me than a fiancée.

The waitress stonewalls me.

Time isn't on my side. It takes only a second to change her will. She tells me my bride-to-be left no more than twenty minutes ago and headed left. I follow the woman's directions. A few miles down the road I see what looks like a person slumped on the shoulder of the road. My heart clenches. Please, don't be Sam.

I pull over and approach the mass. It is definitely male, and he is out cold. He's bound by zip ties and blood oozes from a temple wound. I roll him over to get a good look at him. I get the impression he might not be human. He might be one of Veda's but, honestly, I just don't know. I call Caleb and give him a precise location, descriptions of everything, and arrange for him to collect our new friend. Caleb is maybe five minutes behind me.

I take off again, trying to sense Samantha. My heart is being squeezed. If we had been mated before all of this drama, I would have been able to hone in on her exact location…or I would have sensed her leaving. I could have stopped her.

'You know why she wanted to wait, son. She loves you too much to put you in danger. She knows her odds of survival are low. Despite what you think right now, this escapade is her way of protecting you. She has a selfless nature when it comes to the ones she loves. She's completely devoted to your preservation.' With that, Morta's voice withdraws.

Thanks for the vote of confidence, Mom, but I have too much on my plate to contemplate my mate's intentions. All I have room for is finding her and getting her home safely.

She's stopped again. About thirty miles ahead. Maybe there is another traffic jam. Let's hope luck is with me.

I need a distraction. I call Caleb. "Did you pick up our new cargo?"

"Oh yeah, I got him. I added a few restraints and tossed him in the back seat. What possessed you to zip tie him?" His amusement is apparent.

"I didn't. Samantha did. She got him good. I can't wait to hear that story. If she remembers it when I get to her." I chuckle a little. "She's stopped about thirty miles or so ahead. You flanking me in case something happens?" I ask, but I know the answer.

"Fuck yeah, Brother! I always have your back. Let's get my crazy sister back to the house!" Caleb is fired up.

It eases my concern a little that Caleb has embraced Sam as his sister. I thought it would take longer. Him being there to witness her gift, I think, changed his mind about her. She's not even transitioned yet and she has done something none of us has ever seen before: released a spirit from this world.

Focus. Reminiscing isn't helping. Traffic is letting up as I get closer.

I spot her car and my optimism plummets. The windshield

has been kicked out from the inside and the driver-side window is busted out. Blood smears the broken glass left behind.

It takes all my willpower not to pull over and inspect her car, but I feel her receding at a pace too fast to run. She must be inside another vehicle. I call Caleb and relay the information and quickly hang up. I check auras around me. She's close. There is a plumbing van starting across the bridge, about seven car lengths ahead of me. I see green. I found her!

My elation dies as fast as it arrives. The van swerves right and hits the bridge rail. The driver corrects the vehicle, but swerves again, harder. This time, the van rolls as it hits the rail, goes over, and drops into the rushing river.

I don't think. I jerk my car over, slam on breaks, reach the rail, and dive.

The water is fucking cold. The river's current is too strong, even for a well-trained swimmer. Lucky for me, I know none of it can kill me.

No one from the van is surfacing. I dive and search for it. I spot it ten feet away and reach it in seconds. Thankfully, the van's lying on the side that hit the rail. I reach the side door and yank it open. Both men are unconscious. Sam is gagged and handcuffed to the seatbelt. Her feet are cuffed but not to anything. I pass a hand over one of the wrist cuffs. It falls open and I free her from the belt. I grab her and kick hard toward the surface. Caleb is in the water with Jacob, heading to the van I just vacated. I break the surface and swim to the closest bank. I lay Samantha on the ground and start CPR. Caleb joins me a few minutes into my attempt to revive her. He pushes her hair off her face. His fingertips graze her face, then he kneels next to me and rests a hand on my shoulder.

"You just extricated her, didn't you?" It's a rhetorical question.

Caleb places his fingers on her neck, then bows his head, tears falling. I stop trying, force my hands under her body, and lift my would-be mate. I climb the bank and reach the side of the road as

Jacob pulls up. The men from the van are secured in the cargo hold of his SUV. I get in the back and cradle Samantha as Caleb reaches for the open door.

"Please don't hate me, Brother."

"I don't hate you," I whisper. "I hate myself."

Caleb slams the door and steps back.

It's a somber drive to the manor. Samantha was cold when I pulled her from the van, but she gets colder as I hold her. I check for a pulse. After a minute, I imagine I feel a faint flutter. Maybe there is hope?

'Laine, you knew she might not make it. It is still early. Her human form has to die for her to transition. Her human soul is free to leave. Have patience, my son. What is meant to be will be,' my mother's voice cuts through my misery.

'How will I live without her? I don't want to.'

'Patience,' is all she offers, then leaves.

When we arrive, I send Vanessa to a store to pick up some clothes for Samantha. Jacob and Caleb help me carry a bed down and place it in the living room so I can stay with her even through meetings. I also light a fire and warm the room.

I take some of the clothes Vanessa acquires into the upstairs bathroom, bathe Samantha, then carry her downstairs and place her in the bed. I pile blanket upon blanket on her. Nothing I do warms her. I sit on the floor next to the bed and hold her hand while I tell her about our culture, all the leathoes I know who are related to me, and describe all our friends. I describe my childhood. When I finally sleep, it is with my head on her hand.

TWENTY-THREE

Samantha

TRAFFIC IS A NIGHTMARE. WHAT POSSESSED ME TO USE THE bridge? I never go to Kentucky. I must be crazy. Or maybe I know that no one will expect me to head this way.

While stopped in traffic, I shift into park and grab my map to consider alternate routes. Distracted by the map, I don't notice the men who surround my car. They smash in my driver side window and start yanking me through the opening. I kick and fight as much as I can. Why isn't anyone coming to help me? The drivers of the cars around me don't have phones out and aren't screaming for help. It's like they don't see me. My faith in humanity is officially lost.

I'm hauled to a van a few car lengths behind my car. As traffic starts to move, we pass my poor car. I don't have much fight left in me. Better to save it for one last go when an opportunity arrives. My captors are talking to each other, but I am preoccupied. My tolerance for handcuffs is pretty high, so I know I can strain against them without killing my wrists for a hot minute. But these dumbasses secured me to the seat belt. I slide my hands down the length and pull out as much of the belt as I can so I have as much slack as the van offers.

My captors are deep in conversation about what to do with me before they turn me over. My rage unleashes. I'm tired of being used by men! I work my way to the middle of the rear seat, between the driver and the passenger, and swing my arms together to hit them both. I catch the driver in the temple and the passenger in the left eye. The van swerves into the guardrail. The passenger window explodes upon impact.

I'd rather die than be used for sex even one more time. The driver rights the van. His correction slams me against the door. I try the handle, but the child lock is engaged. I ignore the passenger and go after the driver again. He loses control. We hit the rail, the windshield shatters, and the van goes into a roll, sending us into my watery grave. At least I'm the master of my own death. My terms. I'm the direct cause of it. I picture Laine's face as we fall. I feel sated by his love as we sink. I don't have a reason to fight. I know I'm handcuffed. I have no lung capacity to even attempt to hold my breath. I accept my fate.

I'm freezing. Colder than when I hit the water. There's pressure on my chest and someone on my lips. CPR? Well, I've done this dance a time or two before. At least they know how to do it properly, because I know a few ribs are broken.

Someone moves something off my face. My hair? My subconscious's piercing scream resonates in my brain and disappears. What the fuck? My mind is not only quiet but is now empty. I'm being lifted.

What if my captors escaped and are taking me to wherever they were taking me? I try to fight but I can't move even a finger. I should be freaking out, but my mind is blank.

Later, we are moving. In a car? I hear muffled voices. Someone is holding me tight. How long have we been in the car?

After a while, I realize we aren't moving anymore. I'm carried and then place something soft and comfortable. The comfort doesn't last long. I am picked up and placed in liquid. It's scorching, burning my body. The heat lasts for minutes, hours, days, I don't know. Eventually, fabric slides across my skin. Someone is dressing me. The settling of soft fabric atop my body startles me. Are they going to have their way with me? I try to leave my body before they hurt me but can't picture any place to go. Fabric is placed over me. Lots of it. I smell wood burning and listen to the crackle of a fire. My hand is being held. Someone kisses my face then my hand. Someone begins talking.

The blackness takes over, freezing me further.

THE DARKNESS IS WELCOMING. NOT EXACTLY HOME, BUT MAYBE like Grandma's house.

I am colder than ice. Frostbite must have set in. I still hear the fire and know I am covered by blankets, but this cold freezes my marrow. How long have I been like this? I try to move, again, without success.

My imagination conjures the only thing I have left to hold onto. Laine. His beautiful blue eyes and his strong hands holding onto me. His body is my personal asylum. I wish I had left him a note, to tell him how much I love him. I've never felt so much at home like I do when I am with him. He makes me feel cherished, not an object to be owned and controlled.

In a whoosh, the cold leaves my body. In its place, molten lava flows through me.

I'm in hell.

I knew I was beyond broken and my luck was horrible, but hell? Really? What did I do in my mortal life to deserve this judgment? I need a word with whomever is in charge. If I thought I was burning a minute ago, the temperature just went up. Someone is holding me. Their body is next to mine, cradling mine against theirs. The embrace is possessive and protective, not threatening. Only one man on this green earth makes me feel safe when he touches me. Laine! Laine must have me. Are we burning together? No! I left to keep him safe! I want to scream; I want to run away. He can't be here.

Then he whispers in my ear, clear as crystal, "Samantha, keep fighting. Come back to me. Please. I can't do this without you. Please come back."

I try opening my eyes. I still don't have control over my body. I want to breathe deep and cuddle as close as I can to him, but I can't do either. What if this is what I will be like from now on, locked in my own head, unable to move? What if they assume I'm dead and they bury me? The thought terrifies me.

I relive the choices that got me to this point. At least, I got to know true love before I left. Silently, I say my goodbyes to Laine and to my mother. I accept that I am dead. I haven't been breathing. I can't feel my heartbeat and I can't move.

I savor the time I have left until I officially depart this world.

TWENTY-FOUR

Laine

______

HER BODY HAS BEEN FROZEN FOR COUNTLESS DAYS. I'VE LOST track of time, since I haven't left her side except to use the restroom or take the world's quickest shower. I give her a sponge bath daily. I wash her hair and brush it until the fire dries it.

Nes came and helped me shave her legs and put lotion on her, something I never would have thought of doing. Nes even showed me how to braid her hair. Nes painted her nails. Actually, Sam has had a manicure and pedicure a few times daily. Nes has used every color ever made, at least twice.

Caleb comes over every night and reads aloud to us. I think he harbors an unfair amount of guilt. I know we only do what we are told, that we don't kill anyone, but the tasks still make our jobs hard at times. I know he feels responsible for killing my mate. If I were to take my life, he would be consumed by guilt.

My mother told me to be patient, and I am trying. We know Sam isn't out of the woods. According to our mother, Sam's only reached the second level of transformation. Nona is monitoring. She can't see what will become of Sam, but she can see into the oven, so to speak. I know she said she can't reach Samantha to talk to her, which makes this whole process worse. Samantha is alone. I don't know how to help or if I can. I do what I know comforts her. At night, I climb into bed and hold her close.

Yesterday, when her body went from freezing to fire in seconds, I shot out of bed. I pulled the covers off her as fast as I could, and I doused the fire in record time. I put cold compresses on her and patted her with cool water, but nothing helped.

Jacob is finally here. He had to sedate Samantha's stepfather to prevent the man from breaking his own hands to escape the restraints. As Jacob talks, he seems enthralled with Samantha.

"Look, Laine! Look! Watch!" his amazed excitement startles me.

I look in the direction he points. I am at a loss as to what I should be seeing. Then I see and can't stop watching. Every cut, every bruise, is slowly healing.

"We will be next door at Caleb's if you need us." Jacob tugs Caleb's arm.

I nod but don't shift my attention from the progression of Sam's healing. Within an hour, she looks better than new. She has color back.

I climb into bed and hold her. I'm not sure how she will be once she regains consciousness, but I am positive she will come out of this. I just hope she still wants me and that her personality isn't altered.

What if she wakes and she is no longer green to me? What if she sees she has options and prefers someone else?

TWENTY-FIVE

Samantha

Something inside me moves. Kind of like a flutter, but getting stronger. What is that?

I've been without a heartbeat for so long I don't recognize it, at first. Breathing burns my lungs. I'm being held. Laine has me, I can smell him. I inhale and snuggle closer. He seems tense. I can't bear the thought of him grief stricken.

"Get out of your head, Laine," I whisper against his chest.

His body goes rigid. He's bare chested.

I rest my hand next to my face, right atop his heart. A bolt of lightning seems to pass through my hand. Laine's body jerks and he shifts far enough away to look down at me. "Welcome back. You made it through. How do you feel?" His words wash over me. They're the best medicine ever.

"My hand hurts. I guess I should have waited a bit before moving."

He lifts my hand to his lips and kisses my palm. "I missed you."

I smile. "I missed you, too."

"Really? You missed me?" he sounds disbelieving. "Why did you leave the house, Sam?"

"I was trying to spare you from a fate worse than death. Ryan has disposed of anyone who has ever shown interest in me. He might bury you in a cement slab and drop you into the ocean. He's ruthless. I can't be in a world without you in it. Sometimes, death is better than living." I pause, waiting for a response. In the ensuing silence, I add, "Bad lapse in judgment."

He chuckles softly and lets out a sigh as if he's been holding his breath.

"How long have I been out?" I ask.

"Honestly, I've lost track of the days. If I had to guess, I would say a little over a week." He tightens his embrace. "I thought I had lost you."

The buzzing in my head is gone. So far, my breathing is fine. Have I transformed? Am I now like him? My head is quickly filling with questions. I try to arrange them into order of urgency. "What happened to my captors? What did they want?"

"We don't know yet. Caleb and I have a hunch that they are siquinters. We have them in a holding room with your sedated stepdad."

"Holding room? Where is that? Could be what?"

"Caleb's basement is escape proof and pretty uncomfortable. The toilet is a hole in the corner and that is it. No comfort. No blankets. Total deprivation. It's what they deserve. I can't remember the last time we actually needed to use it." He kisses my cheek. "The siquinter is another race that lives among humans. I'll tell you more about them when you get your strength back. Little bits of information at a time seem to help you remember."

"I'm not special. Why does it seem the whole world is after me?" I choke on a sob as I bury my face in his chest.

"Sam, you are special. I don't know why all these things are happening, but I will always protect you. Hopefully, after the dust settles, so will all this crazy shit." He strokes my hair.

"So, I'm done? I made it?" I am worried this is the calm before the storm.

"You will have one more task to perform in order to become a leathoes, an extricator." He plays with my hair as he speaks.

"What will I have to do?" I hold my breath, waiting for some horrible, gruesome task.

"You will have to extricate. Your first extrication will be a sort of test to see if you are capable and if you are strong enough for this."

"What happens if I fail or can't?"

"I don't know. We've never dealt with a half human before."

TWENTY-SIX

Laine

——————

She's here! She made it through her transformation. I am elated. My heart can beat again. She's different, but still the same. She feels stronger. She looks healthier. She looks radiant. "Do you want anything, Samantha?" She must be starving.

She shifts to sit up. Despite being immobile for over nine days, she is graceful. She doesn't require my assistance, though I stay close in case she does. She stands, arms slightly extended, as if making sure she can balance. Without drawing attention to my shift, I take up a position behind her in case she stumbles. Samantha turns and bends down to make the bed.

"You don't need to do that, Love. I will do it after I make you something to eat." I step closer and pull her to me, my lips finding hers. Sam wraps her arms around my neck. I scoop her up but pause. She really needs food.

Sam kisses my neck. "Take me upstairs, Laine. Please. I will eat in a bit."

I've missed her and I want her now, but I don't want to hurt her. She needs to eat and drink. She grabs my hair and finds my lips again. I should stop this. I need to take care of her.

"Now, Laine," she demands against my lips.

I growl and set off for the stairs. I take her to my room—our room—to what is now forever our bed. I lay her down on my side and climb in with her. She sits up so she can take off her tank top. As she tosses it aside, I slide my hands into her long, soft curls. I deepen the kiss. I can't get enough of her. Her fingers find the button on my jeans and gets it undone. I get out of bed long enough to shove my jeans and boxers off. I stop on my way back into bed.

"Do you want me to use something?"

"Huh? Like toys or something?"

I laugh a little. "No, like protection. You've changed. Things are different now."

She searches my eyes. I can see her brain working. As much as I want her, I want her to call all the shots, for now.

"No."

It's the only word I need to hear. I reach down and slide her cotton shorts off. While she was unconscious, I didn't bother putting underwear or a bra on her, I didn't see the point with how her temperature kept changing. I cover her with my body, not bothering with covers. I start at her lips and kiss my way to her breast. I play with the one as I lick and nip at the other. After spending some time there, I trail kisses down her ribs, stomach, and hips. I look up to gauge her reaction. She looks happy, so I move my hand to test her. She's so ready for me.

I didn't get to go slow last time and now I just wanted to savor that she is here, that she's made it so far. My fingers slip into her as my thumb presses her clit. Sam arches off the bed. She turns her head and moans as I take my time. I keep a steady rhythm, and finally remove my thumb to lean down and put my tongue there instead. I lick and suck until she calls my name and tenses. I still my fingers until she is back on Earth.

Retracing my path, I kiss my way to her lips and remove my hand. Using my knees, I make room for my body. I kiss her neck as I enter her slowly. She wraps her legs around me and tries to make me sheath myself faster but I pull my hips away.

"Please. Laine, please. Take me," she says breathlessly.

I lick her neck and chuckle as I shake my head. We might not be mated yet, but I will treat this as if it were our mating night. Slowly, I lower myself completely into her. She was made just for me. She's perfect. I don't move yet. I take her lips with mine again and she grips my shoulders. Sam threads her left hand into my hair, while mapping out every part of my mouth with hers. Before this, we hadn't spent much time exploring and learning each other. I think quick sex is what she is used to or what she is comfortable with, but I want her to enjoy everything in our lives, starting with our sex life. She trusts me, and I know what signs of trouble to watch for. I pull back slowly until I'm almost out, then slide back in quick and hard. She moans against me. I continue this pattern for a few more strokes until I can wait no longer. I pull Sam close and roll without breaking our contact until she is on top of me.

She breaks away and sits up. She braces herself with one hand on my shoulder and grabs my hand with the other. She is concentrating hard, finding what makes her feel best. She pulls up and slams back down on me. It is an amazing feeling. After doing that a few times, she removes her hand from my shoulder, leans back, and reaches for my thigh to steady herself. Moving her hips with purpose, she is the most beautiful woman I have ever seen. I press my thumb to her clit, sending her over the edge. She collapses onto my chest as I find my own release.

As I come back from my high, I pull the blanket over us. I want to stay inside her as long as I can. I don't want to break the contact. Her eyes are still closed and she hasn't moved, but I know she isn't scared.

"I love you, Laine," she whispers against my chest, her hand resting on my heart.

"I love you more." I hug her. Her body relaxes into sleep. I want to join her but decide to be responsible and move her so she is laying on the bed.

I get up and make sure she is warm and cozy. I know I could ask David to make us a meal, but I want to feed her. I want to take care of her.

The kitchen is vacant when I get there.

"Would you like me to make you and Ms. Harris something to eat, sir?" David asks from the doorway.

"No, I got it, thanks, David. I appreciate it. Take the rest of the day off. Really. I don't anticipate us needing much." I like David. He is a good friend and has been serving me for centuries.

I quickly realize I don't know what my mate likes to eat. Shaking my head at myself, I think back over my observations of her. She isn't a picky eater.

I remember her saying that chicken and dumplings is her favorite, but I don't have a clue how to make that. Tuna. She ate a lot of tuna. I whip up some tuna salad and locate the crackers. I grab a can of soda on my way back up the stairs to her—to *our* —room.

TWENTY-SEVEN

Samantha

I KNOW I AM SAFE IN LAINE'S ROOM AS I FALL ASLEEP. I DON'T
know how long I sleep, but I wake up fast when I don't feel him
near me.

"I'm here. It's okay. I made you something to eat," he says as he
closes the door and walks over with a bowl, crackers, and a Coke.

If I didn't love this man before, I love him now. He knows me
so well.

He sets the food on the nightstand.

I smile at him as he sits on the bed beside me. "You are going
to allow me to eat in your bed? Crackers get all over."

"First of all, this is our bed, and you can do anything you want
in it. Why would it matter if some crumbs get in the bed?" Laine
laughs as he asks. "Linen can be cleaned or replaced."

My past is fuzzy, but I do remember why crackers should not
be eaten in bed. Once, when I had the flu, I had crackers in bed
one night with my soup. Ryan's rage was terrifying. He tossed my
tray off the bed. The food hit the wall. He grabbed me out of bed
and shoved me to the floor. He backhanded me when I started to
speak. He backhanded me again when I started to cry.

My mind fades to black.

"Sam!"

My eyes refocus on Laine. I was looking at him when the memory came. His face is white, like he has seen a ghost.

"I'm sorry." I shake my head to clear it. "I don't know what that was."

"I saw everything."

"What?"

"While you were looking at me, when the memory came to you, I saw it. As if it was a movie playing between us."

"No," I whisper. "That's not possible."

"The crackers triggered the memory, didn't they? Or was it me saying you could eat in bed?"

"I don't know. It might not be a true memory. Sometimes that happens." I hope my imagination is wicked and puts most of these thoughts there on its own accord. No one has such bad luck. Do they?

"Sam, try to remember something else. Concentrate. Look at me and remember something. Anything."

I search back for something nice. I recall the child I helped at the playground. I cradle him and kiss his forehead and tell him everything is okay. I hold him until his mother comes to get him.

My memory transforms into my own mother kissing my head while I lay in a hospital bed. Tears stream down my face. I think I'm thirteen or so. She quickly exits the room as Ryan enters. He closes the door and then steps closer to me. The threat remains unspoken. It is always the same one. He will hurt my mother, maybe kill her, and she is all I have. I turn my face away from him as the tears keep flowing. He pulls the blanket off me and pushes the hospital gown up. He already has what he needs out of his pants, ready... My mind goes blank.

Tears are streaming down my face now. Laine's lips are on mine, gentle but strong. This man, who somehow can see my past, who knows how broken I am, still wants me, loves me. I don't deserve him.

I open my eyes as he pulls away. Tears wet his cheeks. Are they mine or his? I reach to wipe away the moisture there. I try to recall the end of what I had just shown him, but it's gone. Again, I concentrate and try to recall the memory from the kiss my mother gave me. The kiss comes back. When she leaves the room, my head goes blank. My quick inhale of breath makes Laine's eyes snap to mine.

"What's wrong, Sam?"

"It's gone. There is nothing there. I can't recall the memory past my mother leaving the room."

"Try another one. Maybe it's just too old for you to hold onto."

I scan the room. I don't know what I am looking for. Nothing here holds any bad memories. Then my eyes jerk to Laine's, and I am transported to the day Ryan came to pick me up from here. I tense. I know he can't get to me again, but the memory's too recent. He's at the door. I need to keep Laine safe. I rush to calm the monster at the door. To placate him until he is away from Laine.

I remember the pain of my finger getting broken, him forcing himself down my throat. The pain from the bruising that caused. Him making me clean up. Trying to keep my soda down as he touches me under the table. Him telling me about the hotel reservation. His threat to make Laine disappear. His admitting to somehow causing the accident that killed Nick. The smile on his face as I came out of the stall, the sharp pain in my head as I hit the floor. The pain from him violating me, again.

My mind goes blank.

Laine is kissing me again. He doesn't stop. He lifts me so I am sitting on his lap. He is the best medicine I have ever had. He stops and pulls away a little to look at me. His strong arms hold me in place.

"Try to relive that memory," he says softly.

I tremble at the request. I don't want to go back there. His eyes hold mine as he strokes and plays with my hair, his embrace never loosening.

A shaky breath, and I do as he asks. The memory came to me easily a moment ago. So much trauma was likely to stick with me forever. While still looking at Laine, my gaze gets lost in the memory. It is hazy. Incomplete. Like a burning camera reel. The events aren't totally gone, but they're spotty. Only a few pieces really stand out.

Laine's lips press mine. Now his kiss has demand in it. I let him take over, to take my mind far away from its dark thoughts.

When he pulls away, I kiss under his ear and lick his neck. I have no idea if my transformation upped my libido or if Laine sparks such passion. I'm inclined to think it has a lot to do with Laine and some to do with the other. I smile when his boxers prove no match for his need. I open my legs to accommodate him, closing my eyes to focus on the sensations. His hands slide up my back and he holds onto my shoulders. There is nothing soft or slow about this. He just knows what I need, when I need it. The second time is over as quick as it started. Both of us are breathless. I smile as I nuzzle his neck.

"Sam?"

"Hmmmm?"

"Try to remember that last one again."

I slowly bring my face up to look at him. My confusion and pain must be evident.

"Please, Baby. I have a theory. I know it is painful, I don't want you to hurt anymore. Trust me. Please?"

With a heavy sigh, I watch him and try to recall the hell I went through less than two weeks ago. Ryan came to the house to see me. What happened next can be summed up in one sentence, but no picture comes to mind. The shock that washes over me makes me shiver.

"What have you done?" I whisper to my mate, as he holds me and watches.

"I don't know. I just didn't want you to experience pain or have those horrible thoughts anymore. I'm sharing the burden, sort of."

"My memories are now in your head?"

"No."

"I'm lost."

"Mates can share the burdens of anything that happens in their lives. Anything you go through, I can take the pain from you if it's too much, and vice versa. Since I wasn't there for your childhood trauma, I can take the pain or memory and make it disappear. Since I was around for the latest attack, I can't completely erase it, but I tried to do as much as I could. Did it help at all?"

"How do you know so much about mates?"

He shrugs. "It's common knowledge for us. I just didn't know how exactly it works or how your memories would look afterward. I just went with the flow. If I concentrate, I can handle the older memories with minimal effort. The worse of your memories demand a physical effort to replace the bad with something good."

"They are gone."

His eyes widen. "Gone? Like totally gone?"

"The only thing I remember is my mother kissing my forehead, then nothing. And the other can be summed up in one sentence in my mind, but no visual reminders."

"I guess it works on instinct. No one has ever told me how to take the pain from my mate. In all honesty, I never thought I would have a mate. My sister and mother have been trying to find someone for me for over a century."

"Why?"

"They want our line to continue. We are losing numbers. Which is bad for humans and leathoes."

"Why didn't you want a mate?"

"We can procreate with anyone who isn't mated, but I didn't

want to settle. I wasn't ready to have children, so I avoided social engagements." He pauses to look at me. "Then I started following you, as part of my assignment. You are an interesting person in a mundane world. We have so much in common. But you had a fiancé and I didn't want to come between that. Then when he died, you were so closed off. But you never were sad over it, you were lonely. From the first night I started following you, your aura had streaks of green. I thought it was from the yellow and blue mixing, but they got darker as I kept on task. Then when I was at your house, I noticed more green than usual. After we had sex the first time, the green eclipsed all other colors.

"I was so scared when I pulled you from the van. I thought I didn't get to you in time and you were dead. Then when you began your transformation, I was terrified you wouldn't have any green to your aura; that you weren't actually meant for me."

"Can you see my aura, now that I am no longer human?"

TWENTY-EIGHT

Laine

____

"To be honest, I've been too afraid to check."

She makes her way to my closet. She comes out wearing one of my shirts and goes to lay on her side of the bed.

"Love, you need to eat. It would comfort me to know you aren't starving." I retrieve the food from the nightstand.

"Thank you."

We sit in silence as she eats.

My thoughts wander. I transferred her pain. That only happens between mates, right? I should check her for an aura. Doing so would save me from all this worry.

"Laine?" Her brow is furrowed as she tries to get my attention.

"Sorry. Got lost for a second. What do you need?"

Sam leans toward me and places her lips on mine. For reassurance, I'm sure, but she gets my full attention. She pulls away and lays down.

I wasn't ready for our contact to end so quickly.

"Laine, what happens if you mate with someone who isn't… what? Destined?"

"It's not done. You can have kids with unmated leathoes, that is pretty normal. But once your designated mate is revealed to you, that bond can't be broken. It's too powerful."

"Can you not read my emotions now that I've transformed?" she asks drowsily.

"No idea. It wasn't easy when you were human because you could hide it, which you did often." I chuckle a little.

"How do you check an aura?"

"On a human, you just need to concentrate on them."

"Hmmmmm." She falls asleep. She looks so peaceful. I concentrate on her. I hold my breath while I wait to see if I can see her aura. My heart drops. There's nothing.

Sam rolls onto her side and whispers my name. It's a direct hit on my heart. I lay next to her and pull her close. Might as well savor her company while I can. Since she isn't mine to claim anymore, I will have to relinquish her soon.

I don't know how much time has passed, but something tickles my arm. Sam is trailing her fingers up and down my bicept. I open my eyes and look at her.

She flashes a coy smile.

My heart is too broken to return a genuine smile.

Her hand instantly stops. "What's wrong?"

I close my eyes and struggle with words. "You don't have an aura anymore. I can't see anything."

"Okay. So, what does that mean?"

"It means we can't be mated, Sam."

Her smile dies.

Brown cascades in a swirl around her. I stare in shock upon seeing an aura around a leathoes. The only aura we see is on our mate. My heart hurts seeing her emotional aura without the green.

Unshed tears brim in her eyes.

Blue streaks through the brown. She closes her eyes and the tears fall. Rays of gray shoot through the blue and brown. I reach for her face and wipe away the tears. She opens her eyes. Pink laces through her colors. She leans into my touch and the colors vanish as fast as they came.

"If we were still in my world," she whispers, "I could marry whoever I loved, not who would make the best offspring."

"We can stay together until you find your mate, Sam."

The pain is palpable as Sam gets up and goes into the bathroom. She turns on the shower.

I'm realizing this is her go-to move when she needs space and time to think.

'Son, what did I tell you about patience? Do you not trust your mother? We will be by later to discuss with Sam how her next stage will go. Your assignment is complete. Your tasks will resume today.'

'Yes, Mother. I understand.'

The water is turned off. Sam opens the door, dressed in jean shorts and purple tank top. She walks around the room gathering her things, ignoring me.

"What are you doing?"

"I'm moving back into the other room. Clearly, my transformation did not improve the bad luck that shadows me. If I have a shit draw of cards for this almost-immortal life, I will find a way to die." With that, she leaves my room.

I am too shocked to respond before the door shuts.

I walk to Sam's door and knock. I know she won't answer, but I have to try. "Sam, the mothers are coming later to talk with you."

"Thank you, Laine."

TWENTY-NINE

Samantha

———————

I PUT AWAY THE THINGS I HAVE COLLECTED FROM LAINE'S ROOM. After everything is in its proper place, I decide to change into something more suitable for a meeting with the mothers.

Vanessa filled my closet while I lay dying. Reminding myself to thank her, I pull on a new pair of jeans, a pink, low-cut tank top, and a gray see-through cover up with little pink roses on it. I finish the outfit with my black flats and head downstairs. My hair is down and wild, but taming my hair is the last thing on my mind.

Fresh air. Yep. I need to get out of the house and take a walk.

Laine's car is gone when I get outside. I head toward the wooded area at the back of the house. If I don't take care, I can easily get lost, but at this point, I really don't care. My anger is back with a vengeance. I'm tired of life taking from me. It isn't ever something I can actually control.

I run deep into the trees. Finally, I stop at a fallen oak to catch my breath. My breathing. How long have I been without my meds? I test myself. I breathe in and hold my breath. The panic doesn't come. While experimenting with my new-found lung capacity, I don't see my mother approach.

"Samantha?" she asks cautiously.

I turn toward her, fury still my only emotion. I close my eyes as I try to reign in my temper.

"Child, whatever is the matter?"

I visualize my last few minutes with Laine. When I open my eyes, my mother nods.

"You need to have patience. Laine has been told the same. Your human form has died, but your human soul hasn't left your body. Your soul can leave at any time, but it hasn't. Mentally, your final transition test will not be easy. You need to prepare. As soon as your human soul leaves, things will be easier for you."

"When will my last test come?"

"I don't have an exact time, but soon."

"Do you know what I will have to do?"

"Yes. That is why I am here. To guide you on how to complete your first task."

Nona extends her hand. I go to her and take it. She leads me deeper into the forest. We walk in silence until we come to a clearing. A lake fills the middle of the field. On the far right, close to the lake, is a stone bench. Releasing my hand, my mother walks over to the smooth, cold stone and sits. She stares across the lake, not really focused on anything, probably waiting for me to join her.

With a heavy sigh, I follow her path to the bench and sit.

I lose track of how long we sit there. It's long enough for my rage to dissipate.

Finally, I turn to my mother. Her eyes are closed. I don't know what I am supposed to do. "Mother, aren't you supposed to show me what I need to do?"

My question hangs in the air.

Her eyes remain closed.

I hear people approach. I stand, ready to run or fight. I might not be human now, but I am not about to let my guard down. The area around the bench soon fills with people I recognize. Vanessa smiles as she stops a few feet away. Jacob joins her, his face anxious. The woman named Elvia that I met briefly a few times joins them, beautiful as always. Lotti and Morta enter the clearing, walking hand-in-hand, but they stay farthest away. My heart sinks that I don't see Laine. My gaze returns to my mother. Her eyes are open and staring across the lake. Tears stream down her face, but her gaze is hard. I follow her gaze.

The air leaves my lungs. The world falls away. Hatred courses through me. Laine and Caleb approach from the far side of the lake, dragging my tormentor between them. Part of me is shocked that I'm not scared or threatened, that I don't feel the need to run. Instead, my all-consuming rage makes me fear that I will harm innocent people when it is unleashed.

As the men get closer, my blood boils to ash in my veins.

THIRTY

Laine

____

I HATED LEAVING SAM EARLIER TO GO DO MY THREE TASKS, BUT I needed to get those out of the way as fast as I could. During the drive back to the manor, I'm alone with my thoughts. My heart hurts. I have never resented being an Elite or leathoes, so today is a first for me.

'Laine, are you done with today's tasks?' my mother asks.

'I just got done. Is everything okay?'

'I need you and Caleb to meet me.' Her voice leaves my head.

I pull out my phone and shoot a text to my brother. *Where are we meeting?*

My place, I guess.

Making the next right, I head to my brother's house. Less than twenty minutes later, I turn into his drive, park, and leave the car.

Caleb and I never knock. We practically live at each other's homes. I walk in. He's pacing in the living room. He must read the curiosity on my face because he shrugs and continues pacing. I join him, having nothing else to do. We don't have long to wait. Our mother appears in the doorway.

"Boys, I need you to do as I ask for the next hour or so."

"Of course, Mother," Caleb says.

"Always," I agree.

"My sister is on her way. I have a few questions for her, and I need you to remain silent but vigilant. Is that clear?" She looks at each of us in turn.

We both nod once. She walks to Caleb's front door and opens it. Our mother's estranged sister walks into the house. Caleb and I share a sideways glance.

"Thank you for coming, Veda. I wouldn't have asked if I didn't have to. I know how busy you are." My mother sounds sincere.

"Think nothing of it, sister. My quarrel is not with you. I just prefer my solitude. My temper gets the best of me too often." The young woman chuckles. She appears to be around twenty years old and looks nothing like the mothers. Her bronzed skin doesn't come from the sun. Her braided black hair hangs in a thick rope that brushes her waist. A blue ribbon is tied to the end of it. She wears dark blue, hip-hugging jeans with a black leather belt. Her T-shirt hangs off one shoulder and has a local band branded on the front. She's short and curvy, but once I really look at her, I see danger oozing from every pore. A shiver runs down my spine.

Veda turns to Caleb. "Take me to them. Let me put your mind at ease."

He looks at our mother for clarification. "I asked Veda to tell us if the men in your hold are hers or not." Silently she adds, 'We need to figure out if we have to dispose of them.'

Caleb nods, turns, and leads us toward his basement.

When he opens the door, the only light spilling into the basement comes from the kitchen light behind us. Caleb quickly rectifies that. As the lights come on, the prisoners attempt to cover their eyes. Their restraints make that an impossible feat.

Their cell is pungent. Half of his basement looks like a jail you'd find in Mayberry. When we bought this place and remodeled, I wondered if he had watched too many Andy Griffith reruns.

Caleb unlocks the barred door and Veda sweeps into the cell.

The men cower. No one speaks as she looks them over. Ryan keeps his head down, but he is alert. The sedation wore off hours ago. "This one, he will be mine, but not quite yet." She trails the nail of her index finger down Ryan's bruised cheek. She strolls to the next prisoner. She gets close to him. He towers over her by more than a couple of feet but keeps his head down. She grabs his chin to force his head up. He doesn't resist.

"What are you?" her voice is deceptively sweet, but to a trained ear, it contains authority and malice.

He doesn't answer. I expect her to resort to violence to make him answer, but instead she releases his chin and caresses his cheek. He leans into her touch, but still he does not speak.

"Ah, my sister, you have here three siquinter. Perhaps you can let them stay longer. They may prove useful later."

"Caleb, if you would, Son, please keep these three until we tell you otherwise."

Caleb nods.

"Your sons are the strong, silent types, Morta. Do they possess tongues? Can they not speak?"

"They can, they just have no reason to."

Veda studies Morta for a second then looks at Caleb. She takes her gaze off him to turn her attention to me. She appraises me for a long moment, then a slow smile creeps across her face.

"Oh Laine, you are about to have one hell of a ride," she says with a mix of glee and threat.

"Enough, Sister, we will meet you shortly."

I expect Veda to get pissed off, but she doesn't. She slowly turns to my mother, nods, leaves the cell, and heads up the stairs.

"I am proud of you both," Morta says. "Now, we have much to do. You both need to get the human presentable enough to go home. You promised to do as I ask. Please trust me." She meets my dumbfounded stare. "Laine, trust your mother. I have never done anything to hurt you."

I bow my head. Part of me feels shame, but mostly I feel

defeated. I want to kill him. I don't want him to walk free, ever again.

Caleb presses my shoulder.

I close my eyes in pain. When I open them, I enter the cell with my brother to do as we were asked.

I halt before Ryran. "If you so much as think about fighting or trying to escape our hold, we will kill you," I growl at the disgusting human. "Do you understand?"

His glaring gaze searches mine. He neither nods nor replies.

Caleb and I each grip one of Ryan's arms then wave a hand over a wrist cuff. Ryan's chains fall away. I'm prepared for Ryan's hard jerk, and Caleb maintains his grip. With some difficulty, we get Ryan's arms over our shoulders and force him to walk in the direction we want him to go.

"Laine, we're going to the lake. Do not change his will and try not to drag him. Take your time, we're not in a race." She starts up the stairs, but pauses and says over her shoulder, "I will see you there in a bit."

It is not an easy task to get the uncooperative, heavy, worthless human where we need him to go, but Caleb and I manage.

Finally, we emerge from the trees that border the lake. Why are so many people here? We stop and look at each other, mirroring each other's shock and confusion.

Caleb and I march Ryan around the lake to join the group. I feel Samantha's aura before I see her. When I finally spot her, she appears to be on fire. The flames are red and yellow. As we get closer and she sees us holding onto her personal devil, she ignites into a blue inferno.

Caleb staggers. "Holy fuck."

I look at him. "You see it, too?"

"I see it, I feel it..." He holds out his arm. The hairs are standing up and he has goosebumps.

"How are we able to see her aura?"

"Brother, I'm not trying to, she is projecting that. If you have seen it since I extricated her, then her human soul hasn't left her."

"If I didn't know her history, hadn't seen her memories… hadn't known about the shit this thing has done to her, I would almost feel sorry for him."

"You've seen her memories? How is that possible?"

"I shared her pain. I saw what she lived through and what is stuck in her head." I keep walking. We have almost reached them. The temperature gets colder the closer we get, despite Samantha's fire. We stop twenty feet from Samantha.

'Let him go,' Morta silently instructs us. We drop him immediately. He falls to his hands and knees. 'Back away and do not interfere.' She gives me a hard stare.

I bow my head, but my gaze snaps to Samantha.

'Nona will hide us all from the human's sight, so do not touch him or Samantha. Do not speak. This is her test. If you interfere, she will die, Laine.' My mother's stare bores into me, but I don't look away from Sam.

THIRTY-ONE

Samantha

NONA SMILES AT ME. 'THIS IS YOUR LAST TEST, MY DAUGHTER,' SHE says in my head 'He will not be able to see anyone but you. I'm sure Laine told you, he will appear as a solid color to you. Whatever your favorite color is, he will be that. You are to touch him and complete the extrication for your transformation to be complete. If you fail, I will not be able to help you. I cannot see the outcome. Just know, I love you very much. I have faith in you.'

I'm standing with my feet apart. I don't know when that happened. Probably when I saw Laine. I can't think about that right now. My rage is consuming. Electricity has replaced all the blood in my body. I close my eyes to collect my thoughts. Wrong move. Ryan might have been a captive for a couple of weeks, but he is still ruthless. He is up and in front of me in seconds. I open my eyes, just as the back of his hand strikes my face. I slowly turn my face back toward him. I'm so much more now. I'm stronger in all aspects.

"You whore. You think he will protect you and want to keep you? I told you, Sammy, I don't share. I'm going to kill him in front of you, but not before I force him to watch us first."

His sneer tips me over the edge. I grab his throat. I am smaller than him, but that makes the thrill that much better. Horror is all that shows on his face. I tilt my head to contemplate what exactly I want to do. It wouldn't take much to kill him.

No! I want him to suffer. Remembering that this is my test causes me to pause. Why should I extricate him? He deserves to be forced to relive his last moments for eternity, and for me to do the honors. His fear is palpable as I slowly smile.

'Samantha, sometimes death is worse. If you kill him before his time, it could mess up another innocent human's fate. If you don't extricate him, he can kill you after his death. Don't give him that power,' Nona pleads. 'Trust in the process. The rewards outweigh all the bad. I promise.' My eyes whip to hers. She appears pained by the entire encounter.

I turn back to Ryan and speak low, "You will leave here. You will never touch me, contact me, or harass me ever again. Laine doesn't share. If you test my threat, I will kill you. I am going to release you. I dare you to touch me again." My fury is getting hard to control.

I concentrate on loosening my grip on his throat. Finally, my hand unwillingly complies. Before he can run or come at me, I touch his arm, concentrating, imagining my touch is a knife opening his body at that spot. He shivers and his arm erupts in goosebumps.

"Run. Get out of my sight," I say through gritted teeth.

Ryan falls to the ground, one hand on his knee, the other on the ground. He is trying to gauge if I am serious. I step closer, malevolence thick in the air between us. He makes the right choice. He leaps up and takes off through the woods without looking back. As quickly as my loathing and anger flared, they disappear. I close my eyes and take a deep, cleansing breath.

THIRTY-TWO

Laine

———————

THE WIND IS KNOCKED OUT OF ME AS I WATCH SAMANTHA complete her final challenge. Her eyes are closed, her anger gone. So is the blue fire. In its place is the most vibrant, radiant green I have ever seen. No more yellow. Death can't touch her now that she is part of his team. My heart starts to race. I want to run to her, but I have not been given permission to move.

"Very good, Samantha. You've completed your transition. How do you feel?" Nona asks, worry laced through the pride in her voice.

"Mother, may I have some time to myself? I need to process all of this." Sam glances sideways at her mother. Nona gives a small smile and nod.

Sam takes off toward the path Caleb and I used earlier. Not quite the same route Ryan took moments earlier. She's running. I want to go after her. What if she changes her mind and goes after Ryan? What if he finds and hurts her? I don't know if she has her meds with her. What if she gets into trouble?

My mother stands with her back to me. 'You may go after her,' she says without turning.

I take off. I run as fast as I can. Sam isn't in my line of vision. I slow so I can scan my surroundings. Can I sense her if we aren't mated? I stumble to a stop, panting, and close my eyes. I visualize Sam and experience a jolt as my body reacts. My heart is telling me to go left, so I do. I walk quickly, but slow as the vegetation becomes dense. I hear her but I don't see her. Then I do. She's kneeling on the ground, hunched over, her hands covering her face as she sobs. Shouldn't she feel liberated? I search for her emotions. Gray now laces through the emerald.

Without hesitation, I go to her, scoop her off the ground, and cradle her. She tenses, and brown joins the swirl of colors around her. Her arms tentatively encircle my neck. She buries her face against my neck and sobs wrack her body. My embrace tightens as I carry her toward the manor. I remain quiet. She will talk when she's ready.

She weeps the entire twenty-minute walk back home. I would think that much crying would exhaust a person, but Sam doesn't seem to be anywhere near done. She never lets up. My shirt is soaked. I war with myself on what I should do. She is really starting to worry me.

'She's been through a lot today. My daughter is partly in shock, but mostly in mourning. Not for the scum and his worthless life, but she has lost a great deal. She needs time to realize what she has gained. Guide her. Have patience. Though you might not understand her feelings, try to empathize.' Nona's voice resonates long after the last words are spoken.

"Sam, Love, it's going to be okay. I got you," I whisper as I carry her up to our room. I bypass the bed and head straight for the bathroom. "I'm going to run you a bath, okay?"

She nods against my shoulder. I set her on the counter to turn on the water. Her head is down and she's still crying. I frame her face with my hands and use my thumbs to wipe away the tears. I tip her head up and kiss her eyes and cheek. I hesitate to kiss her lips. Finally, she opens her eyes and looks at me. The color of her irises puts an evergreen forest to shame. Her anguish is palpable.

"Would you prefer to be alone?"

She searches my face. She seems lost and frail, completely opposite from the woman on fire at the lake. I take a half step back and drop my hands from her face.

"No," she says so softly I almost don't hear her.

I'm frozen in place. I don't know what to do for her. I turn around and turn off the water. Turning back, I decide to help her into the tub. I start to pull off her cover-up. Her eyes don't leave mine. She slowly starts to help me undress her. Soon, she is naked, but she doesn't move. I pick her up and place her in the tub. She brings her knees up, lays her head on them, and hugs her legs, like she might shatter at any second. I grab a loofah and start to wash her. I don't bother washing her hair, I know she just washed it a few hours ago. The ends are wet because her hair is so long. I step out of the bathroom for a second to grab a towel and one of my shirts. After the tub drains, I pick her up with the towel, carry her into the bedroom, and place her on the bed. Sam still isn't talking, and it hurts to see her in this state.

I slip one of my clean shirts over her head and she reaches for the sleeve openings. I use the towel to dry the ends of her hair and her legs. She scoots toward the headboard and arranges the blankets as she lays down. I climb in and caress her face. She closes her eyes and the room temperature plummets.

"Sam, talk to me. Please. I'm so worried about you. Let me in."

She glances at me before gazing at the comforter. "I'm dead. I died. The last human moment I had was touching the one person I hate most in the world. I could forgive myself more if the touch had killed the bastard, but I wasn't allowed. I didn't get to reach one of my goals while I was alive. I don't know where I belong or who I belong with. I've gone numb, I'm too cold and dead inside. I thought I was strong after the excruciating pain I experienced while my body died. I felt powerful when I held Ryan by the throat. Even though I burned with rage, I was frozen inside. I'm surrounded by people, and I'm alone. I am healed completely but I am more broken than ever."

"Sam, look at me."

She resists, but only for a moment.

"What do you see? Concentrate. Try to feel me, to sense me in your mind."

Her eyes strain with concentration but soften quickly. "Laine, is this how you see me?"

"How do you see me, Love?"

"You have a slight haze around you. If you have this all the time, I might need Tylenol. The haze is off putting. Like when my eyes get tired from looking at a computer too long."

"Do you see colors in the haze?"

She studies me as she laughs softly. The laughter stops abruptly.

"I think while you were in the middle of transition, things got a little mixed up. You still had a human soul, but you were no longer human. I couldn't see you as a mate because you were in between this world and the next." I smile broadly, waiting for her to catch up to what I'm saying. "Sam, did you hear me? You are my destiny."

"Can you still see what I feel?"

A second passes. "Sometimes. It's like it was before, but you have an amazing way of projecting your emotions. It's terrifying and awe inspiring. I think it's a mix of you being human for so long and being an elite."

"If I couldn't be your mate, I would have left to live with the sisters."

I'm confused. "We still could have lived together. We could have had kids and—"

Sam cuts me off, "Until your true mate came along and you loved her more. It would have killed me."

"We never have to consider the 'what ifs,' ever again." I pull her close. "Now we can spend forever together. Losing your humanity isn't such a bad thing, Love."

She turns her head and meets my gaze. I am almost blinded by her bright emerald green tipped with white. Her lips brush mine.

"Laine?"

"What?"

"I love you." Her mouth is soft against my mouth as she speaks.

"I love you more." Her kiss sears me, but I want everything she gives.

We are interrupted by my phone's jingle. It's my brother.

"Can you come over to my place?" Caleb asks.

"I have Samantha with me. Do you want me to leave her here?" I frown at the thought of letting Sam out of my sight.

"No, bring her."

"Sam," I say tentatively, "we have to run to Caleb's."

Without looking at me, she nods.

I reach for her hand. I expect her fingers to be cold, but they are warm.

We throw on clothes then head hand in hand to the car.

Caleb welcomes us at the door. His concerned regard of Sam mirrors my own. Finally, his eyes lock on mine and I give a slight cautionary shake of my head. I'm at a loss on what to do to make her feel better.

As Caleb and I carry on a silent conversation that only twins can, Sam walks ahead of us to explore.

"Stop watching me as if I'm about to break," she calls back. "I have a lot to process. Please, bear with me. I would say I'm only human, but that term no longer applies to me." She wanders around the living room, an expression of deep concentration on her face.

THIRTY-THREE

Samantha

 On my second loop of the living room, Lotti walks through the door. With purposeful strides, she reaches me in seconds. "I realize you have had a lot to deal with and for that I am sorry. My reason for coming today is to discuss your captives." She pauses and looks at the twins. "As you both know, Veda identified those three as siquinters. Now, we need to decide what to do with them. I would like to try to get information from them, but it might be risky."

"What is a siquinter?" This new world is exhausting.

Lotti offers a wane smile. "Luck and Opportunity, who are beings like my sisters and me, created a race of fairies and pixies. Not like the ones who sprinkle dust and help you fly. Siquinter are much more brutish. Perhaps I should show you what I mean." Lotti extends her hand and gestures for me to walk ahead of her. Caleb leads the way.

As we enter a basement, warning bells sound in my head and my stomach becomes queasy. When I can look away from the jail-like cells, I blink in shock to see a completely normal rec room, complete with an impressive bar and pool table. People are clustered about a dart board and pinball machine in the far corner.

"Laine," Lotti says, "you may make the introductions so we can proceed."

The players stop what they are doing and advance. I back away until my shoulders hit the wall. Laine enters my line of vision and reaches for my face. "No one here is going to hurt you, I promise. Come meet the rest of our unit." He steps aside.

A small woman extends her hand. "I'm Isadora. I'm so happy to finally meet you!" She has a smoker's voice, but the slight grate is reassuringly familiar. She's much shorter than me, with shoulder-length, gray hair. Her plump form reminds me of my grandmother, which causes a stab of pain in my heart.

"Hi, happy to meet you, too," is all I can choke out as I try to reign in the rush of loss for my grandmother.

A woman I am familiar with comes forward, accompanied by two women. Elvia has an infectious smile. "Hey, Sam. These are my adopted sisters." She gestures left. "This is Lucinda." The older woman wears heavy makeup and her blonde hair cascades from a high ponytail. She gives me a genuine smile, which I return. "And this is Katerina. We all call her 'Kat.'"

Kat starts toward me, her hand extended. Her blonde hair has a red tint and falls past her shoulders.

I notice that the men in the room stand stock still, which makes me uneasy. Laine must have noticed their odd behavior, too. Tension rolls off him in waves. I look at him. He's staring down his colleagues like they are sworn enemies.

"Um…Lotti? We might have a problem here." Thankfully, my voice doesn't contain any of the fear I feel.

"Boys!" Lotti barks out the single word as if it were a command. To my utter astonishment, all five heads whip around to look at her. The tension leaves the room.

"Come here, Samantha, I want to try something." Lotti gestures for me to join her. She opens a cell door.

Who has a jail in their basement?

I follow her in but remain near the open door. All three men are chained to the wall with wrist irons. Six pairs of steel eyes stare at me. The prisoners aren't human.

My breath catches as I try to wrap my head around what exactly is in this cell.

Each easily stands eight feet tall. Despite the empty trays at their feet, all are equally emaciated. The beings' shiny skin is varying shades of black and purple. They would be beautiful if their hands didn't terminate in long, black spike-claws.

A hand presses the middle of my back and a shiver races down my spine.

"Do you recognize them, Love?" Laine's gruff voice asks in my ear.

My laugh is strained. "I've never seen creatures like this in my life. Why should I recognize them?"

"These," he points to the first two, "are the men who were in the van with you. The other is the one I found on the side of the road."

"Laine, they're not human. The men who snatched me were human."

"Come closer, Samantha," Lotti commands. "I want to see if you can be of further use to your rightful race."

Laine encourages me forward a step.

Hesitantly, I comply. "What do you want me to do?"

The creatures' eyes follow my movements.

"Child, what did you do with the spirit you released?"

Surely, my mother relayed that information to her sisters.

Nodding my newfound understanding, I close my eyes and center my thoughts. Then I open my eyes and approach the prisoner closest to me. It strains toward me and gnashes its teeth as if to bite me. I dodge its teeth, catch the sides of the creature's thin, angular face in both hands and press tightly. Its skin is cool. An ear-splitting shriek rips from the poor thing and its body goes limp. The black and purple pigments drain from its skin, replaced by vibrant orange and pale yellow. The creature's form shifts slightly as the sharp angles of its body soften. The transformation doesn't make it look less frightening. I am grateful it's restrained.

Its cellmates strain against their restraints. Their shrieks and clicks give the impression they are yelling at their fallen colleague.

"What just happened?" I look at Lotti.

"That, my dear, is another facet of your gift. These are siquinter. They are a race separate from humans and leathoes. When they walk amongst humans, they take on human aspects. Luck's siquinter are neither good nor bad, they are just beings sent out to do the work they were created for. They divvy out good and bad luck. For each stroke of good, a bad is created and given out.

"Opportunity, on the other hand, got lazy and lost control over his. Not all of Opportunity's siquinter are corrupt, but the ones in this cell are. You're wondering why they look different now." She paused. "As humans require the sun for survival, so do the siquinter. It is how they can maintain their disguises. The other day, we asked Veda to validate if these were hers or not because your stepfather was in this cell with them and they had had enough sun to keep up their human façade."

"So why are these creatures chained?" I ask.

"Veda is our fourth sister. She and I do not see eye to eye. We avoid each other as much as possible. Veda and Opportunity go a ways back. Sometimes they team up. They make a mess of things when they do so, which annoys me to no end."

"That doesn't answer my question," I say softly.

"These siquinter are power hungry. Their sole purpose is to wreak havoc on humanity. We call the corrupt ones 'faeries.' I'm not sure why these three went after you. Never has a siquinter bothered one of our kind. Perhaps they thought you were easy prey, but this is a new and disturbing development.

"These are chained because they tried to grab a leathoes, and because I wanted to test you further. We can't be too cautious." Her mouth settles into a grim line.

I'm almost afraid to ask, "What did I just do to that one?"

"You cleansed it of its corruption. Pure siquinter are referred to as 'pixies.'" Lotti watches the other two, who are still shrieking and clicking and struggling to free themselves.

"Would you like me to do the same to the other two?"

"Let us ask them, shall we?"

"You want to give them a choice?" my voice is pure astonishment.

"Samantha, sometimes we want to change but lack the discipline, and sometimes we embrace the darkness inside. Why not let them decide their own paths?"

I step toward the next prisoner.

It stops struggling and lowers its head.

I bend my head and peer into its eyes. They are the color of brushed steel. They are mesmerizing. Finding my voice after a long moment, I ask, "Do you want to change or are you happy like this?"

It raises its head slowly, closes its eyes, and tips its head down as if awaiting to be knighted. I repeat the actions I took on the first one. This one doesn't make a sound even though it, too, convulses and slumps to the floor. When I reach the last one, it rears to full height and glares. It flinches from my upraised hand.

"Why won't you let me help you?" I keep my tone soothing even though my heart is pounding.

The creature's eyes search mine.

Can it understand me? Do these beings talk?

Of course, we talk, stupid human.

I flinch.

You can hear me while I am in my true form? What are you? Human, leathoes, or something else? its voice sounds male and contains a trace of awe.

"I was human. I died. Now I am leathoes. I'm the only half-human to make it this far," pride laces my words.

"Samantha, are you communicating with it?" Lotti asks in a hushed voice.

"Of course. Can't you hear him?"

She and Laine shake their heads.

"Only primes and subprimes can speak to siquinter in their natural form," Lotti explains. "All we hear are his shrieks, caws, and clicks."

"The siquinter can only speak English in human form," Laine says. "It's part of their mimic ability. They don't change into humans or speak the language, they are just really good at changing how others see and hear them."

Turning my attention back to the being in front of me, I ask, "Why won't you let me help you?"

Who would I be if I let you alter me? he sounds scared, lost.

The question hits my heart. I completely empathize. My mind replays the same fears I have about Laine sharing my pain. "You wouldn't be alone, your companions have changed. I imagine you will feel lighter of heart. You will begin a new chapter in your life." I smile.

If I stay like I am, will you still be around? the question floats through my head and hangs there.

I'm intrigued. "In what way?"

I enjoy conversing with someone outside our pack. To be seen as I truly am and not have to hide. This is all I know. I prefer to stay in the state I am currently.

"That depends. Do you wish me harm?"

At one time, I did. We do love the delicacy of human flesh from time to time. But now, I rather prefer your company.

"If you prefer, I will not change you. I do not know what my companions' plans are for any of you. Do you have a name?"

Bramwell, leader of the siquinter, at your service. His smile reveals perfect white rows of sharp, pointy teeth. *I am honestly shocked to meet you.*

It's unnerving to not feel scared as he extends his long, sharp-clawed hand. Automatically, I step closer and shake his hand. It's as cold, hard, and shiny as the rest of his body appears.

Pleased to meet you. I'm Samantha Har—

Laine pulls me backward, turns me until I face him, and cups my face in his hands. He searches my eyes, his brow and eyes creased with worry. "Is everything okay? Is he threatening you?"

I purse my lips and silently count to five. I'm still counting when my new friend, Bramwell, asks, *What is that other humanoid saying?*

I pull away from Laine and turn toward Bramwell. "You can't hear his thoughts?"

You are the first human or leathoes to ever interact with any of us while we are in our true form.

"Lotti, what are you going to do with these siquinter?" I ask.

"I have no immediate plan for them. Do you have a suggestion?"

"You gave them the option to change. I think you should give them their freedom," my answer is immediate.

She inclines her head.

As my fingers touch the metal of the lock, the shackles pop open. I release all of their restraints.

"Ha!" I whirl to face Laine. "That's how you kept getting into my locked room! I thought I was crazy."

"It might be a trick I've used once or twice."

Laine grunts as I elbow him in the ribs, but his grin doesn't fade.

Upon turning back to my newfound acquaintance, I'm alarmed to see the cell empty. Laine slips a hand around my waist and urges me toward the door. After a couple of moments, a wave of exhaustion overtakes me and I hang my head. Laine steadies my steps as we make our way out of the house and to the car.

The events of the day return front and center. I feel like such a traitor, not only to my race but to my gender, for letting Ryan go, for not ending his life so he can't hurt anyone else.

I barely notice when we arrive at the house or that Laine carries me upstairs. Detachedly, I notice I'm now wearing one of Laine's black T-shirts. My lips find Laine's, my hands grip his shoulders, and I pull him down onto the bed beside me. My thoughts stay dark even while kissing him.

Laine unexpectedly pulls away. "What can I do to make things easier or better?"

He's always trying to make things right for me. I'm horrible. I never do anything for him.

"Sam, talk to me."

"If I think of something, you will be the first to know." I roll away from Laine and drape my arm over my eyes.

The water is cool on my skin; I love swimming. My mother is some-where on the upper deck tanning, lost in a novel, I'm sure. I wear one of the bikinis bought by my parents. I never get to pick out the clothes I own. New clothing simply appears in my closet or in my dresser. It's been that way all my life. It hadn't occurred to me that it wasn't normal to not pick out my own style. I once went to the mall with a friend and came home with a sweater and new tennis shoes. They never made it past the front door of the house. Ryan took the bags from me and hauled me down to his basement. I can't remember what happened, but I remember I never wanted to go shopping ever again, and I never hung out with that friend after that day.

The sun on my face goes dark. Someone is blocking its warm rays. A shiver runs through me. I open my eyes. Ryan is standing on the deck looking down at me in his pool.

No! He is supposed to be at work!

"I took the rest of the day off, Sam. I wanted to spend quality time with my children." His smile is threatening.

My brother is gone, attending some camp Ryan found for him. My heart stops and my blood runs cold. I look over his shoulder to the upper deck to see if my mother is still there. She leans against the railing, looking down, watching the exchange. There is no emotion on her face.

"Get out of the pool and come inside, Sammy."

I paddle away from him.

"Tsk tsk tsk. Oh Sammy, you think I won't be able to get to you? Make this easier on both of us and get out of the pool." He doesn't even try to hide his arousal as he grits his teeth and issues his command.

"Samantha, get out of that pool this instant and do as your father says," my mother calls from her perch.

I stare at her in disbelief. Looking around, I realize there is nothing I can do. We live too far away from other houses to be able to run or scream for help. Ryan's smile gets bigger as he sees the realization hit my face. He starts to undo his belt and takes off his pants. My shoulders fall as I slowly wade to the pool ladder and climb out. He yanks me up by my arm and shoves me onto the scorching deck. I yell as I hit the hard surface and the hot pavement scorches my skin. Quickly, I silence myself. He enjoys my screams, so I don't make another sound.

He reaches for the ties on my bottoms as he licks his way from my neck to my bikini top.

I search out my mother. She stands on the deck above, passively watching. Tears threaten my vision and I turn my head away from her. I close my eyes and the drops fall. I struggle to mentally escape to a secluded island where no one can find me.

I wake with a start and sit up. How long did I sleep? My mind flashes the last remnants of my dream. I bolt from bed, slam the bathroom door, and reach the toilet just in time. My stomach won't stop convulsing even though there is nothing to expel.

A cool cloth touches my face.

Instinctively, I jerk away.

"Samantha, it's okay. It's just me." Laine kneels on the tiles beside me.

"I'm sorry." My voice burns my throat.

He pulls me close and deposits the wet cloth on the counter. He picks me up as he stands and carries me into the bedroom.

"Did you have a bad dream, or did you remember something?" he asks as he sits on the bed, not letting me go.

"It feels like a memory. My mother watched as Ryan did what he wanted with me. Normally, when I remember anything to do with my mother, she is ignoring what I'm telling her, or she leaves me alone with him. In this memory, she just stood there, emotionless. She even yelled at me to listen to my father, knowing full well what he planned to do." Talking about my deranged parents is harrowing.

"Would you like me to try to take the memory away?" his longing and hope are evident.

I consider his offer. If he does that, would I lose a part of who I am? On the other hand, if I keep that horror and more and more memories return, how will I endure? If this keeps on, it might make me physically sick to be intimate. That thought seals my decision. I nod.

Laine's arms tighten around me as his lips capture mine.

Warmth spreads through me, as if I have just downed a double shot of whiskey. I wrap my arms around him. I'm home.

He licks my bottom lip and I open to let him intensify what we have already started. He lifts me off his lap and onto the bed, not taking his mouth off mine. He slides his hand down my body, pushes aside the hem of the shirt I wear and rests his hand where I need him most. He smiles as he kisses me. He has proof of how much I want him.

When he removes his hand, I groan in frustration. He shifts his boxers to free himself. I open my legs and he lifts my shirt to expose my breasts. He flicks one nipple with his tongue as he enters me. Breath leaves my body. I wrap my legs around his hips and arch off the bed. He pumps frantically, like he is desperate to find his release. He reaches down, strokes me, and then adds the pressure I need to fall off the earth. He falls with me.

When I return to reality, Laine is laying on me, panting and sweaty. After a few minutes, he raises up and kisses my neck. "Can you recall anything that upset you earlier?"

"Mmmmmm, I don't want to try, I have other things in mind." I run my fingers through his damp hair.

"How am I supposed to know if I did it right if you won't attempt to recall the memory?"

"Oh, I know you did it right." I giggle. "You're telling me you only did that to alleviate the nightmare I had?"

He chuckles as he nuzzles me, tickling my throat. "I don't need a reason to take you, Love."

THIRTY-FOUR

Laine

WE DON'T LEAVE THE BED FOR HOURS. IT IS NEARLY TIME FOR OUR morning meeting when we finally get our fill of each other. We shower together quickly.

I pull on jeans and a black T-shirt, then we rush downstairs to the car and head out. "Where is the meeting?" Sam asks as she stares out the windshield.

I grab her hand and squeeze.

She looks over at me in surprise.

I smile, bring her hand to my lips, and kiss it. "We're going to the diner. It's our usual spot."

"The diner that we met at?" she asks incredulously. Her eyes match the rich green of her T-shirt, which hangs off one shoulder. The silver design on the front displays her Hogwarts house. Her jeans hug her curves. My mind wanders to happier places than work.

Nodding as I watch the road, I keep her hand in mine until we reach our destination.

"What if your coworkers don't like me?"

"Sam, you know almost everyone. Don't be nervous." I release her hand and step from my car. She's already out. Old habits die hard.

I slip my arm around her waist and we enter the diner. Not everyone is here, but that isn't uncommon. The meetings aren't mandatory. Jacob and Vanessa are just sitting down. Elvia already has a drink in front of her. The waitress returns, takes our drink order, then leaves. Samantha studies the menu. She hasn't eaten anything except tuna salad since her change. She won't starve to death, but she could weaken and put herself at risk, which eventually would put me at risk. Caleb walks in just then and takes the seat opposite me.

THIRTY-FIVE

Samantha

—————————

"WHO ELSE ARE WE WAITING ON?" JACOB ASKS.

"I think this is it for today," Caleb answers as he grabs a menu.

I look up from the menu. "How many typically come to these gatherings?"

Caleb and Jacob chuckle.

That grabs my attention. I tilt my head to study them, unable to understand the humor in my question.

Caleb's eyes dance with mirth. "This is the most people we have ever had. Elvia typically isn't awake until later in the day. You and Vanessa are refreshing additions. It's so nice to see pretty women instead of these morons."

I flash a smile at him and return my attention to the menu.

The waitress returns and takes our orders. After she is out of earshot, I ask, "So, what do you do at these meetings?"

"Kind of touch base and relax a little before we face our tasks," Elvia's voice is light and airy. She truly is the epitome of beauty. "Sometimes, we meet for dinner. Just depends on if we want company afterward."

"So, you never work together?"

"Not usually. If something happens that results in high casualties, then we're likely to run into someone. But since we have about twenty-four hours from the time we get the order to get them completed, most of us complete our assignments hours before an event happens." Elvia turns to Vanessa. "What on Earth made you decide to pair those teal heels with that orange wrap dress? I never would have thought of that. I would have played it safe with black heels or flats."

I don't hear Vanessa's answer. I'm too busy pondering Elvia's information. While it helps to know that we receive assignments so far in advance, some critical piece seems to be missing. Before I can puzzle out my discomfort, our food arrives. My head goes empty as soon as my plate is placed before me. Whoa. I didn't realize I was so hungry. My mind flashes to this morning, to getting sick. I don't remember why I got sick. Something about swimming. I pace myself so I don't get sick again. Laine is watching me, not touching his food. That realization stops me mid-bite.

"Sorry, I'm just elated that you're eating." He smiles and stabs a bit of his biscuits and gravy.

I finish the bite on my fork. Pancakes have never tasted so delicious. Typically, breakfast food is not something I enjoy unless I make it for dinner.

Idle conversation continues as I eat, but I don't know what to say so I remain silent. I mull over Elvia's earlier explanation. My fork is halfway to my mouth, when I drop it to my plate. Laine is in the middle of saying something when the loud clink causes him to turn toward me. He grasps my hand under the table. I return his squeeze, stand, and leave the restaurant. I need a few moments of fresh air to think through the idea that just sprang to mind.

After a few minutes, Laine joins me.

"Are you okay?" He lovingly caresses my cheek.

"I know what would make me infinitely better. What I really need." I hold my breath for a moment. "Has Ryan passed on yet?"

"No."

THIRTY-SIX

Laine

———

"No, he hasn't died yet?" she's asking for clarification.

"Correct." I frown while waiting to hear what scheme she's planned.

"I want to be there. I want to see him die, to see the life fade from his eyes." She grips my arm as she speaks.

"That isn't a good idea." I place my hand over hers.

"Laine, I need this closure. I need to know he really is dead. It will ease my conscience."

Her words impale my heart. "Why does your conscience need eased? You did nothing wrong." This might be a hurdle we will struggle to overcome. As willing as I am to take all her horrible memories, I know she is worried that my doing so will change who she is. She might be right. I have no idea.

"I sent him out into the world to unleash his evil upon some other girl. At least, I knew that I could live through it. For the last few years, from the texts and phone calls we exchanged, I know he restricted his depravity to my mother, since she was the closest he could get to me. I have no idea what kept him from coming to my house over the last five years. He knew Nick and I didn't live together. Everyone knew Nick and I were friends rather than lovers. He even knew it. Nick didn't pose a threat until we got engaged. Ryan knew about the engagement before I told…" she trails off, lost in thought before her grip on my arm tightens. "Nick must have called Ryan and asked for my hand. My time was up when the accident happened. I was supposed to have perished. Please, Laine, please, I have to see him die."

I sigh. "Sam, are you completely sure?"

"Laine, can I ask you something? Please, I need your honesty." She is scared and determined, yet still manages to remain sweet. I'd find a way to give her the stars in the sky if she asked for them.

"I am always honest with you, Love." I brush a kiss on her lips.

"Do you know how he will die?"

Her question catches me by surprise. I pull away and gaze down at her. She still holds my arm, but she isn't gripping it.

"Yes."

"I need to witness it," she whispers.

"Okay, Love." I urge her toward the car and open the door for her. She gets in quickly. I get in, start the car, and note the time. "We have four hours to get some work done before we need to head to his ToD."

"ToD?"

"Time of Death. Sorry, you'll soon get used to the lingo. You and I will work together until you feel comfortable going it alone."

"How many do we have to do in a day?"

"Depends. The same number of people don't die every day." I flash a smile. "The most I have had in one day is nineteen. The average is maybe ten. The least I have had is three. But with two more extricators, our number of assignments should drop a bit. There are eighty-eight counties in Ohio. We take care of a fourth of those. Other groups, disbursed around the world, take care of all humans."

"How do you know where to go and who to touch? I'm not

sure I can do this. Maybe I could if they were paraded in front of me, so I didn't make a mistake, and didn't get lost. My sense of direction is the absolute worst. I'm terrified of getting lost, alone," terror leaks into her voice.

"I promise, Samantha, I will stay with you until you are ready to handle assignments on your own."

"What if I am never ready to do it solo?"

"Then you won't ever do it alone and we will spend lots of time in each other's company. You will get bored with me quickly and want time away from me."

She slaps my arm as she giggles. "I will never get bored with you. You're my favorite person."

She knows exactly what to say to ease my anxiety. "Okay, so now you need to take a calming breath and concentrate. Let your mind go blank. Now imagine the shape of Ohio. I want you to imagine it cut in half horizontally and cut in half vertically. Do you see the southwest portion? Hone in on that. Concentrate on it. Now, do you see any points showing in your mind?"

She's concentrating. Then her face relaxes a little and she opens her eyes. "Oh, that is seriously cool. Okay, I have three on my map and they are pretty close." She seems excited but apprehensive.

"I have five, all pretty close." We head toward mine so she can see how we operate in the field. She saw Caleb when we shadowed him, but I'm not sure if she remembers all of it.

We drive for about ten minutes and stop at a shopping center. Sam and I enter a little boutique for children. She pretends to shop while I approach a younger woman trying to wrangle two small boys. I feel Sam's eyes on my back.

THIRTY-SEVEN

Samantha

—————————

MY HEART IS IN MY THROAT AS I WATCH LAINE APPROACH HIS target. She is so young. She has small boys that need her. When Laine passes her, she turns to look at him and he brushes his fingers down her bare arm. She gets goosebumps. He drops his hand and heads toward the door. The woman shakes her head and gives a confused look around. Her children have calmed down. She goes back to searching through a rack of boys' shirts. I turn and walk out the door.

Laine is walking down the strip toward a pet store. He enters, knowing I am following. I enter and head toward a parrot cage. The store is crowded. Laine is at the counter talking to a cashier. She looks up something in the computer and shakes her head. As he turns, he touches the hand of the older man behind him in line. Watching closely, I see the moment the twinkling spark leaves the man's amber eyes.

As Laine makes his way toward me, my head snaps to atten-tion. One of my targets is in this store, too. Laine stops as soon as he sees my reaction. I glanced around at the people close by. None of them are it. I walk past aisles and stop at the last one. My gaze rests on a little girl. She can't be older than six or seven.

Laine comes up behind me, his arms encircle my waist, and he holds me tight, giving me strength. I disengage his arms and approach the child. She is watching the fish in the tanks. I kneel next to her. She turns to me and it is like staring into a mirror to the past. I stumble to my feet, reeling from the shock of how much she looks like I did. She reaches for my hand and then goes back to watching the fish. I don't know how long we stand there like that. Finally, she releases my hand, and, starting at her forehead, I run my fingers through her long, curly brown hair. She smiles up at me.

I head toward the exit. Laine's arm encircles my waist, holding me up as we leave the store.

Laine guides me in silence. When I get outside, my lungs finally take the cleansing breath I need.

"Laine, my love, please tell me she doesn't live the same hell I did."

He comes to stand in front of me, cups my face in his hands, and I search his eyes.

He says softly, "I don't know what her past is. I only know how she will pass. All humans die, Love. You can't stop it. We help them escape the hell this world becomes after death."

"I hope she doesn't suffer," I whisper.

He releases me, takes my hand, and leads me back to the car. "She looked how I imagine any daughter we have will look," he says factually, but there is an emotion in his voice I can't place.

"My heart broke having to extricate a child who looked just like I did at that age." My thoughts are still scattered.

We set off toward a hospital. I stay in the car. He can finish quicker if he doesn't have to manipulate humans' minds to get us both through the hospital's security.

He is back in the car within minutes. We take off again. This time, we end up at a nearby fast food restaurant. We head in and I get in line to order. It occurs to me that I have no idea what Laine likes to eat. Turning to ask him, I discover he isn't behind me. I spot him. He's handing money to a rough looking, middle-aged man. The man sits at a booth by himself. It is evident he is homeless. He quickly stands and hugs my mate. Laine returns the man's hug. When they separate, Laine offers the man his hand. The handshake gives the man a visible chill but doesn't affect his smile.

It's finally my turn to order. I play it safe and order two burger meals. As I pay, Laine steps up behind me and places both hands on my hips. I flinch.

"Sorry, old habits die hard." I smirk. Realizing what I just said, I close my eyes, exhale, and shake my head.

We grab our food and head back to the car to eat. After we finish our meal, I collect the trash and get out to throw it away. When I return, Laine says, "We have about an hour before we need to head toward Ryan's ToD." He still seems worried about taking me.

I close my eyes and visualize the map Laine instructed me to make. My last two tasks are together. Laine drives and I tell him where to turn. Like a compass needle, I am drawn to the right location. We pull up to an apartment building. My mind knows where to take me. Laine is trailing me. For support? I raise my hand to knock on a door, but Laine pulls my hand away, shaking his head. He tugs me down the hall a ways.

"You need to know how to change a human's will. Do you remember when you looked for my aura? These are your tasks so you shouldn't have to concentrate hard to see theirs. Whatever you see, you need to visualize their aura as the brightest white you can imagine. They will trust anything you say, for at least a few minutes. Do you understand?" His expression is serious.

"Yes." I return to the door and knock. The door is a typical wooden apartment door, but the sound of my knock echoes in my head.

THIRTY-EIGHT

Laine

———————

I AM SO PROUD OF HER. SHE WORKS AS IF SHE HAS BEEN extricating souls for decades. She gets inside the apartment with no issue. She is in there for a few minutes. When she comes out, she has tears brimming. She looks defeated and exhausted. I have an urge to take her home. She doesn't need to witness her tormentor's demise after this latest devastation. I hold her close as she cries against my chest. I walk her back to the car. She sits on the seat, her feet on the pavement, and holds onto the inside door handle for support. Her head is bowed and she is breathing slowly, trying to regain control of her emotions.

"Love, what happened?" I stroke her hair.

She doesn't answer fora few minutes. Finally, she looks up at me. "That was my assistant and her fiancé. She is the only person I know here. She is the closest I have to a friend."

"Do you want me to share your pain?"

She studies me before her attention returns to the ground. "Is it normal for mates to share so much pain or so many burdens?"

"I have no idea. The gift is a resource provided by the mothers, so I have never questioned it. It's there to use if we need it."

"I don't want to forget her. I'll hold onto my memories for

now. But thank you for offering." She pulls her legs into the car and shuts the door. I quickly get in and start the car.

"Can you see what happens to them?" Her quiet voice is full of sadness.

"Car accident, what else?" I don't know how to be empathetic with answers like this.

"Will she suffer?" She looks at me, her eyes pleading for the answer she wants.

I compress my lips as I try to see what is destined to happen. Hmm, well that is interesting.

Sam is watching me, waiting for an answer.

"No, none of them will suffer. The woman I extricated earlier will be the cause. Her kids aren't with her."

That doesn't seem to make her feel better. I really suck at being empathetic. I am at a loss on most of this human stuff.

"Will their loved ones be able to see her at the funeral?"

"Huh? What do you mean?" She totally has me lost now.

"At the funeral, will they be able to see her to say goodbye?"

"What's a funeral?"

She looks at me as if I am completely insane.

"What?" I demand.

"You mean to tell me the grim reaper has no idea how humans mourn each other?" her incredulity matches her smirk.

"There is no such thing as a grim reaper. Humans have wild imaginations." My tone is defensive.

Sam leans over and kisses me. "We need to get going, Laine."

"I still think this is a very bad idea, Sam."

She gives me a hard glare. The temperature in the car drops as she watches me. Does she know she is doing that?

With a defeated sigh, I throw the car into reverse, back out of my parking spot, and head to her requested destination. The cold disappears as I drive. We pull onto Sam's street. Using minimal effort, I shield our presence from any nearby humans. Cars line both sides of the narrow side street. We park one block away and walk to where all this began.

As we approach her little house, we hear shouting. Items are being broken. We cross the lawn to a side window and peer in. Ryan is tossing her house. I wonder what he is looking for.

"The deal was, I would have Sammy again!" He is furious.

"And you did have her. You didn't specify how long you wanted her. Half of your requests have been met, adequately."

I know that voice. Veda.

"I didn't get to finish when I did get her! How is that fair?"

Veda's laugh is malicious, haunting. "Stupid man, life isn't fair."

"What did you call me?" Ryan steps toward Veda, raising his hand, ready to backhand her as I have seen him do to Sam. Hatred flares for this human.

He never lands the blow.

With a flick of her wrist, Veda grabs Ryan's hair and bends his head close to her. "Don't let my look fool you, child. I can end your existence on Earth and your eternity in my domain can begin this second if you try me further." Her voice is cold.

Ryan's eyes widen.

Veda releases him and walks out of the room.

Ryan grabs a crystal vase off the mantle and hurls it after her.

Beside me, Samantha tenses and gasps.

I follow her gaze. Leah, Samantha's mother, stands framed by the open front door. Ryan storms to her. She doesn't cower or flinch. She holds his gaze.

"Why are you here?" he demands.

"My daughter invited me to visit her. Alone." Satisfaction settles on her face.

His eyes narrow. "I've been in town for over two weeks," his voice holds steady.

Leah steps back toward the wall. "What have you done to her now, you sick fuck?"

"Nothing I haven't done before. But now I have to bide my time and get her alone, away from that boyfriend of hers." He is almost talking to himself.

"Why can't you just leave her alone? You like them younger; she's too old." Leah sneers.

"I do like them young, but Sammy will always be mine. You get what you want out of our marriage, I want what I'm entitled to. She is mine!" he bellows.

Leah looks around at the destruction. "What on Earth are you here for?"

"Evidence."

"For what?"

"To get her away from her boyfriend. Nowhere safer than county jail." He winks.

Leah picks up a fallen accent lamp and smashes it against Ryan's head.

He goes down. He's out, but probably not for long.

Leah starts looking around. Something must have caught her eye. She stoops and touches Ryan.

I can't see exactly what she's touching. She stands up with handcuffs in her hand. She pushes one arm of the metal restraint to swing through the other and open. With a devious smile, she handcuffs one of his hands behind his back to the opposite ankle.

Sam shivers. "Ryan's favorite way to incapacitate. That is so uncomfortable, and no way out."

I know she speaks from experience. I slip an arm around her and pull her close. I kiss the top of her head then return my attention to Leah. She's searching the house. She comes back from the kitchen with lighter fluid.

I knew as soon as Sam extricated him how he would die. I might not like that Sam is going to witness this, but I'm excited to watch Karma work his magic.

As if on cue, a tall blond man joins us and halts next to Sam.

"I do love a good barbecue, don't you?" the man whispers.

I incline my head. "Good to see you, old friend. It has been too long. Your handiwork, as always, is amazing." I press Samantha's back and jostle her to get her attention. "This is my mate, Samantha. Sam, this is Karma."

Sam appraises the blond. "Karma is a man." She holds out her hand. They shake.

"Of course, I'm a man! I can fuck anyone. Haven't you heard? I'm a bitch!" His laugh rebounds off the house, but no one inside seems to hear him. "Only people I want to be heard and seen by will see me. Never worry, reaper."

The scathing look I send him can't be helped. He knows how much I hate that word.

With another laugh, he vanishes.

Sam appears astonished, but movement inside the house catches our attention.

Leah squeezes the bottle and streams of liquid hit the bastard. She makes sure to really soak his pants. The container is finally empty. Leah locates a dish cloth, shoves it in his mouth, and secures it there with a scarf from a pile of random items Ryan created.

Ryan starts to stir and wakes. His eyes are first confused, then flash murderously at his wife.

THIRTY-NINE

Samantha

MY BREATH CATCHES. I LOOK AT LAINE. WHEN I LOOK BACK, I notice other family members peering through other windows. The mothers are here. So is Jacob and Caleb. My heart is in my throat that they came to witness, either on my behalf or in support of me. Watching through the opposite window is a woman I have never seen before. She stops watching my mother and focuses on me. Her cold eyes seem to see into my heart. Her eyebrow arches as she flashes a smile devoid of warmth. It's more like a threatening grin.

Her attention returns to Ryan, almost as if he's a steak coming to her table after a weeks-long liquid diet. Her expression is unnerving. Reluctantly, I return my gaze to the spectacle in my living room.

"Oh, Ryan, would you like to speak?" my mother mocks him.

Who is this woman? When did my mother get courage?

He glares.

"Tsk tsk tsk, you need to learn better manners. Or I should say, 'You should have learned better manners'?" She voices a derisive laugh.

He searches for something he can use to free himself.

"For once, you are going to shut up and listen to me," her confidence doesn't waver. "I have never understood your infatuation with my daughter. I don't know if it is her, or that you think you have absolute control over her, but it stops now. I thought when she turned eighteen and moved away that would be the end of it. Clearly, I was wrong. I have been wrong my entire adult life. I should have left at the first sign of anything potentially harmful to her. I was selfish. I stood by and did nothing. I called her crazy when she came to me for help."

I watch in absolute shock as my mother lights a cigarette in front of Ryan. My mother has hidden her smoking from him for as long as I can remember. He abhors smokers.

"After a while, you stopped hiding it from me." She takes a long drag from her favorite vice. "I think it was a thrill, a high for you, to violate and abuse my daughter in front of me, knowing I was stuck in this marriage. Any man that got too close to her, you managed to find a way to make him disappear. I can't let you do that again. For the first time in her life, Samantha has found someone she truly loves. She's happier in her messages to me. She told me you were in town." Another drag. "She didn't elaborate, but I know your game. I bet you've already done something unspeakable. Well, I hope it was worthwhile, because that was your very last."

If looks could kill, my mother would have been dead a hundred times over.

She doesn't seem affected by his glare. He holds no control over her anymore. I can't help but wonder where her newfound bravery came from, and where it has been my whole life.

My mother turns to look out the window where Laine and I watch and takes a few short puffs, then turns the half-inhaled cigarette around to see the lit end. Her face breaks out in the most terrifying smile I have ever seen. My heart chills.

Ryan scans the living room again and fixes on the lighter fluid can laying on the rug.

Laine's embrace keeps me standing, but his arms and chest aren't enough to warm me.

"Ryan, I just want you to know, I never loved you. I loved the lifestyle you provided. I realize now how badly I treated Sam." She takes a drag of her cigarette. "I hope you burn in hell, and we don't meet in the afterlife." She turns back to Ryan and flicks her cigarette at him. He tracks it through the air with a disbelieving stare.

Leah backs toward the front door and stands with one hand on the doorknob.

Flames engulf Ryan before I can blink. His muffled screams don't faze me. If this had been any other human on Earth, I would have rushed in and attempted to help them.

I step out of Laine's hold and move left. I halt at the edge of the window, where I can watch Ryan's face. His skin is burning. Some parts are starting to split open. Detachedly, I realize the fire is spreading through my small house, but my eyes don't leave my stepfather's flaming mass. His strangled screams have stopped, but he's still convulsing. I know he isn't dead.

Part of me knows there is something wrong about wanting to remember every detail, but the realization doesn't stop me. I want to remember the heat emanating through the window as the fire begins to consume the house. To remember the scent of bonfire and honeysuckle, from the flowers blooming along the side of the house. My eyes refuse to leave Ryan's charred form. I need to retain every second of his death, from the first lick of fire on his skin to the roaring wildfire. I strain to hear his last breath and record every sound my ears pick up.

I know the exact moment Ryan passes. The watcher from the opposite window now stands over Ryan's lifeless body. Her jeans, shirt, and even her hair are intact. How is she able to enter the house and not burn? She reaches down and yanks something from Ryan's body.

I blink.

She has vanished.

I turn to ask Laine if he saw her, but he isn't nearby. Looking around, I spot a cluster of people in the yard. Even the mothers are joined in conversation; everyone except Nona and Laine. Nona remains at the window looking in, her face grave. She appears lost in thought. Out of the corner of my eye, I see Laine. I head toward him but stop before I reach him. Laine faces Leah. Neither is talking. My mother isn't even looking at him. He runs his hand down her forearm. He doesn't step away from her but stands and studies her face. After a long moment, he turns and meets my eyes, his mouth set in a grim line.

Realization smacks me hard in the face. My shock must show because Laine cusses under his breath and starts toward me. Instinctively, I step back.

A hand grips my arm. It isn't Laine, who's still a yard or more in front of me. I start to react aggressively, but my arm is released as suddenly as it was gripped. I turn my head just enough to keep Laine in my peripheral and see Nona by my side, her face anxious.

"Don't fear those who love you, Samantha. There is nothing to be afraid of when it comes to your mate. He loves you more than his own life. You're a vital part of his existence. I know this is a lot to process, my daughter. You have been so strong and brave your whole life, through all of this. I'm proud of you." She pulls me into a tight hug. I hesitate before returning the hug, I've got so much whirling through my head. She releases me and offers a small smile before she disappears, like the woman in the house. Staring at the spot she vacated, I don't notice Laine come up beside me until his arms encircle me.

FORTY

Laine

____

I AM TRULY IN AWE OVER SAMANTHA'S CALM THROUGHOUT THE entire ordeal. The apprehension I felt at bringing her melted when Sam saw everyone and appreciation radiated off her. I gave her my support until she didn't need it.

"You just extricated my mother, didn't you?" Samantha's question drips with sorrow.

I tightened my embrace. I breathe in her scent as I kiss the top of her head and then close my eyes. "Yes," I murmur.

She pulls away, wraps her arms around herself, and looks at her burning house.

Sirens wail in the distance.

Samantha takes a deep breath, crosses the lawn, and starts walking down the street.

I follow her, but make sure to give her space.

Sam walks for over an hour, not headed in any particular direction. She stops every so often to observe a family or watch children playing, I wish I knew what she was thinking. Abruptly, she stops and faces me. Tentatively, I come to stand a couple of feet in front of her. As much as I want to hold her, to touch her, I refrain. I'll take my cue from her pace and parameters.

"Laine, I'm lost." Her face reflects her statement.

"Love, we aren't that far away from the car. We can take our time walking back."

Tears fill her eyes. "No, I don't know where I belong. I'm an orphan. I died. No one will remember me. Everyone who would is dead or about to die." She takes a steadying breath. Her gaze sweeps to the sky.

"Samantha, you belong with me. Wherever we are together is right where we belong," is all I can think to say.

She closes her eyes and the tears that had threatened to fall, do. "Laine, I want to go home."

"Sam, your house is gone—"

She runs at me and slams into my chest. Her arms encircle me and she holds on as if her life depends on that support.

"You're my home. I'm lost until your arms make me feel like I'm home. You smell like home. I am going to work on accepting that someone loves me, and that my family won't make you disappear. Please be patient with me. I'm trying. I forget sometimes, but I'm trying."

I put my finger under her chin to tip her head up. "I will spend the rest of eternity reminding you if I need to. I love you."

"If I wasn't meant to be your mate, would you feel the same way?"

"I fell in love with you the night we spent talking at your house. Your mannerisms, your voice, and everything inside your head makes me love you more every day. I am more connected to you as your mate, but I would have loved you without that affirmation."

She raises up on tiptoes to place her lips on mine. She pulls away with a reluctant ghost of a smile. I clasp her hand, bring it to my lips, and kiss the back of it. Keeping her hand in mine, I urge her back toward the car.

The destruction of her house is complete. She looks at the

ruin with detachment. Not stopping, Sam walks on to the car. The ride back to the manor is quiet.

FORTY-ONE

Samantha

Company awaits us when we reach the house. Caleb and Nona are there. It's obvious they came to check on me.

I'm a caged animal in a zoo. Both of them watch me like I will shatter at any moment.

I'm made of stronger stuff. Today's events pale in comparison to anything I have experienced while alive. Losing a material possession has never mattered to me. Are they worried over how I took Ryan's death?

There is something wrong with me. Nothing could have been offered that would have kept me from savoring that scene. Closing my eyes, I recall every detail. When I finally open them, three sets of eyes are watching me with trepidation.

"You're not bothered by the event that happened, are you, my child?" Nona asks hesitantly.

"Which? Losing my house? My mother getting extricated in front of me by my soon-to-be mate? Watching my tormentor's death? Knowing no one will remember me? Extricating the only human friend I had in this world? Dying? Please tell me which event you are referring to, please, so I can tell you exactly how I fucking feel about it." My tone is testament to how close I am to unleashing my anger. "The only thing that assuages my conscience is knowing for a fact that he can't hurt anyone else ever again."

"I realize you have had a lot to deal with, and for that I am sorry." Nona sounds sincere.

"I made sure your body was among the debris in your house," Caleb says, "and that the cuffs were removed from Ryan's body. Also, I had your house labeled an accident."

Using the last bit of restraint I have left, I ask, "How did you do that? Why did you do that?"

"Humans are easy to sway. This way, no one comes looking for you or him. Vanessa suggested that the fire being declared an accident would make life easier for you."

"Please, excuse me." As I walk to the sink to get a drink of water, Caleb and Nona let themselves out.

FORTY-TWO

Laine

————

I THINK FOR SURE SAM WILL COLLAPSE FROM EXHAUSTION, BUT SHE doesn't. After Caleb and Nona leave, instead of letting me take her upstairs, she asks if she can have some time alone. I give her enough space that she doesn't see me but remain close enough that I can watch her.

She makes a fire in the fireplace, pulls a chair up, and sits watching the flames. Her legs are curled under her and her elbow is propped on the chair's arm. Her head rests on her palm. She's blocked her aura. We sit deadlocked for hours.

"Laine," Sam whispers to the void between her and the fire.

I suspect she knows I am near and that I hear her.

"My tormentor is dead. I watched him die. I can recount each facet of his departure from this world." She places her feet on the chair cushion, ankles crossed, lays her cheek on her knees, and hugs her legs as if her life depends upon holding herself together. "I tricked myself into thinking that all the emotions and fears I have flowing under the surface would disappear if he died."

I wait for her to continue. She doesn't.

As I hesitate, unsure what to do, her wall crashes down. Like a boulder dropped into a pond, the first wave, dark blue, hits me without warning. Before I can recover from that tsunami of sadness, the next wave breaks. Its beige pain takes my breath away. I take a staggering step toward her, but a brown wave stops me in my tracks. My heart constricts over her anguish. Regaining balance and senses, I rush toward her. As I kneel in front of her chair and cover her hands with mine, the oxygen seems to leave the room. I break into a cold sweat. My instincts yell to get out, but I won't leave her. The room feels like a tomb. Even the fire flickers and extinguishes. I pull her into a hug. Like a dam bursting, oxygen returns, but Sam is gray. The color clings to her like a shield.

She tenses at my touch. She's drained but restless. It takes little effort to stand with her in my arms. Hesitantly, she slips her arms around my neck and leans her head on my shoulder.

"Sam, what can I do? I feel so useless. You're not alone. Love, are you sure you don't want me to take some of this away?" I tighten my embrace. She's still tense. "Anything you want, I will make it happen. Please, Sam, help me take care of you. I love you so much."

Slowly, the tension melts off her. I would have held her for the rest of eternity, if that's what she asked of me, but she only required about an hour.

She startles me when she finally says, "Laine?"

"Yes, Love?"

"I'm hungry."

Her voice is thick with anguish, but at least she is beginning to function again. Wordlessly, I carry her into the kitchen. David has already retired, and I am grateful for that. I set her on the counter so I am free to raid the fridge.

"Do you prefer something light, or should I find and fix an entire horse?"

Sam gifts me with a faint smile. Her eyes are still haunted by the ghosts not exorcised by today's events. She seems to not trust even herself in this moment. She takes so long to reply that it breaks my heart to see her indecision.

It takes me no time to whip up some breakfast food for a very late dinner. Plating the biscuits and gravy takes seconds. I leave the kitchen only long enough to place our food and drinks on the dining room table. I return, collect her off the counter, and set her in her chair. She stares at the plate in front of her but doesn't pick up the fork. The juice and coffee I supplied also go untouched. I sit next to her.

"Sam, would you prefer something else?"

Her eyes sweep from the plate to my face, as if she had forgotten she wasn't alone. "Thank you, Laine. I don't deserve you. How did I get so lucky?" She starts worrying her bottom lip as if she has more to say but doesn't know how to say it.

"Talk to me Sam, you can tell me or ask me anything. I have never lied to you, and never will."

"What happened in that basement, Laine?"

"What do you mean?"

"Lotti had to step in and stop whatever was going on between you and your colleagues. I didn't even get to meet any of the men in your unit."

"Our unit," I correct, so she understands that she's part of our world. I take a deep breath and let it out. "Have you ever looked at Jacob or Caleb?"

Now it's her turn to appear confused. "Why, of course. What about it?"

"Since your transition, have you seen them differently?"

"Laine, if there is a point, please get to it. I have little patience left today."

"All the men in our unit see the green around you."

"Ugh, let me guess, it's never happened before," her tone is pure annoyance. She pushes away her plate. "I'm regretting more and more that I made it through my transition, or that I had to be anything more than a completely unsuspecting, oblivious human."

Sam stands abruptly and storms out of the dining room and disappears up the stairs. I don't follow her. Encroaching on her space or forcing her to talk to me would do more harm than good, at this point.

Needing something to do to occupy my mind, I gather our plates and clear the table. The dishes take seconds to clean. David will be unhappy that I didn't leave them for him. I shoot Caleb a text to see if he is still awake.

His reply is swift: *What's up?*

Want to come hang out? I have a few things on my mind, and I could use some input.

Cool, be there in a few.

By the time Caleb arrives, I have already straightened up the living room.

"Why are you cleaning? Did David quit?"

"I needed something to do to take my mind off things."

"Is Sam here?"

Caleb is my twin, I love him unconditionally, but his mention of Sam brings home all of my insecurities. My reaction isn't even completely rational. Our race has been spoiled by never having to vie for the attention and affection of the person we should be with.

"Earth to Laine. Man, what is going on?"

Sam choses that moment to barrel down the stairs. She's wearing a pink, knee-length dress, the kind of dress you want your girl to wear if you take her dancing. My mind's eye sees her twirl and her dress lift, swishing around her legs. Sam almost always wears jeans when she goes out; today is not a jeans day. Caleb and I gape at her as she grabs her car keys and rushes out the front door. It takes a few minutes to even register what just happened.

"Where is she going?" Caleb's question pulls me out of my

daydream. Both of our eyes lock for a second before we rush to the door. We reach the driveway just as Sam's taillights disappear through the front gate.

"Should we go after her?" Caleb asks.

"I'm worried about Sam right now. She has endured much today, but she seems to have boundless reserves of energy stored in that small frame of hers. I'm not sure it's a good idea that she's driving."

"Why?"

"She's been awake for over twenty-four hours, and I shudder to think of her in an accident."

Caleb laughs. "Seriously? It isn't like she'll get killed."

"No, but what if her destination got her too close to a vengeful spirit or an accident results in a soul being trapped because this isn't a predictability? Dangers still lurk for all of us, Caleb."

"Laine, she has made it this long in one piece. Samantha has defied all odds. Brother, I know your struggles. I have no intention of trying to steal her affection. I fully intend to stay unmated for as long as I possibly can."

"I appreciate that, Brother." I gaze at the empty driveway and my mind snaps to attention. "I have a new project." I pull out my phone and text Vanessa.

Hey, if you get a chance, could you come by the manor? I have something I could use your help with.

Sure, I will be a little while.

FORTY-THREE

Samantha

I REALLY WANT TO WAKE UP FROM THIS NIGHTMARE. NOT IN MY wildest dreams is this what I pictured for my life. Thinking back to all the fantastical stories I have ever read and worlds I have loved stepping into for brief moments, I regret ever wanting to be a part of those worlds, even for a moment. I'm in hell.

While I drive to where my mother said she was when I texted her minutes ago, my thoughts roam. I know she doesn't have much time, but I have things I need to tell her. I want to hug her one more time.

I search for the last real conversation I had with my mother, face to face. Nothing comes to mind. My memories are too limited. Lost in trying to retrieve long past instances and conversations, I don't hear my phone, at first. I pull into a parking lot and look at the screen. It isn't a number I recognize. I let it go to voicemail.

'My daughter, what are you doing? This is not the place for you,' Nona's voice intrudes.

I roll my eyes and continue my radio silence. Proof yet again that I can't get completely away. I don't see my mother's car here. Maybe she's running late. I'm sure, at this point, Laine is either on his way or already close. My feelings for Laine are strong and true, but I detest being told what to do. My thoughts drift to darker places. What if I had no feelings for him? What if he repulsed me? Are leathoes forced to mate with people they don't know or like? What if I had transitioned and my mate had turned out to be a clone of Ryan? A shudder runs from the top of my head into the tips of my toes.

My phone goes off, saving me from myself.

Change of plans, Sweetie, can we meet in about an hour or so? Your brother has surprised me with a visit at the hotel.

My stomach churns as I type, *Please don't mention me.*

She doesn't answer, and I hope she reads my message and complies. My brother and I have never seen eye-to-eye on anything. We don't agree that the sky is blue, we don't agree that the grass is green, and we have completely different views on Ryan. My brother worships that man; he's his hero. I am the enemy. Sam, the liar, the family destroyer, the black sheep.

My mother and Ryan both think that boy walks on water. He plays his part well. Lucas, never Luke, thinks he is a gift to the world. The universe owes him everything merely because he exists. My parents think I hate him because of jealousy, and part of that is true. He can go months without speaking to them but shows up out of the blue and they fall at his feet. He is never harassed, has been handed everything in his life, and never known a hard day. But my hatred is deeper than that. I loathe Lucas because, despite seeing the abuse firsthand, he doesn't believe what I say, and actually tells people he was beaten as a child. Bullshit. Utter bullshit. No one ever laid a finger on that prodigal child.

The diner I had asked her to meet at is partially empty. This diner seems to be the meeting place for most people. Probably because it's located in the middle of this insanely small town and it has the easiest parking. The food is rather good, too. The waitress, as usual, is quick to take my order.

FORTY-FOUR

Laine

———

"So, Brother, what do you need Vanessa for?" Caleb asks as we reenter the living room.

"Nes has lived around humans. She can explain stuff to me. Sam once said she had goals she never got to achieve as a human. I am going to see if I can fix that."

Caleb looks at me amused. "So, what kind of goals did she have?"

"Has," I correct.

"No, Laine. *Had.* She is no longer human. If she didn't accomplish those goals before she turned, she won't achieve them now. She isn't human." Caleb is factual, but the truth stings.

"Hey, where are you?" Vanessa calls from the entry.

"In here," Caleb and I answer at the same time.

"So, what can I help you with?" Vanessa enters and settles on the other end of the couch.

"I need advice. Sam wants me to join her for— Oh, what is it? What is it called when humans mourn their fallen?"

"A funeral?" Vanessa giggles. "Why on Earth would she want you to go to one?"

"She had to extricate one of her friends yesterday."

Vanessa's expression turns solemn. "You really have no idea how humans mourn or honor their dead?"

I shake my head.

"So, you need me to walk you through what to do?"

"No." I stand and pace the room, trying to figure out what exactly I need. "Nes, what is a human mating ceremony like?"

Shock passes over her face but quickly turns to understanding. "Well, that depends on if you want something small, or a huge celebration. They don't call it a mating ceremony. It's called a wedding." She pauses as if waiting for my reaction.

"Okay, so how do you do one?"

"You wish to marry Sam?" Her smile is incredulous.

"Do you know about her goals?"

"Of course, I know what they were."

"*Are*," I raise my voice.

"Laine, she's already missed her deadline."

"Thank you!" Caleb throws both hands out toward me.

I return a seething glare. "I know she wanted them before she died, but she's still alive, just not human. I want to make her dreams come true, and this is my first opportunity. Help me, Nes. Please."

"Sure, no problem. First, I have to know if you want something big and elaborate or something small and simple."

"Why can't we make one small and elaborate?"

She considers my question. It must be valid since she stays silent for a couple minutes and then flashes a toothy grin. "I guess there is no reason why we can't. So, the next question is, what kind of budget do you have to work with?"

She knows the answer. I'm at a loss on why she even poses the question.

She must see the uncertainty on my face because she says, "It is the next question because most couples have a budget. I'm just going off the shows I've seen. Attending a wedding is vastly different than planning one. I do not have experience in planning one, but I have watched hours upon hours of wedding shows on TV."

I shake my head. "There is no budget. Sam deserves the best. But I do want it to be a surprise, so can you help me?"

"We need to decide who you want to attend. To make things easier, Caleb will be your best man and I will be Sam's maid of honor. What colors would you like to use?"

"Colors?"

"Yes, what colors do you want incorporated throughout the whole thing, or do you have a theme?"

"Theme? Aren't all human mati—weddings the same?"

Vanessa bursts into laughter. She shakes her head as she fiddles with her phone, then she stands and approaches. She holds out her phone. "Look." Page after page, picture after picture are different ceremonies. One has bright colors, another has butterflies on everything, and a good many are outdoors.

"Is holding it outdoors a typical thing?"

"No, it's just a trend right now. You do whatever is right for you and Sam."

Recalling the days I spent observing her, I remember her telling someone that she didn't like camping or anything more than a walk outside. "Indoor ceremony would be best, if we can manage it, I think."

"Okay, we will consider that. Now, what colors?"

"Gray and teal," my answer is automatic. It's something that stuck with me from our first evening together.

"Now, Sam needs a dress. But leave that to me. You will need to recruit David to make a meal for anyone coming. Would you like David or a local bakery to make the cake?"

"Sam hates cake." I distinctly remember her argument with her fiancé over it. She lost the argument. I want this to be everything she has ever dreamt of.

"Okay, so no cake. Would you like something else for dessert?"

"Cookies. Samantha loves cookies."

"Excellent. I will contact the local bakery. What do you want to do about decorations?"

"I give you creative freedom. Is there anything I get to do or have to do?"

"Typically, no. The bride usually does most of the choosing, sometimes the groom gives his opinion or is asked what he wants, but that's rare. Oh! I know! You can pick out your rings. You will need a diamond engagement ring and a matching band for her, and you will need a band that matches hers for you. Actually, come on. Let's go get that out of the way."

I give Caleb a quizzical look accompanied by a shrug. He nods and we leave with Vanessa.

"We'll take my car since I know where we're going and my car is closest." She chuckles as she opens the driver side and gets in. Caleb takes the passenger seat, while I take the back. As she drives, Nes quietly sings along with the radio. We head toward the neighboring town and finally stop in front of a shopping center.

"All we need is right in this plaza. Let's go find rings." She airily walks into a jewelry store I've been inside a time or two on tasks.

"Welcome, how can I help you?" The clerk smiles warmly at us.

"We are looking for wedding rings and an engagement ring." Vanessa exudes confidence.

"Of course. What is the style you prefer, miss?"

"Oh, it isn't for me, it's for my sister."

"Excellent. And which of you is the lucky man?" The woman's gaze drifts up and down Caleb and then me.

"That would be me." I step to the counter to see what trinkets are under the glass.

"Could we see some engagement rings first, please?" Nes takes over.

After countless rings are brought out for me to look at, I spot one that looks like something Sam would wear. Picking out bands was uneventful and not nearly as time consuming as finding the perfect engagement ring. Leaving the shop with three rings and one extra item I just had to get my mate, we set off for the bakery a few stores down.

"Laine, I am leaving the dessert entirely up to you," Vanessa states as we enter. After the owner greets us, my sister informs the small plump man that we are looking for cookies for a wedding.

I know what I am looking for and I feel a little empowered to have a say and a handle on something.

"I will be back in a bit. Take your time, Laine." Without a backwards glance, Nes sweeps out of the store.

We are just finishing up with the order and a time for delivery when Nes walks back in carrying a huge garment bag and a handled bag with a couple of boxes in it. "Ready?"

"Yep, I think we have everything done here." I shake the baker's hand as we prepare to leave.

"What on earth is that?" Caleb points to the large zipped bag Nes is holding up by a hanger.

"This, gentlemen, is The Wedding Dress," she announces as if it were the queen.

"Why is it covered?" I ask.

"You can't see it until the wedding, it's bad luck!" Vanessa grins.

"Ha! What kind of bad luck do humans think happens if you see the dress before?" Caleb has been relatively quiet through all this—human things bore him—but this process has him studying every detail.

"They think seeing the dress before the ceremony will doom the union." Vanessa opens the car and folds the dress neatly on the back seat.

"Doom the union?" my brother and I ask in unison.

Vanessa giggles. "Humans get divorced more often than not, and they like having something to blame the failure on. Seeing the dress early is a big no-no."

'You need to get to Samantha as quickly as you can,' Nona's voice enters my head, and by the looks on my siblings' faces, they hear her, too. 'She is meeting her mother in a few minutes. She's been through so much, I'm not sure how much more she can take.'

We pile into the car and Vanessa speeds away. We are maybe ten miles away from Sam's location when Nona asks, 'Laine, can you change how her mother will pass?'

'I can't. I'm not close enough.' Desperation pierces my heart.

"I'm sorry, Laine. I can't extend her mother's time. I'm just not close enough," my sister says, keeping her eyes on the road.

Nona must be talking to all of us.

My body seems to deflate. For all that I am, there is nothing I can do to get to Sam faster. My eyes dart to the clock on Vanessa's dash. Painfully, I stare at it, wishing I could stop it just long enough to get to her so she isn't alone. Another minute passes. My hands ball into fists and my breath ceases. The last digit on the clock changes once more. I close my eyes and exhale. I'm too late. As the diner where Sam is meeting her mother comes into view, siren wails bring traffic to a standstill. A wailing ambulance and a fire truck zoom past. I pop open the door and jump out. I sprint toward the diner, toward Samantha, my siblings hard on my heels.

The scene is gruesome. A wave of sorrow passes over me. Sam is at the front of the commotion. She's kneeling, holding something. As I get closer, I see Sam is holding her mother's hand. Tears stream down her face and fall on her mother's. She reaches down and strokes Leah's hair. Leah is hardly recognizable. There is blood everywhere. The EMT's pull Sam away from her mother and I'm there to take her into my arms. Sam startles as a piercing alarm sounds next to us. The bus that hit Leah reverses, uncovering the body lying under it. Sam cringes.

"I missed my chance. I knew it was coming, but I thought I had more time," Sam sobs into my chest.

"Sam, do you want to go home?" I stroke her hair.

She nods, her hands going around my neck as I scoop her up and walk her back to Vanessa's car. Vanessa has removed the dress and bag from the backseat. We are silent as we make our way back to the manor.

"Samantha, do you want me to run you a bath when we get home?" There's blood on her hands, arms, and dress.

She doesn't answer. Her gaze is fixed on everything rushing past her window.

"Laine, take her in and get her situated and comfortable. I'll take care of everything else," Vanessa says.

FORTY-FIVE

Samantha

—————

THE COSMOS MUST HAVE THOUGHT I HAD ISSUED A CHALLENGE when I earlier thought I was in hell. I should have insisted that she meet me first and visit with my brother later. Lucas always gets the better end of every deal.

My thoughts turn bitter. He got to hug her, to tell her he loved her, and to say good-bye. I didn't. I haven't had a chance to see my mother in years. She wouldn't come to me and I didn't dare go to her. Guilt hits me hard, and my heart screams in pain.

Laine's arms encircle me, but I don't feel them. I want nothing more than to join my mother. I failed her. I'm a curse to anyone who gets near me. Ryan got what was coming to him; I don't regret his death. But my mother, Nick, and Stacy…my heart is heavy with remorse for their fates.

Laine would do better not getting mixed up with me. There may only be one or two ways to kill us but leave it to me to attract it. My gift comes to the front of my mind. Yep, see, it has already started.

"Get out of your head, Samantha," Laine whispers in my ear. It feels like a lifetime ago that he last said those words to me. With a huff, I realize it was a lifetime ago, when I was human. "Sam?"

Laine sets me on the edge of his bed. I didn't realize we were back at the manor. Poor man is looking at me like I'm about to disappear in front of him. As much as I wish it, I know I won't.

"Laine, what happens if I get hurt? Physically, I mean."

"Nothing." Laine pulls out a pocketknife, opens it, and tries to slice his palm. A light red mark appears and disappears with a blink of my eye.

My quick intake of breath startles him.

He tosses the knife onto the nightstand and kneels in front of me before I can exhale. He captures my face, his eyes searching mine.

"What are you looking for?" I ask.

"I need to know what you're thinking. Talk to me, Sam. Please."

His pleading hits me square in the heart. "Laine, I'm a jinx. You would do best to stay away from me."

His wry smile gives me pause. "Why are you looking at me like that?"

"You aren't a jinx. He hasn't visited this part of town in months."

"What the hell are you talking about?" Confusion replaces most of my coherent thoughts.

"Many myths in the human world are based off beings that are really around them that they can't explain. Those entities are forever changing their appearances. Even The Sisters change."

He's trying to distract me. It's slightly working. "What other things are there?"

"How about I run you a bath, get you into clean clothes, and then explain some of the things humans not only have wrong, but don't realize they're close to getting right."

"Deal." He stands, offers me his hand, leads me into his bathroom, and closes the door. I help him remove my clothes and wait as he fills the tub. Midway through my bath, I catch him leaning against the counter watching me. "Like what you see?"

"Yes and no."

I stop scrubbing and tilt my head.

"You're stunning, Sam. But I hate seeing you like this. So sleep deprived, and none of the emotions coming off you are happy. I wish I knew what to do to make it all better for you."

I break eye contact and finish rinsing my hair. Laine hands me a towel as I stand. Clothes are sitting on the counter for me.

Freshly dressed and feeling moderately better, I make my way to his bed. Exhaustion hits me. It consumes my thoughts as I sink onto the mattress. If I hadn't gotten there at that moment, I would have collapsed on the floor. Laine doesn't get a word out before I succumbed to the darkness.

Laine is wearing a slate gray tux with a teal shirt and a black tie. His beard is trimmed short. His hair is a little long. It falls over his forehead. He's standing at the end of a lane. No, not a lane. A white aisle. Chairs line the aisle. As I look around, I see people I know. Caleb is there, standing next to Laine, dressed in a black tux, gray shirt and teal tie. My mother is there. Leah is radiant. Vanessa stands next to me, shoving a bouquet into my hands. Her eyes glisten with unshed tears.

Music starts and she begins to walk down the white carpet. After she reaches the end, I follow, like a moth drawn to the flame that is Laine. His smile is blinding. I stop in front of him. He takes my hand, and when he releases it, there are rings where once I didn't have any. It's an odd feeling, but not unwelcomed. We turn and walk through a set of ornate doors.

The sun is bright. Too bright. I lift a hand to shield my eyes. I regain vision in time to see Laine's smile fade and become a grimace. As he falls to his knees, a spirit that looks uncomfortably like Ryan exits his body. The spirit flashes a vindictive smile as Laine collapses to the floor. My heart bursts into flames and turns to ash. I fall next to Laine and reach for his hand but it's just out of reach. I can see but I can't move. Tears fall from my eyes as the light in his eyes fade.

'I told you not to get involved with me!' I scream-think at him. 'I knew I would be your demise.'

"SAM!"

Someone has a firm grip on my shoulders.

"Sam, wake up. Please," Laine sounds scared.

My cheeks are damp. Upon opening my eyes, I realize I am crying. Laine's thumbs are wiping the moisture off my face. "You were screaming, Sam. Do you want to talk about it?"

"Laine, I'm terrified of getting close to anyone. Everyone I have ever gotten close to has ended up dead."

"We're different. Nothing will happen to me."

"That isn't true. I saw it. You were killed by a vengeful soul, which killed me, too."

His face is a myriad of emotions.

"I dreamt we were married, connected to each other. The soul killed you and stayed behind long enough to watch me die again. The soul was Ryan. The pain of my heart burning to ash was nothing compared to seeing you succumb to my foolishness. I can't let that happen. Not if I can do something to prevent it." I drop my attention to the quilt that covers his bed and trace the pattern with a fingertip.

"Sam, quality over quantity. If all I had was one night as your mate, it would be better than five eternities without you. But, I'm sorry to say, you are right to worry about Ryan. Since he sold his soul to Veda, he is more of a threat now than he ever was as a human." He tilts my face up to his. His mouth descends on mine, full of purpose and strong emotions. Before he can take the kiss further, I pull away.

"Laine?"

"What, my love?"

"I'm hungry." I hope to distract him while I plan.

He pulls me to my feet so we can make our way downstairs. Vanessa, Caleb, and Jacob are seated in the living room. Their conversation halts when they see me. Vanessa hurries to my side and hugs me. "Oh, Sam. I was so worried."

"I'm okay." I don't hug her back. "I hope for a break from surprises and unpleasantness, honestly."

Laine tenses beside me and Vanessa throws me an apologetic look. My heart sinks to my feet. "Okay, what now?" My voice is weary even to my own ears.

"We will leave you alone for a few." She motions to the two men and they retreat.

My attention turns back to Laine. He's still tense, but his eyes are soft as he appraises me. His attention shifts behind me for a fraction of a second before returning.

FORTY-SIX

Laine

My sister is trying to direct me on how to do this whole human thing, but I'm lost. The ring box feels like a twenty-pound barbell sitting in my jacket pocket. I've never been more nervous around Samantha than I am at this very moment. Lately, she has been firmly against marriage, but, at one time, it was important to her. My skin feels like it is too tight for my body.

Vanessa is talking to Caleb. Caleb turns toward me and mimics what Nes did just seconds ago. He's down on one knee, holding Vanessa's hand. It's now or never. Slowly, I exhale as I sink to one knee in front of Sam. Her eyes narrow, her breath catches, and her emotions are blinding. Pinks mixed with teal. She's mesmerizing.

"Sam, I have no idea what normal humans say, but I know what I need to say. After everything you have endured, past and present, I never want you to feel alone again. You're the most impressive woman I have ever encountered. Your honesty, courage, and strength know no limits. I know you don't need a protector or confidant, but I want those roles in your life. I know beyond a shadow of a doubt, you are who I would follow into the depths of hell. I want to experience everything with you. Sam, I want your life, your world, to begin and end with me, for always. It never crossed my mind to try and help you accomplish any of the goals you set for yourself. So, I want to rectify that oversight. Samantha, please, marry me?" My eyes never waver from hers.

Her tears started falling as soon as my knee touched the plush carpet. Remembering, at the last second, that Vanessa said I had to present her with the ring, I quickly fish the box out of my jacket. I open it for her to see.

Do humans decide if a mate is worthy based upon the type of trinket they receive? Seems a little preposterous. No wonder they are an unhappy species. I corral my thoughts and home in on Sam. I will hold this stance until she answers, even if she says no.

Sam's hands are shaking. Her inner turmoil plays across her face, one emotion replacing the next, replacing the next. I'm not going to interrupt while she makes sense of what she wants. Sam falls to her knees in front of me, her eyes wide and searching mine, her hands gripping my upper arms.

She closes her eyes, pain evident in every facet of her being. Leaning down, I tentatively kiss her, whisper light. I don't want to alarm or upset her more. Sam moans softly. Vaguely, I hear my siblings and Jacob leave the house. Samantha's fingers thread into my hair while the other caresses my face.

"Sam?" I ask between kisses.

She pulls away far enough to look at me. Her voice is full of sadness, "I'm terrified. Laine, I am responsible for so many deaths, please don't make me suffer the next life knowing I was the cause of yours."

"Love, I would be in agony every day knowing you should be mine and that we belong together. I can't live this life without you."

"You don't have to. You said we could still see each other and even have children. We don't have to recklessly tempt the bad luck that's targeting me."

"It's not enough."

She sits on her heels and her shoulders droop. Her wall goes up.

"Sam, look at me."

Her gaze meets mine with the slightest hesitation.

I'm plunged into confusion.

Sam rests her elbow on her knee and lowers her chin onto her upturned hand. "I really don't have a choice, do I?"

"You always have a choice," I sound harsher than I mean to. I run my hand through her hair and down her arm. The contact, as always, evokes electricity. "Tell me I'm not alone here."

"You're not alone, Laine. Why are you doing this?" Her brows furrow. "Are you sure you want so trivial a human ritual?"

"Of course, I'm sure. I'm asking you because marriage was important to you. I will do anything to make you happy, Sam."

She stares past me for a while before her attention slowly returns. "Laine, I'm scared and overwhelmed."

"Love, all I need is your answer. The rest are just details."

"The details are what makes marriage special to human women."

"Not in this house. Details, while important in the moment, mean nothing in the long term."

"Laine." She gets back to her feet and looks down at me. "Ask me again."

"Samantha, will you do me the honor of marrying me?"

She noticeably swallows. Tears threaten to fall, but she finally says, "Yes." She inhales deeply. "I will marry you."

I'm on my feet in seconds, crushing her body to mine, and kiss her for all I'm worth. Sam is the first to pull away, a small smile on her lips. "I'm still hungry."

"I have been neglectful in feeding and watering you." I remove the ring from the box and offer it to Sam.

Her hand trembles as she takes it. Looking from it to me, she says, "It's the most perfect ring I have ever seen." She places it on her palm. "Pick it up, please."

Her politeness slays me. I comply.

"Now, Laine, put it on me." Her whisper is like a prayer aimed straight at my very essence. She indicates the proper finger and I obey immediately.

FORTY-SEVEN

Samantha

WHAT ON EARTH HAVE I DONE? WHAT HAS GOTTEN INTO ME? THIS is completely selfish, but seeing his face light up when I said yes is an image burned into my brain. He hasn't taken his hands off me since.

"Laine, my love, we have a funeral to attend. I would like you to come with me, but if you don't want to, I understand."

"Wherever you are is where I want to be."

If my heart weren't so heavy with grief over losing my only human friend and connection who would have remembered me, his declaration would have melted me on the spot. But here we are, getting ready for a funeral.

I apply minimal make-up and then add the finishing touches. When I leave our bathroom to assess my fiancé, I find him dressed in jeans and a light blue polo. "Love, you can't wear that to a funeral."

He stands before a full-length mirror that leans against the wall in the far corner of the walk-in closet. "A little direction, if you could spare it, Sam. I'm totally lost on what humans expect."

I head to his suits.

"I am not wearing a suit. That is ridiculous," he scoffs. "The dead can't see what I'm wearing. Why does it matter?"

"We wear black to show we are in mourning. We go to pay our respects and get closure. That is the purpose of funerals. We reminisce, we support each other, and we offer assistance to those closest to the deceased. It's that simple."

"Sam, I am trying to be supportive, but, honestly, I didn't know either of them. Their deaths are trivial and inevitable."

His words sting. I am once again reminded that I am the enemy of my former race. Nothing is ever going to be the same. I need to find time to process and accept all of this before our different views on my former race drive me insane.

"Sam!"

I scan the closet before focusing on Laine, who still stands in front of the mirror, tension rolling off him. I reach him in a few steps, slip my arms around his waist, and hug him close. "Sorry, I know this is new to you. It will likely be the only one you ever have to attend. I will go to my mother's, but I am fine going alone. I feel like all I do is worry you and upset you. I'm sorry for that. I will try harder."

He strokes my hair as he lets out a heavy sigh. "Sam, you aren't a burden. I will probably always worry about you. I think it's natural for a mate to worry about the other. I love you, you know that, right?"

"I'm learning to know that. I will never get tired of hearing it." I smile at him as I release my hold and turn back to his clothes. I locate black pants and a black button-up, collared shirt. I hand them to Laine. He leaves the walk-in minutes later looking beautiful and dangerous wrapped in black. A shiver runs down my spine as he approaches. For the first time since meeting him, I am afraid. I know he will never hurt me, but in that one moment, my mind forgets everything my heart knows.

He must have seen or sensed my fear. He stops in his tracks, eyes locked on mine. My mind can't place what made him so frightening, but the fear is consuming. My breathing turns shallow and my heart races. I break eye contact, close my eyes, and will myself to calm.

Arms encircle me and my mind snaps. I fight for all it's worth. The arms tighten, pulling me close. His scent halts my assault. The dam inside bursts and tears fall as I cling to him. Am I always going to be one move away from losing my mind? How can we live like this?

"It's okay, Sam, I got you. I'm here. You're fine." He holds me close, his head resting on mine. His arms stay strong around me.

"Laine, how can you stand to be with me? My mind is like a minefield with no way of knowing where to step without setting me off. You can't possibly want to deal with this day in and day out for all of your days."

"My love, I would do far more for you without a second thought. Please, Sam, please don't give up on us. Who are we to fight kismet?"

Now isn't the time to discuss our future, we have somewhere to be. "We better get going."

Laine reluctantly disengages. I stride to the bathroom to retouch my make-up. The few minutes alone give me time to calm. Finally, I smooth my flared, black, tea-length dress and decide I am fit to get this over with.

We stop for gas on the way to the funeral home. At the funeral home, I squeeze Laine's hand as we head to the receiving line. I say a silent prayer of thanks that the family could have an open casket. From the size of the crowd, the whole town seems to be here. Finally, it is our turn to offer condolences, and to say our goodbyes to Stacy. Her fiancé lies in the next room. They are being buried next to each other. Laine is silent through the entire service. After the viewing is done and people begin to leave, we return to our car and wait.

"Why are we waiting in the car?"

"Now we wait for them to load the caskets. Then we follow

the procession to the cemetery." I reach into the back seat and grab the white roses I bought at the grocery when we stopped for gas.

"What are the flowers for?"

"For the graves. Typically, we put them on the casket before it is lowered into the ground. Some prefer to place them on top of the grave after it's covered." The petals are soft under my touch. I love roses.

"You are my rose. My protected love. Strong and beautiful, but always ready to defend."

Laine's words wash over me, and a smile tugs my lips.

"Giving flowers to dead people seems insane to me."

"Laine, what if we have our mating ceremony and I think some of it is insane or silly? Would you be upset at me for saying so?"

He appears to think hard about what I just said. Good, let him stew on that for a bit. Smugly, my attention returns to the roses. I remove the plastic wrap and start fashioning two small bouquets. I feel Laine's eyes on me. "Why are you staring at me?" my tone is hushed as I complete my task.

"It's fascinating how efficiently you arranged those roses, and yet not once did a thorn harm you."

"Nothing can harm me, as you demonstrated earlier." I hold the flowers up to make sure they are even. "Besides, it could be that the florist removed their thorns."

Laine reaches over and grabs one of the bouquets. Instantly, his hand is pricked by several thorns but not a drop of blood is lost. "See? Only a rose can avoid the bite of another rose," he breathes as his mouth closes on mine. His kiss is full of promise, but he pulls away before it can go farther.

The cars in front of us start to move. I push the button for our hazard lights and instruct Laine to put on his headlights. His expression says it all and makes me roll my eyes.

"Seriously, Sam?"

"Stop arguing. Just do it. If you stop fighting this whole process, I promise not to question any mating ceremony ritual that I find weird."

"Why would I want that? I love when you ask questions. Your curiosity is a big part of who you are. I would never wish that away."

"Fine, then I will reward you when we get home if you are very good until this is over."

He cocks an eyebrow and an amused smile plays on his lips. "Deal!"

FORTY-EIGHT

Laine

———————

THE PROCESSION REACHES THE CEMETERY AND WE JOIN THE CROWD assembled about the gravesite.

I never stopped to consider how humans live and the rituals they adhere to. Watching Samantha living as a human for months didn't prepare me for seeing her as a leathoes interacting with humans. During the months I followed her, she only went to work and then home. Her only interaction was with her fiancé. She never attended a party, wedding, or funeral. Foolishly, I thought she was a standard human, that they all behaved as she did. I was wrong. Samantha is clearly aware of how she is supposed to act and does a superb job at acting the part. My stomach churns knowing what type of training she suffered and what it costs her to play the perfect part. A character in her own life, a protector of everything she felt she had to conceal. My heart aches for the girl she was, a girl so alone and tormented.

A voice calling my name snaps me out of my reverie.

"Laine, you okay? What's wrong?" Sam worriedly peers at me.

I adopt her hushed tone as we leave the ceremony and walk the rows of graves. "Sam, I see your sadness"—I take a deep, calming breath—"but why are you so lonely?" I expect her to take a moment to examine her feelings, but she doesn't.

"Because I am alone. My family is gone, my friends. The only person left on Earth who will remember me in a passing thought is my brother. It's as if I never existed."

She speaks factually. She might feel lonely and sad, but she doesn't shed a tear. Her steps don't falter. The farther we get into the cemetery, the calmer she gets. She now seems peaceful, as if this is her true happy place. Somewhere she can relax without threat of discovery. Sam stops in front of me, dead still, as if holding her breath. A shiver runs through her.

My gaze follows hers. A woman paces in front of a small row of grave markers. She is clearly not of the living. Before I can say anything, Samantha grabs my hand. Walking quickly and silently, we reach the car.

"Laine, we need to get out of here the same way we came. Quickly, please." Her voice is strong but contains a slight tremor.

Without hesitation, I take us back out the way we came. In the rearview mirror, I see the woman standing at the cemetery gates. Her gaze is locked on our car, but she is pulled back to her original spot as we leave the vicinity of the cemetery.

"Sam?"

"I felt her before I saw her. I knew I couldn't help her; she was too angry, too full of pain. I don't know the range they have, so all I could think about was getting you as far away from her as I could, as fast as possible."

Sam is trembling as we make our way back to the manor. I want her somewhere safe and I know I can keep her safe at the house.

As soon as I pull up to the door and shift the car into park, Samantha's door is yanked open. Both of us startle.

"Heya, Sis, I need you to trust me and let me put this on you, K?" Nes is bubbly and excited, a complete contrast to my mate's current fright. Nes doesn't wait for an answer. She snags Samantha's hand, pulls her from the car, and turns her. The last thing Samantha sees before Vanessa blindfolds her is me leaning against my open car door shaking my head in defeat.

I circle the car in a few quick strides, take Sam's face in my hands, and kiss her, slowly putting every ounce of passion I have into it. Vanessa clears her throat a few times, but I ignore her. Finally, I pull away from Sam. "I'll see you in a little bit, my love," I whisper before Vanessa escorts her inside.

The house looks amazing. The entryway is draped with gray and teal silks. Lighting is by candlelight. Candelabras sit on most flat surfaces. All support long, teal candles. The formal dining table is ablaze with white roses. The silk gray table runner contains intricately designed teal embroidery and is accented with crystal goblets and wine glasses. The bone china is white with a metallic-outlined rose, which I'm sure is platinum, as Vanessa wouldn't settle for less than the best. The buffet that sits against the far wall displays the massive cookie collection I ordered. Every cookie I could think of was made and brought. The spread is impressive. I allow myself a bit of pride over the selections that have been made and how everything has turned out.

Nes really can plan a party. Our unit members are the only guests, most of whom have no idea what a wedding is, but they are here to support us. I only hope Sam loves it.

"What's on your mind, Brother?" Caleb slides his arm around my shoulder and squeezes before releasing me.

"I hope this is everything Sam wanted and more. She's had a pretty bad day. I am worried I picked the wrong time to do this."

"What happened?"

"We had that human ceremony, for her dead friend. She was sad over that, but while there we almost walked into a pissed-off spirit. Thankfully, Sam has a longer range for sensing them than I do and we got out without harm, but it shook her up. This morning, she had a minor freak out. I have no idea what brought it on. I got dressed and when she saw me, she literally froze in fear."

"Sounds horrible, for both of you," Caleb sounds genuinely concerned.

I keep my voice low, "I put my arms around her, and she fought me like a wild animal."

"Laine, I only ask this as your brother, because I love you. Are you sure you want to be mated to her? I mean, you could always just be together without being connected entirely."

I can't help but chuckle.

"What's so funny?"

"Sam said the same thing. You know I've never wished to be mated or obligated to anyone. But with Sam, I want to experience everything with her."

FORTY-NINE

Samantha

Nes leads me from where she accosts me in the front drive, through the house, and up the stairs. I trust her. I remember all the insane parties she used to throw back in California. She lives to plan things.

"Nes, what in the world are you doing?"

"Tsk tsk. You will address me as 'Fairy Godmother' today."

"Ha! Like hell I will. What are you up to?"

"Sam! I would never spoil a surprise."

A door closes and Nes guides me over to sit on something firm but soft. "Sam, I am going to have to take off this blindfold for a few minutes. Do you promise to behave?"

"I don't think you are really giving me a choice, are you?"

"Nope!"

She tugs on the knot at the back of my head. The blindfold falls into my lap. I lift the material and glide it through my fingers. The silk is cold, smooth, and beautiful. It looks like liquid silver. I'm tempted to rub it against my cheek but refrain. Instead, I absorb the sight before me. I'm not in my room or Laine's. I'm sitting on the edge of a bed in a room I have never seen before. Hardly surprising. I'm sure I haven't seen a fourth of this house.

The walls are draped in yards and yards of sheer material. Deep gray, crisp white, and, every so often, a vibrant teal pokes through. I feel like I occupy a dream. Vanessa gestures for me to stand, hands me a flute of mimosa, and then shoves me toward a chair in front of an ornate mirror at the far end of the room. "Sit!"

She's so bossy, it feels like old times. "Yes, Ma'am."

She giggles as she goes to open the door just wide enough to admit three women I have never seen before. Each rolls behind her what looks like wheeled luggage. The glee on Nes' face is contagious. Quickly, I stand as Nes begins the introductions.

"This is Natasha, she is your make-up artist." Nes gestures to the first woman who entered. She is a little taller than me and has brilliant purple streaks running through her blonde hair. She is maybe twenty-five. I am immediately jealous of her boldness. I am too scared to put unnatural color in my hair. She exudes confidence, and her make-up is flawless. I know I am in good hands for whatever crazy scheme my sister has planned.

"This is Stephanie, she's going to take pictures throughout the day. Don't mind her, unless she asks you to pose for something, got it?"

I nod as I try and fail to make out the woman obscured by all the camera equipment.

Vanessa directs my attention to another woman. "And this is Ashlee. She is your hair stylist." Nes beams with pride.

"Glad to meet all of you. I have no idea what my sister has up her sleeve. I'm just along for the ride." I smile and roll my eyes at my best friend, now sister.

"Please, just relax," Ashlee reveals a slight southern accent. "Leave everything to us. We don't have time to waste."

"Girls, could you please all come here for one second? Sam, you stay!"

All three woman scurry toward the door and huddle. What the hell are they up to? Straining my ears as much as I can, I still can't hear a word. I flop back into the chair and wait for them to finish their secret meeting. When it concludes, Ashlee approaches and circles behind me.

"If you could style your hair any way you liked, how would you wear it?" Thankfully, Ashlee hasn't touched me yet. "I can't wait to play with all of this. Is this permed?"

"No, it's naturally a curly mess. I typically just wash and go."

Her gaze meets mine in the mirror. "How would you like me to style it?"

"Honestly, I don't know what Nes has planned so I can't tell you what would be best. Nes! Tell Ashlee how to do my hair, please."

Nes comes over, a long, ornate comb in hand. "This belongs to Nona." She hands me the comb. "She wants you to have it. It's platinum. The stones are diamonds, opals, and rubies." She turns and talks to Ashlee. I forget about them. The comb is the most beautiful thing I have ever seen in my life. The five tines have waves in them. The six diamonds are nearly the size of dimes. The six penny-sized opals intertwined in the platinum's knot design are stunning. I turn the comb this way and that to watch the opals' different colors play off the lights. Eight dime-sized rubies are scattered throughout the design in no apparent order. Closing my eyes, I send a thank you to my mother for such a beautiful gift. She doesn't respond, but I am certain she hears me.

Ashlee is back behind me and playing with the tips of my hair. Nes glides over, plucks the trinket from my hands and gives it to Ashlee. Ashlee nods to Nes and begins wetting my hair with a spray bottle.

"Hey, I'm gonna start on your make-up, K? I need to push your chair back a smidge." I see Ashlee nod to her in the mirror and the two of them slide my chair away from the mirror. Natasha then stands in front of me, opening what looks like the Mary Poppins of makeup trunks. "How do you typically wear your makeup?"

"I don't."

She appears utterly shocked that someone might leave her house without makeup. "Okay, so you go for a natural look. I can work with that."

I close my eyes and let them do what they want to me. It isn't going to kill me to let Nes have her fun.

Eventually, Natasha asks, "You want to see the final look?"

I open one eye. "No, I trust Nes. Where to now?" I stand and start toward the door and am accosted by my sister. She might be teeny, but she is formidable.

"Oh no you don't. This is my show. Now, you have a choice, a real choice, but they have consequences. Do you want me to blindfold you or do you promise to keep your eyes closed until I tell you to open them?"

"What are the consequences of each choice?"

"If I blindfold you, you run the risk of ruining the makeup. If you peak after you promise to keep your eyes closed, I will hate you forever."

"I promise to keep my eyes closed until you tell me."

"K, starting now, close them. It will be only me in the next room. I am going to dress you in the clothes I picked out. Trust me, please, Sam. I have never done anything to make you doubt me, have I?"

"No, I trust you."

She leads me somewhere and I stand listening to the zip of a zipper, the rustle of plastic, and the swish of fabric. Nes helps me out of my black funeral dress. It's cold in the room. I see again the woman pacing before the cluster of tombstones. Why was she there? Shouldn't she be where she died and replaying her last moments? She should not have been there. As the image keeps playing in my head, I almost don't notice the brush of cloth as Nes dresses me.

"Brace yourself," Nes says as she pulls something tight around me. A corset? Is she putting me in a corset? Why? Okay. Maybe she is doing another themed party.

"Step…step…there you go. I'm going to have you sit so I can put the thigh highs on and attach them to the garter belt."

Keeping my eyes closed, I arch an eyebrow in question, I know she can see me.

"Chill, you know me. I love being authentic when it comes to anything I do."

She has a point. Finally, I feel the smooth, cool fabric glide over my body. Whatever era she is dressing me for, they had heavy dresses. Maybe she is doing another fairy tale party. Oh good gravy, who does she have me going as if she has to keep me in the dark. Resigned to my fate, I endure the rest. It isn't life or death, it's just a few hours, and I can deal with it.

FIFTY

Laine

____

"You need another drink, Brother?" Caleb asks as he grabs another beer from David.

"No, I'm fine. Have as much as you need." I laugh.

"What do you think happens at these things? What do humans do at…what are they called again?"

"Weddings," I supply.

"Right. Weddings. How long do they last? How do they show they are bound? Why do I need to know any of this? Oh, that's right, my only brother has latched onto a human. Now we get to do all these stupid human things." Caleb takes a long pull on his beer.

I know it's hard for him to care about humans when he's seen them as his job and nothing more. "Well, for one, according to Nes, human weddings last hours. It's like a giant party. They use rings as their symbols of commitment. And you want to know because, even if you don't admit it, you are curious." I grip Caleb's shoulder and jostle him to either perk him up or annoy him. Either would make me happy. Caleb gives me an eye roll and finishes off his beer.

"You should consider having another drink, you're making

me nervous. I can feel the tension coming off you." Caleb already has a fresh beer in his hand and offers it to me.

To shut him up and to give me something else to concentrate on, I take it and sip. "I want to keep my head clear. I want to remember everything from this day. It is important to Sam, and I want it to go perfectly."

"I'm sure our sister is making everything authentically human."

All I can think to do is nod as more of our unit arrive at the manor and come over to join the conversation. They are just as curious as Caleb about this human ceremony but are more open about their curiosity than he is. We are in deep discussion on what a wedding is and bouncing ideas off each other on how some of the traditions got started when I glimpse Vanessa flying down the stairs. I excuse myself and meet her at the last step.

"Oh good, just who I need," her voice is light, but her face is tight with concern.

Fear grips my heart. "What's wrong?"

"I know I said you can't see the bride before the ceremony but…Sam is getting anxious the longer she waits upstairs. So, I really would like to start this sooner rather than later. If that isn't possible, you will need to go up and calm her down."

"We can start right now, if you want."

She lets out a breath of relief. "Thank you, Brother. Too many people accepted invitations to hold the ceremony indoors so that part is outside." She hugs me and rushes to grab Caleb. The sight of Caleb's muscular frame being dragged by a thin girl half his age is amusing until I soberly remember where they are going and what is happening. Jacob apparently got the memo and is already front and center, loitering under the archway Nes erected to adorn my sprawling backyard. Vanessa was annoyed that we couldn't find small children for the parts of the wedding she wanted Samantha to have. That just couldn't be helped. Our race is not reproducing…at least, not members of this sector. I am going to make great efforts to rectify that as soon as possible.

While making my way toward Jacob, to wait for Sam, my anxiety peaks. What if Sam gets this far and her earlier fear returns? What if she decides to sacrifice her happiness and escape, thinking that leaving will somehow, ultimately save me? She's done it once already. What's to stop her this time?

I stand in my appointed spot as my heart hammers, imagining all the things that could go wrong.

Out of the corner of my eye, I catch movement. Our final unit members have arrived. So have the mothers. Even Veda has come. With her is a younger but strikingly similar woman. Veda nods to me. I incline my head. Behind her is the oldest man I have ever seen. I don't know who he is, but I'm sure the mothers will introduce him after the ceremony.

Nes starts to walk down the aisle. Her little black heels make half-circle impressions in the fabric that serves as a carpet. She takes her place opposite me, leaving room for Sam to stand between us. Nes nods to her mother then turns her gaze to the doorway.

As Sam comes into view, my breath catches in my throat. She walks, arm in arm with Caleb, her eyes closed. All our guests stand as the solo violinist starts to play.

Sam's eyes flutter open, and she takes a long moment to absorb the scene around her. Caleb hands her a large bouquet of white roses. The long tail of teal ribbon flutters on the breeze. Her gaze takes in everything, tears threatening to fall. She looks down at her dress, then her gaze sweeps up to lock onto me.

Nothing in this world could have taken my attention off my mate. I chance a peek at her aura. The green is almost eclipsed with brilliant white. Pink swirls in intricate lacework, broken only by one burst of teal. Silently, I plead with Sam to keep walking, to trust me, and complete one of her goals. To let love and destiny be our guide through our lives.

FIFTY-ONE

Samantha

____

I'M DREAMING. HOW HAS ALL OF THIS BEEN ARRANGED AND I NOT notice? There are more people here than I know or have met. A stab of sadness washes over me, stopping me from looking for any of my family.

The gown Vanessa has chosen for me is absolutely, perfectly me. It is the exact dress I would have picked if I had been given the choice. The feeling of being ill prepared hits me hard. I don't have a ring for Laine. I hope the vows she picked for the officiant to dictate are what I would want.

Closing my eyes, I shake my head as a rueful smile crosses my face. That minx. Vanessa prepared all of this and more. The garter belt and thigh highs should have been a tip off. What else has that girl planned?

My gaze finds and locks on Laine. He looks stressed and worried, which is typical when anything involves me. As I make my way to my fiancé, he seems to relax with every step closer I take. It seems a lifetime before I finally reach him. He exhales as if he has been holding his breath for the same lifetime it took me to arrive. Nes takes hold of my roses as Laine takes my hands.

Absently, I glance at who is there to marry us and the shock on my face is funny enough for Jacob to laugh aloud.

"How? There is no way you can legally marry us." I am not questioning, I am stating.

"Online. Did everything online. We are very resourceful when it comes to pleasing our women." There is something in his tone and the shift of his eyes that make me file that away for later reflection.

"Is this anything like you imagined, Sam?" Laine's voice is strained, nervous. I want nothing more than to reassure him he is acting exactly like a human groom, but I refrain.

I rescan everything around me, my hands still holding Laine's as he waits for my verdict. "No," I breathe. His shoulders droop and his eyes close. Leaning close, I add, "It's a million times better." I place my lips on his.

Vanessa clears her throat. With great annoyance, I release Laine and resume my place. His hands once again take mine as the congregation sits down. Vanessa hands Jacob a small piece of paper, and the music finally plays out and stops.

"We are gathered here this day to witness and celebrate one of life's greatest events," Jacob reads from the little card. "A happy marriage does not just happen, it is created. Remember the little things mean so much more than all the big things. To stand together to face anything this life brings your way, you are forevermore a team. Always remember you don't have to be the perfect partner, just be the right partner for the other." After a few seconds, he turns his focus to Laine. "Now, if you would please repeat after me..."

"Actually, I wrote something of my own, if that's okay."

My usually confident man is in unknown territory, trying to find his footing, and doing an amazing job, which, at once, makes me grateful and proud.

Taking a deep breath, Laine centers himself. "I vow to always protect your mind, body, and soul. I vow to endeavor to never make you cry. From now until the end of my days, I will strive to not only make you happy, but to provide everything your heart desires. Samantha, you are an interesting person in a mundane world. From this moment on, my heart is yours." His hands tighten on mine.

My heart melted as soon as I opened my eyes and saw all he and my sister had planned, but that experience pales in comparison to how it melts now.

"Would you like to say something before I continue?" Jacob's question is so quiet I almost miss what he said.

Searching for the words I want most to say, I find my mind knows exactly what I need to say. "Laine, I vow to try every day to show you how much you truly mean to me. I vow to work toward being the woman you deserve. I promise to always be cautious and conscientious in all of my actions. To always guard you above all else. I promise to never go to bed angry or upset. I can assure you, I will never lose my sense of humor. I will strive to forgive and forget, but, most importantly, to let go of the things I cannot change. I will always tell you I love you when the sentiment crosses my mind, to the point that you will tire of hearing it before long. I will always remind you how much I appreciate everything and anything you have ever or will ever do for me. I will never take you for granted. From this moment on, my heart is yours and only yours."

After a grueling day, my burden is instantly weightless. My smile can't possibly get any bigger. The electricity that once flowed through my veins is replaced by warm, soothing waters; my happiness, overwhelming.

"Now, if you would repeat after me." Jacob pauses and looks at Laine. "I, Laine, take you, Samantha, to be my lawfully wedded wife. To have and to hold in sickness and in health; for richer or poorer. In good times and in bad, I vow to honor, love, and cherish you from this day forward for as long as we both shall live."

Laine looks so insanely pleased with himself at having accomplished the repeating of the vows, it almost makes me giggle. He slides an intricate diamond band on my finger and secures it with a kiss.

"Now, Samantha, your turn. Please repeat after me." Jacob winks at me, drops a wedding band in my hand, and continues, "I, Samantha, take you, Laine, to be my lawfully wedded husband. To have and to hold, in sickness and in health; for richer or poorer. In good times and in bad, I vow to love, honor and *obey...*"

My expression must say it all. Jacob succumbs to laughter as I finish exactly how Laine did, not repeating Jacob, at all. "I vow to honor, love, and cherish you from this day forward for as long as we both shall live."

Jacob still hasn't fully recovered from his fit of laughter and all I can do is giggle at the confusion on my husband's face. Deftly, I slide my husband's wedding band on his finger.

"Why is he laughing?" Laine is miffed to be out of the loop. "Jacob, what's so funny?"

"He tried to pull a fast one on me and get me to vow to do something I would never do." I quickly grab Laine's hands before he can wrap them around Jacob's neck. "Love, it was all in good fun. No harm done. Humans are not actually bound by any of this. Many marriages last less than a year. Many people marry many times in their life. It's okay. This is unimaginably perfect."

His mouth crashes against mine. There's nothing subtle or chaste about his kiss. He was done being restrained by propriety or whatever Vanessa told him his decorum should be.

"Hey! I didn't say you could kiss the bride!" Jacob objects, but his protest falls on deaf ears.

By the time Laine is done thoroughly staking his claim on me, my head is dizzy.

"Come, my love, you need to eat something." He draws me back up the aisle. As we near the house, he sweeps down and scoops me into his arms. I emit a squeal of surprise. He carries me into the house.

The decorations are, of course, all Nessa's creations. The woman loves a good party. In another life, she was a coronation planner, I'm certain.

I know exactly what Laine planned or decided and what Vanessa handled. One of the options for dinner is chicken and dumplings. Its inclusion on the menu touches me deeply that he remembered something so trivial from what seems ages ago. There is also a make-your-own-chili-dog station, which makes me laugh. After mingling for a bit, we are told it is time for the first dance. I'm curious to see what my husband has picked for our song. He doesn't disappoint. It's a waltz. Thankfully, Laine knows how to dance and leads me expertly, so it looks like I know what I'm doing.

"You're my favorite," I tell him. I had vowed to share sentiments when they crossed my mind.

"Your favorite? Your favorite what?"

"You, my husband, are my favorite person in all the world. My most favorite thing, ever. Whenever I am asked, 'What is your favorite?' you will be my answer."

"Husband? That's what I am now?"

"Yes, this marriage makes you my husband." My contentment can't be contained.

"What are you now?"

"I'm your wife."

"What is your favorite book?"

"Ah, Mr. Knightley, are you testing your wife?"

The gleam in his eye does not go unnoticed.

"Ours is my favorite story, but you are my favorite book."

"Ms. Harris, you are quick."

"Not Miss anymore, and definitely not Harris. Not now, not ever again."

"Do married people always change their names?"

"Depends on where they are from. In some parts of the world, the husband's last name and the wife's last name make up a hyphenated last name. Sometimes women choose not to change their names, and I'm sure, a time or two, a man has changed his last name to his wife's. Since I detest my last name and all that comes with it, I happily relinquish it. I'm honored and exceedingly happy to be Mrs. Knightley from this moment on."

"Come, I want to show you the cake." His happiness almost makes me forget how much I hate cake. Memories threaten to surface around the reasons I hate the dessert, but my husband's elation quiets all of them. His hands frame my face as his stares into my soul. "I would never have something you don't like near you on our special day." His lips brush mine as he releases me and ushers me to the dessert table. Where people would have a tiered cake, our celebratory dessert is comprised of giant cookies separated by little pillars. Regular-sized cookies encircle their tiered cousins, and the rest of the table is decorated with much smaller cookies. Every cookie imaginable must have found its way onto this table.

"I am the luckiest girl in the world." My body melts into his as I hug him for all I'm worth.

As guests approach to talk to us and get dessert, I notice that others pair off to dance to the classical music that's still playing.

"Sam, follow me." My husband takes my hand and leads me up the stairs. Not one person seems to notice. He rushes to our bedroom door, quickly opens it, pulls me inside, and shuts the door.

Laine reaches for my neck and tips my head up to gain access to my mouth.

When I can do so without insulting him, I pull back and look at him through my lashes. "I have no desire to take off my dress or to be done with our wedding yet, husband. So, I offer a compromise." I reach for his belt and loosen it.

"I don't care about the party downstairs."

"Oh, that is obvious, my love. Soon, we will go back downstairs and mingle some more, and as a reward for doing what I want, I will give you something you want." I arch a brow, grace him with a half-smile, and pull down his pants as I sink to my knees.

I reach out to stroke the only thing he is interested in using right now. He emits a soft moan. Using that as a signal that he agrees to my proposal, I sheath him completely while swallowing around him. I slowly pull back, then use my tongue to apply pressure as I slide him back in. With one hand, I cup his balls and with the other, I grab his base. Now, I'm moving quickly and adding pressure until he is close. He is concentrating hard, trying to make this last as long as possible. Well, that won't do. This is where I am most in charge. Swallowing hard and bearing my teeth sends him over the edge.

When, at last, he is finished, I release him.

While he regains his bearings, I lick him clean before regaining my feet. I start to brush past him to enter the bathroom, but he grabs my wrist. Before my mind can jump somewhere dark, his warm mouth meets mine. The dark creeps back into the recesses of my head.

"Love, let's go back down to our party." His voice is husky, his desire for more, evident.

Smiling, I nod and lead him to the door.

As we descend the stairs, a woman falls to the living room floor. As we reach the first-floor landing in a rush, a scream, ripped straight from the soul, reverberates off the walls around us.

FIFTY-TWO

Laine

THE ENTIRE PARTY—EVERYONE—FREEZES. I KNOW WITHOUT thinking, one of our own has gone down. "Jacob!" I shout. People surge toward the collapsed body.

"Right here, Laine. Everyone, back up!" Jacob hurries to the woman. She's laying on her side, one arm extended above her head, the other limp across her middle. Her light brown hair covers her face. Jacob kneels next to her and brushes the hair off her face. Her eyes are open, shocked, in pain, but not seeing. She isn't moving. Instinctively, I reach for Samantha and sidestep until I'm shielding her from Megara's lifeless body.

"I'm taking the unit to my house to figure out what went wrong. The sisters left after the ceremony, so all that's left is the group. I will report back as soon as I know what transpired." As Caleb speaks, the air around Megara's body shimmers. Her body slowly disappears. "We will honor her after we get all the facts together."

Samantha and I stand aside as everyone files through the front door. Sam's hand finds mine as we close the front door behind the last guest. With little effort, I pick her up, hold her close, and take the stairs two at a time.

I set her down outside our closed bedroom door, press her against the wood, and kiss her hard. While we're kissing, I grope for the doorknob, turn it, and sweep her into my arms before she has a chance to stumble backward. I kick the door shut on the way in, stride to the bed, and place her on the edge. As I reach out to grab ahold of the dress, Sam's raised hand stops me.

"Laine, please." She gingerly stands up.

"What, my love?" I would give her the moon, this second, if she asked.

"Honestly, I have not a clue how to get out of this gilded cage, but I don't want to ruin it. Would you please help me get this dress off before you have your way with me?" her voice is husky but strained.

My fingertips touch on the back of her neck as I tilt her head up to look at her better. "What's wrong, Sam?"

"That woman, she's dead, isn't she?"

"She is. But it isn't her death that has you troubled, is it?"

"No." She doesn't elaborate.

For once, I am torn between letting her work out her issues and pulling her out of her head.

Deciding to distract her, I trail my lips from her mouth to her neck. Her body begins to react.

"Sam." A tug on her hair comb sends her curls tumbling down her back. "My love." I turn her so I can inspect the dress while I ponder how best to free her mind from the dark. I press kisses on her neck while I tug on the ribbons along her back. They loosen the dress gradually, which releases her body. When there is no more ribbon to let out, I find a zipper. With one drag of the metal down her back, her body is free of the heavy dress. The sight before me nearly stops my heart. Sam wears a white garter belt, white thigh-high stockings, and heels. If I wasn't already trying to get her into our bed, I would be now.

I turn her around. "Wife, please, get out of your head. Come back." I bury one hand in her hair as my mouth explores hers.

With my other hand, I pull her close and hold her in place, not giving her the chance to pull away.

Her mind is completely on me; I've got nothing but time with my mate.

Somewhere over the course of a few long hours, we finally let sleep consume us.

I WAKE TO MY PHONE GOING OFF. I SNATCH IT OFF THE BEDSIDE table before the ringtone wakes Sam. "Hey Caleb, what's up?"

"We have a problem. I can make it over in a few minutes. Is that enough time for you to get dressed?"

"See you in a few."

Carefully, I slip out of bed. Samantha's had little sleep during the last few days. I want her to sleep as long as possible.

After I yank on a clean T-shirt and a pair of pants, I check on her. She looks so peaceful. As much as I want to kiss her before I leave, I refrain. I don't close the door all the way, afraid the click of the latch will wake her.

My front door opens as I reach the bottom step. Caleb pats me on the shoulder as we make our way into the living room.

"So, what went wrong? What happened?"

"Megara was expecting, so our loss with her is great."

"That is unfortunate. What happened to Jeremiah?"

Caleb is silent for a long moment. "A task was reassigned. He left after the ceremony to complete it." He pauses. The hesitation heightens my weariness.

"Caleb?"

"His task was a reassignment from someone who was meant to be in a different part of the country. The task decided, last minute, to attend a funeral of their relative or something..." His voice trails off. His eyes widen as he stares at something behind me. I know it's Sam.

"The woman pacing the tombstones," her voice is low, "was

angry. I think us being there angered her more. Their anger gives them power, doesn't it?"

I turn. "No, Sam," I start, but Caleb interjects, "Yes, Samantha. The angrier they are, the more power they have."

"If I hadn't left the funeral party, or if I had not gone at all, then she wouldn't have been so enraged that she had the power to kill one of us." Sam migrates toward the kitchen.

"It is unfortunate that she took three with her when she released." Caleb stops talking when he sees me flinch. "What's the matter?"

"Samantha blames herself for their deaths. She might refuse to mate me, or wall herself inside the manor, too fearful of doing anything that might harm me."

"She might do both," Caleb whispers.

"That isn't helpful!"

"There is nothing left to do. The bodies have already shimmered. We can honor them this evening."

My thoughts race over what course Samantha will choose. I take a few minutes to gather courage to face my wife. Then, with weary purpose, I enter our kitchen.

FIFTY-THREE

Samantha

My mind whirls. I haven't experienced this much buzzing since I died.

I head to the kitchen bar and sit on the first barstool I reach, my back to the doorway. I'm too lost in thought to remember Caleb and my husband in the living room. My husband. I got married in this house, just hours ago. A few hours ago, we had two more leathoes than we do now. One was pregnant. I'm a curse. A curse with nowhere to run.

That's not true. Laine isn't mated to me. I vowed till death do us part. I'm not alive. I died. That is a human ritual. I'm not human. I can still save him. My earlier plan, to live with the mothers, can still happen.

"My daughter, I feel your pain." Nona's arms encircle me.

Familiar words flood my head, *No matter how bad or how old, a girl will always want her mother.* I turn and my arms encircle her as my tears start. I have no will to stop the sorrow that flows through me. Guilt is overwhelming, anguish, a close second.

She releases me when my tears stop falling. "Samantha, my child," Nona says, "you cannot live in fear. You aren't to blame for any of this." She steps away.

I can't focus on what Nona is saying. All the negativity and doubts I've had over the course of the last month crash over me in waves. My blood is ice mixed with electricity. I don't hear Laine enter. I don't notice him until he wraps his arms around me, which silences the buzzing in my head. His presence doesn't ease the emptiness I feel, like it once did. A hole exists where my heart was.

"Samantha, can you talk to me?"

When I turn my head toward Laine, I glimpse Nona, in the far corner of the kitchen, staring out the window.

Calm has descended. I have no more tears to give. I wiggle out of Laine's arms, cross over to my mother, take her hand, and stare out the window. After a few minutes, Nona looks at me. "Samantha, it is very rare for your race to be killed. It is so rare, we keep all the dead in one place. This is not your fault. You did not do anything wrong. I see everything you are thinking. It serves no purpose if you stay unmated. Your new husband would not want to live in a world without you. If you doubt me, ask him."

There is no need to challenge what she says. I feel the same way.

"I see you feel the exact same way. Embrace the happiness offered to you. Love is the most beautiful gift this life gives. I told you once before that you would be instrumental in helping to raise our numbers. I meant that. It will make things so much easier on everyone if you do what your heart says. Now, my child, your husband and you have a few things to set in order." She looks past me. "I will be by later tonight, Laine."

The air shines around her. I finally witness my mother vanish.

"Sam, Love, are you okay?"

"I'm cold, husband. But it isn't my flesh. My body is hollow and so cold."

Laine's arms encircle me from behind. He has become a crucial part of my existence. I'm not sure how I feel about that.

He murmurs in my ear, "Wife, would you do me the honor of being my mate?"

Closing my eyes, I lean my head back to rest against his chest. He stays silent while I consider what Nona just said. I love that he understands my needs before I do. Laine, my husband. He truly has been by my side since my world fell apart. Actually, long before my world shattered. He puts my needs above his own. He is always thinking about my comfort. Can I deny him the one request he has made of me if it saves his life in the long run?

"Sam, if anything happens to you, I will never be able to go on."

"Laine, that simply isn't true. What if years and years from now we have children? Surely, they will give you reason enough to live. It would be irresponsible of us to mate and risk us both succumbing and leaving them alone."

His arms tighten around me. "My love, it really is unusual for our race to die. You and I will be more careful if that makes you feel better. We will always complete tasks together if that's what you wish. Tell me what will make me acceptable to you and I will do it. I love you, Samantha, more than anything."

Silence falls over me as my thoughts flit by in snips, eluding my attempts to capture and examine them. I give up trying to call my mind to order. "Laine, I love you. You have done so much to make me happy. Things I never would have thought to ask you for. I would do anything to make you happy. I'm just so scared. The thought of anything happening to you hurts." I let a few moments pass. "Take me back to bed, please. I am exhausted."

He picks me up and cradles me close as he returns to our room. I'm half asleep as he situates me under the covers. My sleep is dreamless beside him.

Hours later, I feel rested enough to stir. Alarm turns into panic when I realize I am alone in the room. The panic gives way to self-annoyance. I've never needed anyone before, what's wrong with me? Shaking my head, I climb out of bed and head for the bathroom. After a quick shower, I slip into jeans and one of my husband's shirts. I sweep my hair into a ponytail and then get to work cleaning the bedroom. Mindless busywork calms my nerves. As I finish making the bed, Laine returns.

"Sam, the servants will clean all of this. Don't trouble yourself, my love."

"Why? I'm capable of picking up. I like feeling useful and having something to do."

"Sam, we have tasks to do, and we have to honor our decommissioned later tonight."

"Laine, I trust you."

"I'm sorry, were we in the middle of a conversation?"

"I've been thinking about us." I stare at the bedspread, waiting for him to respond.

Waves of tension pour off him. "What have you decided?" he almost sounds exasperated.

I can't blame the poor man. I run hot and cold in a nanosecond.

"Samantha?"

My eyes meet his. "How soon can we be mated?"

FIFTY-FOUR

Laine

To say I'm in shock is putting it mildly. "I... Um, well, I guess as soon as tonight, if that is what you truly want."

She nods as she bends to smooth the bedcover once more. "What do I need to do to prepare?"

"Nothing. Everything is arranged by the male. The mothers will attend. It typically is a very small gathering, quite the opposite of the human's idea of a joining of two people."

My desire to go to her and hold her is overwhelming, but her aura keeps me from touching her. She is a slow swirl of every color.

"Sam, don't do this if you don't want to. We have all the time in the world."

The colors fall from her, like a heavy coat slipping off her shoulders. It isn't her wall, I can still see the green.

"Sam, talk to me. The faster you get it out of your head, the happier you will be."

"There are no guarantees in life. Not as a mortal, not as an immortal with an asterisk. Not even the mothers can tell us what will be. I want to make you as happy as you have made me. You aren't asking me for anything more than I wanted in my former life. I am too tired to fight my heart anymore."

I open my arms to her. She crosses the room and melts into my embrace. "I understand what you meant when you said I feel like home. You feel like home to me, Sam."

Standing here with her is where I could spend the rest of eternity, if allowed, but we have obligations and I have too much to do. "Come, the morning meeting starts in under a half hour, and then on to our tasks. How many do you have today, my love?"

She closes her eyes for a moment. "I have two. Why do I have only two? I thought you said we would have upwards of ten a day."

"The number of deaths in a given day changes. Some days you can have one and another you could have twenty. It just depends. Some leathoes transfer, more get tapped, then you have those who get suspended tasks. Like when I was tasked to teach you and keep you safe. Circumstances warrant the halting of tasks for some of us."

"Oh."

"Do you prefer to go alone, or do you want me to go with you?"

Before she can answer, Vanessa rushes into the room.

I roll my eyes. "Don't you know how to knock?"

"The door was wide open. Learn to shut it and I might knock. Sam's coming with me today. She needs some serious girl time!"

Sam grants Vanessa a radiant smile as she disengages from me. Vanessa pulls Sam behind her as she runs out of our room and down the stairs. After they leave, my phone goes off. Nes is texting me.

U have time 2 get everything done that needs 2 be done 4 2nite text u when omw bk l8r

She texts like that because she knows I hate it. She's right, though. It's a good thing I only have eight tasks today. Shaking my head at the thought of everything I have to get done, I head for our meeting. Halfway there, I text Caleb.

I'm skipping the meeting today. I'll see you later tonight.

Ha! First time for everything. You do know the meetings are just to hang out? See ya tonight!

Luck is on my side. My tasks are clustered together today. Five are in a hospital on the same floor. Two are in a fast food restaurant, and my last task is in the same shopping center I have business in. I'm not big on shopping but I have to get this part right. I still have the bracelet I bought when I got our wedding rings. I never had a good chance to give it to her.

One of our race owns the regional store where we purchase special items required for our ceremonies and rituals. I ordered Samantha's ceremonial cloak the day she passed her final test. Thanking my forethought, I stop by the store, pick up my special order, and head back to the manor.

"We have a small problem," Caleb announces as I step through the front door.

"Glad to see you, too, Caleb. Why are you in my house?" I kick the front door closed, careful not to drop the box I carry.

"One of the agents is on his way here right now."

My head jerks up. "Why?"

"Honestly, I am not sure. But I do know they mean to question you and Sam. Just wanted to give you a heads-up so Sam doesn't freak out when one of them shows up. Hopefully, they knock and don't shimmer like the mothers."

"Can agents shimmer?"

Caleb laughs. "I've never seen an agent arrive, so I have no idea."

"Thank you for the heads-up."

"I'll leave you to it, then. I'm happy for you, Brother."

Samantha and Vanessa make it home about an hour after I do. No sooner have they closed the door behind them than a knock sounds. Vanessa shoots me a curious look as I go to open it.

"Laine Knightley?" a short, bolding man asks, his voice strong and confident despite his lack of stature. Beside him is an average sized woman with curly brown hair. She has a friendly face, a striking contrast to her partner.

"Yes. How may I help you?"

"I am Agent Allen, and this is Agent Ahonen. May we come in?"

I step aside to let the man and woman into the house. My attention darts to Vanessa, who looks worried. She isn't looking at the agents; her gaze is on Samantha, who looks like she is about to lose it. I grab Sam's hand and squeeze. Terrified emerald eyes find mine.

"Sir, perhaps you should tell us why you are both here. Based on your titles, I am to understand you are from the Agency of Death and Chaos."

"Of course, my apologies. The ADC is investigating the circumstances around the decommission of Jeremiah and Megara Vaughn."

I kiss the top of my wife's head and lead her into the kitchen. Agent Ahonen follows behind Agent Allen.

I turn to Sam as she takes a seat at the bar. "The ADC is a band of leathoes in charge of keeping peace and order amongst our kind. Their devout members are powerful enough to carry out their duties. They vow to never mate and they can never extricate." As I finish my explanation, I turn back to Agents Ahonen and Allen. "My wife is learning about our kind. I needed to explain what you do."

"Okay. So, Mr. Knightley, do you know how he came to ruin?"

"I was told. The mothers and our entire unit were here at the manor most of yesterday."

"Why?"

"Samantha and I had our wedding yesterday."

"You had a what?"

"My mate is half human. We had a human mating ceremony

yesterday. It lasted most of the day. Jeremiah was here for the initial ceremony, but I honestly can't tell you if I saw him or when he left. I was preoccupied. We didn't know anything was wrong until Megara expired in the middle of the living room."

"I heard that the last-minute task he was assigned was located in a cemetery about thirty miles east of here. Some said you had a close call in the same area, is that correct?"

Samantha says, "Yes. I was at the cemetery early yesterday morning."

"You did not have any tasks yesterday, I checked. Why were you there?"

"I was attending a funeral."

"Another human gathering?"

"Yes."

"Curious. Do you harbor resentment for the leathoes part of you?"

Clearly taken aback, Samantha's anger flares. "Sir, as I am very new to this part of my life, I don't know what you are getting at, but I do think I know what you are implying. I did not know Jeremiah or Megara. I had not been introduced to them. I do not know the ins and outs of how any of this goes. I have no idea where our tasks come from or how to do much of anything except extricate. Are you investigating their deaths because you think foul play is involved?"

Agent Allen scrutinizes Sam. "Yes, Miss, that is exactly what I think."

"After the funeral, I took a short walk. I felt her before I saw her."

"Sam's range is a bit longer than usual leathoes. I know that if she didn't have that little extra, we would not have gotten out of there ourselves."

"Your range is longer?"

"I have no idea what you are talking about. Range of what?"

"Love, the range of feeling when a spirit is near."

"Oh. Yes, I can feel them. We were about seventy feet away from her. I could feel her anger."

All of us look at her, astounded by her disclosure.

"Your range is impressive. Almost twice what the rest of us have."

"Samantha is half human, but she is also an Elite."

The little man's mouth opens in shock. Recovering his manners, he quickly genuflects and stands. His partner mirrors his actions.

Sam looks at me, her brows knit in pure confusion. She appears alarmed.

"Thank you both for your time. I will send you a full report once it is completed. I will disclose, we are almost positive their deaths are the work of The Plague."

Nodding my understanding and dismissal, they quickly leave the room. Vanessa escorts them out. The front door opens and then closes, and I breathe a little easier.

"Doesn't everyone know you are elite?" Sam asks as I bend to kiss her.

"Honey, everyone in our race knows who Caleb, Vanessa, and Laine are. But no one was told about you. We knew Nona had a child, but only our unit was told about you a few months ago. Because you were human and mortal, we couldn't risk something happening to you. Except Jacob, no one knew about you while you grew up. Even he wasn't told everything. He only knew you were half leathoes, not who your mother was. Not all leathoes are good. The Plague is a group that wants to eradicate all humans. There's more than just The Plague to worry about. Many beings and creatures live around and interact with humans every day, but humans are blind to them and easily persuaded."

"Bramwell." She hesitates. "The Plague? Work with Veda?"

"Yes, beings like Bramwell. There are others you will come to know in time. Veda works alone. She doesn't like to share credit for anything she cooks up. Not all leathoes are extricators, but most are. Come, my love, we have a ceremony to prepare for." I pull her with me. I retrieve the large rectangular box I wrapped earlier and hand it to her. She carries it into the living room, sits in the chair nearest the fireplace, and rips off the paper. Carefully, she slips off the lid and lifts away the tissue paper. She strokes the exposed material then looks up at me, her confusion evident.

I grab the top of the garment, pull it free and hold the cloak up for her inspection. She sets aside the box, stands, and glides a hand over the silk, stopping to run her fingers over the intricate trim. The black silk brocade is embroidered with tiny red roses and has a crimson silk lining. The loose-fitting hood is mostly for decoration. She examines the intricate clasp, which is white gold and diamond encrusted. Only the best for my mate.

"What is it?"

"Can't you tell?" I grin.

She traces the design in the brocade as she shakes her head.

"It's your cloak. I had it made for you the day you passed your final test."

"Cloak? Seriously? I thought humans get reapers all wrong."

"We aren't reapers, and don't always wear a cloak. This is why mating ceremonies are small and private. The last big one brought too much unwanted attention. Some of the men imbibed way too much. One thing led to another, and now humans think The Grim Reaper wears a tattered black cloak, carries a scythe, and is some sort of skeleton."

"Well, I agree you don't look skeletal, but you are giving me a cloak. Do all leathoes own cloaks?"

"Of course. We wear them for rituals and ceremonies."

"I am kind of sad you don't have a mystical weapon."

"We use a scythe. For rituals and ceremonies."

"See! Humans didn't get it all wrong," Sam says indignantly. She tenses and her gaze bores into me, "If The Plague hate humans, why would they kill or attack a leathoes? Aren't leathoes one of their own?"

"I'm sure, when we get the report, our questions will be answered. Come, I have a few more things for you."

"I don't need anything else. This is beautiful. Thank you."

"I know I didn't have to do it. I wanted to."

I drape the cloak over my forearm and lead Sam upstairs. I pull a garment bag from my closet and offer it to her. Tentatively, she takes it.

FIFTY-FIVE

Samantha

I'M NOT SURE HOW I FEEL ABOUT LAINE GIVING ME THINGS. UNTIL recently, I hadn't noticed how well off he is. This house is insanely massive and ornate. He has several cars. He owns a few acres of land. There are at least three live-in servants.

Money has never been something I aspired to have. Living meager, I was able to enjoy life, but still had to tell myself no on some occasions. As I lay the garment bag on the bed, I hear Laine riffling through something in the bathroom. I unzip the garment bag and find a floor-length black chiffon dress. It's flowy, loose, and beautiful.

"Laine, do all the cloaks for special occasions look like this?"

"No, my love. The men wear solid black ones with plain closures. Our women wear solid black until they're mated. Mated women wear colors that correlate to their mate's family colors, or a color he decides he wants her in." He steps into our bedroom carrying a small rectangle box.

"So, which is mine?"

"I picked the color that your aura most often shows. It is a huge part of who you are."

"What does red mean?"

"Red is anger. Even when you are scared or upset, there is always red mixed in."

"Husband, I don't think that is either a compliment or a good thing."

"Either way, it doesn't matter. It is what I picked." He smiles and winks as holds out the small box.

"Laine, I am realizing more and more that you have more money than sense. I'm not comfortable getting so many extravagant gifts."

"Sam, you're Elite. Your mother did not bring you into this life penniless. You will have to ask her about those details, but even if you had nothing, we are together. What is mine is yours."

"I don't want your money. Financials have never been that important to me."

"Stop worrying and open your present."

Gracing him with a withering look, I comply. The box contains the most dazzling diamond tennis bracelet. "Laine, I'm not used to having such pretty things. I love who I am. I don't want to lose myself to all this finery."

"You don't like it?" His dismay makes me feel a million times worse.

"It's gorgeous. Just please know, going forward, that I'm easier to please than this. I don't need things. I value and love you giving me your time and attention. Those are the two most precious gifts you can give to anyone."

"How so? Presents take thought and effort."

"But time is something no one can buy. It means the most to me because we are only given so much time in our lives, and someone deciding I am worth spending some of theirs on is the gift I most cherish."

He takes a few steps to me and places a molten kiss on my lips. "I will leave you to get dressed. Come downstairs when you're ready." With that, he exits the room, closing the door behind him.

A quick shower and a few minutes wondering if I am making the right decision leads me to no other conclusion but to follow through with my commitment to Laine.

The dress fits perfectly. It hugs my breasts, and the hem skims the floor. It flatters my curves. I was not provided shoes and wonder if I have any that will match this outfit. Worry assaults me. I decide to forgo shoes.

I unclasp the cloak and twirl the heavy, beautiful thing around me with great flourish. I've seen that move done thousands of times in movies and always wanted to try it. After I fasten the clasp at my neck and pull the hood up, I make my way downstairs to join my mate. My foot lands on the last step and my brain floods with the promise I made Laine, which seems like a hundred years ago. I swore not to question anything about this ceremony.

Oh, this is going to be interesting.

FIFTY-SIX

Laine

____

I BREATHE A SIGH OF RELIEF AS I SEE HER DESCEND THE STAIRS. There is not a creature alive who rivals my mate's beauty. The dress I had made for her is perfect. The cloak, made of the finest material, compliments her in every aspect.

The mothers have arrived, so the ceremony can begin, as have Caleb and Vanessa, who will witness and contribute as needed. Curiously, Jacob is here. Not that I object, he is a very good friend, but he looks a little troubled. Maybe after the ceremonies we can find a moment to talk.

Sam stands at the bottom of the stairs, apparently unsure of what she needs to do or where she should go. I extend my hand to her and relief replaces her confusion as she approaches and takes it. "Ready, Samantha?"

"As ready as I will ever be."

"Good, let us get started."

I lead Sam to the backyard where just yesterday we were married. I expected her to be nervous or tense, but she seems peaceful.

The frail old man from the wedding is standing in the back-yard, the full moon his backdrop. From the rear of our small group, my mother says, "My son, this is your grandfather, The Father of Time. He will be performing your mating."

Father Time's white hair hangs down to his knees. His white beard stops just short of his waistband. His cloak is not the solid black men wear but appears to be woven of mist. Its colors swirl, passing through and around each other: black, purple, dark blue, and brown, each following its own path. The colors are incredible. He is thin, almost to the point of emaciation. His scythe looks as old as he. Two chains drape his neck and one wraps his ceremonial weapon. His frail hand pulls his hood into place.

A cold shiver threatens to run down my spine, but I manage to control my reaction. I don't want Samantha terrified of what is to come.

Nona hands her daughter an ornate scythe. Sam looks like she is trying hard not to speak. Suddenly, I remember her promise not to question anything if I behaved at the human thing she took me to.

Morta brings me my scythe. Everyone in the gathering dons their cloaks. They pull their hoods into place before holding their scythes vertically in front of them.

"Step forward, let the ceremony commence," the old man's voice is purposeful and commanding.

Samantha and I approach and take our place before him, facing away from the witnesses. My brother approaches and places my long black cloak on my shoulders then fastens the closure. Caleb steps away.

"Laine, prepare yourself," the old man commands.

I brace myself.

"Samantha, retrieve your mate's essence."

Nona steps close and whispers in her daughter's ear. The blood drains from Sam's face as she looks from the weapon to me. Her eyes flash and her anger peaks. I catch her eye and nod once. Sam places the tip of the blade at my heart, pauses for a second, then applies pressure. The blade slips into my body and pierces my heart, sending a jolt of pain I knew was coming after seeing other ceremonies. Chancing to look at her, I see she is scared to continue. I reach for her scythe and help her force it down and out of the side of my body. Her astonishment at seeing the blue swirl of smoke clinging to the metal makes me smile.

She eyes me as I place the tip of my blade at her heart. I'm not sure if I should go quickly to lessen the pain or go slow so she remembers every aspect of this moment. As I think it through, I feel pressure applied to my handle. Sam's eyes not leaving mine, she pulls the blade into her body in one hard jerk. I can see her working to internalize the pain as much as she can. Slowly, I move the blade down and out of her side. Her essence is bright golden, light emanating off it. I'm mesmerized.

FIFTY-SEVEN

Samantha

"Now, Laine, help your mate as we recite the binding," Father Time instructs as the witnesses draw closer.

Laine brings his scythe up to touch mine and the smoke clinging to each attracts as if they are magnets. They don't mix, they literally start to swirl in front of us.

"Now, my love, repeat what I say." Laine brings one hand up to caress my face as he says, "My heart is your heart." The colored smoke stops circling. Instead, each lengthens side by side like pieces of ribbon. "It beats only for you." The tail of each color begins to knot with the other. "My life is your life." The blue encircles the gold, slowly twisting itself around the gold. "My soul is your soul." The people around us, I notice, are softly chanting. "Without you, I'm nothing. Without you, I'll die." As I conclude the final word, the ribbons of smoke knot at the top. The joined ribbons hang before us, giving me time to hear the witnesses. They chant, "Forevermore entwined."

"Now, Samantha, grab my wrist as I grab yours. Don't let go until I do." His right hand grabs my left wrist, palm flat against my pulse. I copy his hold. The twisted smoke proceeds to wrap around our hands. Laine looks at me quickly. As he does, my wrist feels like it catches fire. I want to jerk away but Laine has a death grip on me. Panic threatens to overwhelm my senses. "Samantha, I got you. Almost done. You're doing perfectly. I'm so proud of you." His whisper is only for my ears. "Now repeat, 'forevermore entwined.'"

As the phrase leaves my mouth, Laine lets go of me, but only for a second. His arms crush me to his chest and he kisses me thoroughly.

Eventually, he ends the kiss and presses his forehead to mine. "I love you so much, Samantha. Although I want nothing more than to take you into the house and fulfill my duties, we do have one more thing to take care of."

I giggle for a second. "What else do we need to do?"

"We have to visit the vaults."

"I'm not even going to ask. Lead the way."

The walk to Caleb's is shorter than I anticipated. Behind his house is a cave-like recess in a massive hill. A metal door spans the entrance. Caleb presses his hand flat against the door and it swings open. We step inside and the candles in their sconces ignite. It's magical. I love it. Until I remember this is a place for our dead. The remembrance sobers me.

We descend a long, narrow staircase and reach a circular room containing stone beds. There are rows of leathoes. They appear to be sleeping. My heart sinks. There are at least seventy-five stone slabs. "Laine, when did all these people die?"

"Jeremiah and Megara were our seventh couple to die. The rest died alone. When leathoes die, we remain in the state you see here. We've had one hundred and eleven leathoes deaths since the inception of our race."

"Humans decompose. Eventually, we turn to dust."

Laine looks at me appalled. His expression is almost comical.

"Well, leathoes freeze in their death state."

"So, what do we do to honor them?"

"Watch and copy me." He raises his scythe and rakes it

through the bodies horizontally. I do exactly as he instructed. The Sisters come forward next and kiss the cheeks of both bodies.

Instinctively, I reach out and run my fingers through Megara's hair. It is then that I notice a strange mark on my left wrist.

"What is this?" I extend my hand palm up to show Laine my wrist.

"My mark is the crescent moon. I marked you with my mark."

His mark is intricate and beautiful. Swirls adorn the inside curve of the crescent. The entire mark is about three inches from top to bottom. "Do I have a mark?"

"Of course." He exposes his wrist. "See the lightning bolt crossing the moon at an angle?"

"That is my mark? Well, that's fitting. I sometimes strike without warning, and I can't be stopped or bottled." My mark is solid and rigid. Almost too harsh to mark Laine's perfect body.

"It is really fitting then." He leans down and brushes his lips against mine.

"Laine, I hate to interrupt. Could I talk with you for a second?" Jacob is tense.

FIFTY-EIGHT

Laine

Excusing myself from the mothers and Sam, I join Jacob. "Of course, what's wrong?"

Jacob gestures for me to lead the way.

I head for the stairs. We climb the long staircase in silence. I wait for Jacob to speak. When we leave the crypt, we walk side by side toward Caleb's house.

"Laine, I have known for some time now that Vanessa is my mate. But I didn't see a reason to rush into a joining." He glances at me as he speaks then quickly goes back to looking at the stone floor.

"That's awesome! Surely, you didn't think I would be mad about that?" I grin and slap him on the back.

"No, of course not. It's just that sometimes she isn't green to me. Like, the green shuts off or flickers."

"What? That isn't possible." My elation fades.

"I don't know what to make of it. I do love your sister, Laine, but not always seeing her green has me questioning the knowledge we have about our race. Are we really deteriorating that much? I'm not sure what to make of it. It has me worried."

We reach Caleb's house and enter. Jacob finds glasses as I grab a bottle of whiskey. I pour two fingers into each glass.

"For the time being," I say, "let's keep this between us and keep a close eye on her. Maybe it's something small. Maybe you don't see her as a full mate because she isn't fully tapped to extricate yet. Maybe she's been exposed to humans for too long." I tap my glass to his and we down our drinks.

"I can keep an eye on her. I think it is all I can do right now."

The back door opens and closes and I hear multiple footsteps in the kitchen.

We nod to each other and go to join our companions. I'm anxious to find my wife.

"Thank you for listening to me. I appreciate it."

I nod at Jacob, enter the kitchen, and spot Sam right away. She isn't alone, and I'm shocked to recognize her companion. He doesn't attempt to disguise his true nature.

Vanessa collides with my shoulder but keeps walking. She doesn't even acknowledge me. I watch her walk away as Sam and Bramwell join me.

"Laine, Bramwell thinks we need to be careful of Vanessa," Sam murmurs.

"When did you get here Bramwell?" I'm trying to hide my shock at seeing him in his true form. "It's only Vanessa," I reply distractedly. "She's probably really tired or something. She planned all of this rather quickly."

"Bramwell senses something sinister going on."

"Jacob and I have agreed to keep an eye on her. Thanks, Bram." I wait for Sam to translate and then pull her by the hand through the door to head home. The breeze catches her cloak and it billows behind her. The sight is burned into my brain forever.

The walk is quick, the night is crisp and clear. "The stars are out tonight."

"They are beautiful." Sam is breathless as we walk. "You can see so much out here. Nothing like where I grew up. The sky is amazing."

David has the door open as we reach the front door. We take the steps to our bedroom two at a time, but halt when we see Vanessa.

She stands at the top of the stairs, her expression blank. She doesn't say a word. She's blocking the way to our room.

"Hey, Sis, you okay?"

"Nes," Sam says. "Hey, you don't look so good. Do you want Jacob to check you out?"

She throws Sam a deadly look and launches herself at my mate. I leap in front of Sam. Vanessa's body slams into mine. Our collision knocks her to the floor. Her head hits the wood and, after a second, Vanessa's eyes focus. She starts to cry.

Jacob rushes up the stairs and sees her lying in the hall, crying. His look to me says, *See what I mean?*

"OH, SISTER, YOU ARE ABOUT TO FACE THE CONSEQUENCES OF YOUR actions." I laugh as I watch my minion enter my niece. It will take a bit of trial and error to bring her under my control, but anything worth doing is worth doing well.

Centuries of patience are finally paying off. Sooner or later, I knew the chance to get even would come. That heartless bitch, taking the only man I truly loved and destroying him because he preferred me. She thought she had the last say. She has no idea what I am about to unleash on her precious dears.

Seeing my young niece fight against herself while appearing to fight with her family is the sweetest thing I have ever seen.

"Mother, the siquinter knows."

My dutiful daughter is anxious for me.

"It matters not. It isn't like he would tell anyone."

I resume concentration, fighting to get the results I need from this vessel. No matter how long it takes, I have accomplished the hardest part. The rest will come. No one has patience like a woman scorned.

Sneak Peek

Sneak Peek at Chain Reaction

BY TARAH SCOTT AND EVAN TREVANE

What you won't find in the history books.

Chapter One

October, 1942

Tension fermented in the air like a sour mash whiskey. By chance, skill, stealth, and deceit I had kept my secret. But tonight, I strode down the halls of Chicago University's Eckhart Hall with a feeling my time had run out.

Every evening I reported for duty as The Manhattan Project's head of nightshift security not knowing what I missed during those midday hours when I lay dead to the world. Along with the bizarre sleep that immobilized me, the strange infection raging through my body made me dislike food and drink, stopped my smoking habit cold turkey, and switched me into permanent high gear. The worst part was the dread I barely kept at bay, knowing the people I worked for would turn me into a lab rat if they discovered the truth.

My gut coiled tighter as I entered Security Chief Lopez's office at six o'clock sharp. Lopez stood in front of his desk, hat in hand, while rifling through a stack of files. He looked over his shoulder and our eyes met.

I halted. His bloodshot eyes told me something was wrong even without the uncharacteristic loose tie and rumpled black suit. He straightened and raked strands of greased hair over the bald spot in the back of his head.

"Pierce," he said, "there's been a security breach."

Relief washed over me. This had to be a repeat of the one and only *security breach* we'd had a couple of weeks ago. In a fit of depression, Miss Therese Hance, a mathematics major here at Chicago University, had written a poem. I still recalled the verse verbatim:

DEAR LITTLE NEUTRONIAN WHO LIVES ON A NUCLEUS IN AN ATOM OF MY knee, if you do not stop jumping around, you are going to cause an atomic blast and blow up the universe.

WITH THE TOP-SECRET RACE TO BEAT THE GERMANS TO THE FIRST nuclear chain reaction going on at Chicago University, the poem hit too close to home. When Miss Hance's professor, Dr Albert, found the poem on her desk here in Eckhart Hall—Dr Albert had some vague awareness of the research going on—he passed the poem along to Oppenheimer, and Oppenheimer panicked. Lopez and I barely prevented the scientists from having a collective nervous breakdown.

I gave Lopez a *not this again* look. "Which student wrote another poem? Miss Hance didn't know a thing. It'll be the same this time." Then I added before he could reply, "Don't tell me you bought into the story about how her studies in group theory gave her a subconscious knowledge of the scientific research being conducted here."

"We intercepted a radio message north of the Ontario border

last night." Lopez grabbed the folder and extended it toward me. "The code-breakers say the message contains the correct amount of Uranium 235 needed to sustain a chain reaction."

"The true U-235 amounts?" I blurted, mechanically reaching for the folder.

Our big edge over the Nazis was the knowledge of how little Uranium 235 was needed to start a chain reaction. Of the two isotopes of uranium, U-238 and the rare U-235, the Nazi's head scientist, Werner Heisenberg, believed they needed a uranium concentration of ninety percent U-235 to build an atom bomb. According to our head scientist, Enrico Fermi, only a twenty percent concentration of the rare isotope would reach critical mass. The disparity was enough to keep the Germans busy doing nothing but enriching uranium until we drove them back to Berlin. But we had to attain the first nuclear chain reaction to ensure victory.

I dropped my stare to the folder and forced my fingers to close around it as Lopez's hand fell away. A bona fide breach here at Chicago Pile One? No one in the outside world knew what was really going on in Eckhart Hall's *Metallurgical Lab*. The real liability lay a block away at Stagg Field. The scientists were building an atomic pile in an abandoned squash court beneath the field's west grandstands. Damn it, I'd warned Lopez someone would get suspicious at seeing scientists constantly running between Eckhart Hall and Stagg Field, briefcases clutched so tightly their knuckles turned white. Suddenly Miss Therese Hance's poem didn't seem so farfetched. Who else had noticed strange activity at Eckhart Hall?

"Who else besides the CP-1 scientists have this information?" I asked.

Lopez's mouth thinned. "You, me, and General Groves."

Groves and Lopez were above suspicion. The transmission had to have come from one of the fifty-two scientists working on the project. They all understood the ramifications of an atomic weapon in the hands of a madman like Hitler. I couldn't believe any of them capable of selling out their country, much less the rest of the world.

I swung my gaze up to Lopez's face. "If the Nazis find out Heisenberg's equations are wrong…"

"And the Nazis get their hands on the correct equations…"

We both let the unsaid words hang: *The US could lose the war.*

"Any leads?" I asked.

"Nothing. I rang your apartment an hour ago when the report hit my desk, but you must have been out."

I nodded. Here was the reason for the dread I'd experienced tonight. A crisis like this could draw attention to the fact I was always *out* during the height of daylight hours. My service during the Great War combined with my position as a detective on the Chicago Police Force had gotten me through the security check for this job. Keeping a low profile had kept my secret safe —until now.

"What are our instructions?" I asked.

"Sit tight and observe until the spooks finish their investigation." He nodded at the folder. "It's all there. I've already requested a list of the scientists who have access to the U-235 information, as well as a few other topics so the librarians can't guess who or what we're after."

"When will the report be available?" I asked in a tone I hoped didn't show my disbelief. Waiting for our counter intelligence experts to mull over mounds of information wasn't General Groves's style. Groves was the kick-ass type who single-handedly spearheaded the construction of the Pentagon, the world's largest office building.

"When they're ready," Lopez said. "We've got to catch this guy, but can't chance alerting the scientists to the possibility we have a spy. Any panic, and the university might discover this isn't the harmless metallurgical laboratory our government claims. Those bleeding heart academics will strip us naked and toss us ass first to the media wolves. In the meantime, we go on alert. Our inside network is working to pinpoint where the information originated."

Suddenly, the folder felt like it weighed a ton. I'd never expected to be holding one of these super secret reports. My thirty-nine years of age made me ineligible to fight this war, so I'd consoled myself with the knowledge Chicago cops were needed to keep the streets safe here at home. When I'd been attacked in the alley eight months ago, I'd put my life on hold while I hunted for the fiend who attacked me. Now, I'd set aside my search in order to aid the war effort because I was even more afraid of Hitler's Nazis and Mussolini's fascists gaining control than I was of what I had become. The longer I put off finding out who infected my body with this sickness, the less likely the chances I'd be able to reverse the disease. I hadn't allowed myself to think about what I might become if the disease ate me alive.

"We can't let those bastards win the war," I said.

Lopez's mouth thinned. "I have to fly to Washington. You're in charge while I'm gone."

"Me?" I forced back shock. "What about Banks? He's your dayshift second in command."

"You're head of nightshift. Groves says you're in charge when I'm not here."

My mouth went dry. Lack of seniority enabled me to do this job. I wanted to ask when he would return, grill him on every tiny detail in the red file I gripped, anything, to keep him talking and here at CP-1.

His gaze bored into me. "You got this handled?"

"Yeah," I replied.

Without another word, he donned his hat and disappeared out the door.

I stared at the open doorway and muttered to the empty room, "As long as I can find the leak before sunrise."

Chapter Two

I HAD READ ONLY EIGHT OF THE ELEVEN PAGES OF THE *EYES ONLY* report when I got the call. Two minutes later, I stood outside the closed office door of Dr Leonard Heinrick, stopped by the smell of cold blood seeping from the room. A lot of blood. What stopped me wasn't the heightened sense of smell that aroused boyhood memories of the way my father smelled when he returned from the slaughterhouse where he worked, but the stomach-churning odor of decaying blood.

I fought back a rising panic. Why the hell hadn't Lopez caught a plane an hour later? As head of security, he should be standing here instead of me. At the very least, he should have locked down the lab and given me authority to run my own investigation. Instead, he'd tied my hands and left me waiting for information from the eggheads.

Movement on the other side of the door's frosted glass startled me from the dread and I recognized the blurred form of Officer Of the Day, or OOD, Colonel McHenry. I opened the door. He stood near the desk in the cramped office and turned, revealing the mutilated body of Leonard Heinrick. He lay on his back, arms at his side as if at attention. Blood had pooled in his right eye socket. Crimson stained the front and sides of his starched white shirt where his throat had been cut, and over a quart of blood had puddled on the floor under his head.

A chill snaked up my back. The precision throat slice reminded me of the way Lawrence 'Lucky Larry' Fiato liked to kill—when he had the time to enjoy his work.

"You didn't touch anything?" I asked in reflex as I forced my legs to carry me forward. The stench of dead blood made me want to vomit. Week-old hamburger would smell better.

McHenry marched to the door, quietly shut it, then faced me, hands clasped behind his back. "I secured the crime scene, then called you from the office next door."

I didn't know what *secured the crime scene* meant—the Army wasn't known for doing things like the Chicago PD. I swallowed back rising revulsion as I unbuttoned my suit jacket and squatted beside the body. The disease flowing through my veins made me crave warm, living blood. *Dead* human blood made my gut roil as if I'd taken a nosedive in a Douglas A-24 Banshee.

I made as close an inspection of the body as possible without disturbing anything. Nothing obvious was missing. Heinrick's wallet bulged in his front pants pocket and the Prexa Swiss-made Chronograph Manual watch he wore was still strapped to his left wrist. No other wounds were visible, but forensics would have to tell me what his backside looked like. The rotting odor I knew Colonel McHenry couldn't smell forced me to choke back a gag. I'd seen my share of blood and death. At fifteen years of age, my six-foot height and sprouting beard got me into the Army during the Great War, where I saw enough death and dismemberment near Maginot Line in France to last a lifetime. Now I couldn't get past the violent aversion to cold, *dead* blood.

But I'd have to deal with my loathing in order to find the killer. The stabbing to Heinrick's eyes indicated torture and the slice to his neck was professional. A trained killer had infiltrated the sterilized ranks of Chicago Pile One. I had to work fast. Espionage, torture, and murder mounted a greater problem than being out of communication during the midday hours when I lay unconscious.

We couldn't afford to draw attention to the lab with the kind of security found on military instillations, so we kept security light. I'd strapped on the Colt .45 General Groves had insisted Lopez and I keep in our desks in case of emergency, but neither McHenry, nor any of his civilian-dressed officers—we had to make the daily business look like a typical university operation—carried weapons. A policy that had to grate against McHenry's military mind. Yet strangers didn't enter Eckhart Hall without notice. So how had someone waltzed into Heinrick's office noticed?

I stood and walked a circle around the corpse. More important than the how was the why? Scientists had reasons to be jealous of one another: status, projects, publications, and occasionally romance created friction among them. But these motives seldom led to murder. Was Heinrick's murder related to the security breach or another matter altogether? The easy answer was that Heinrick had passed on the priceless U-235 information, then outlived his usefulness. But I had a feeling there'd be no easy answers.

I steeled myself against the nausea, squatted again, and drew the stench deep into my nostrils. In two seconds, I knew Heinrick had been dead approximately four hours. "You were killed around quarter after six, Heinrick," I murmured.

"How can you tell?" McHenry asked.

I looked up, having forgotten him. "Hypostasis." I drew an imaginary circle around Heinrick's eye with my forefinger. "See how pink his skin is here? That's an indication the blood is settling in the lowest parts of his body. The pinker the skin, the earlier the time of death." I glanced at McHenry, not adding that hypostasis commenced approximately six to eight hours *after* death and isn't fully pronounced for eight to twelve hours. Truth was, I couldn't explain how I knew the age of dead blood, and I'd grown tired of trying to understand the strange ability.

I dropped my gaze back to the bloody neck. "Just a guess. The coroner will have the final say."

"Security is on full alert," McHenry said. "We're on lockdown. If the killer is still here, we'll find him."

I nodded, not saying, *If he isn't one of the staff or military personnel.* Inside jobs were the hardest for military police to accept. Traitors in the midst of patriotic zeal hit hard.

I rose. "I assume none of the evening staff are missing?"

"No."

"You have someone checking on the day crew?" If the murder turned out to be an inside job, he could be in Canada by the time the day shift showed up and we discovered him missing.

"Banks is on it," McHenry replied.

"How about the office?" I asked. "Anything missing?"

"Don't know. Security still has to inventory the contents of the safe."

I glanced at the combination safe by the desk where Heinrick stored his classified documents. What McHenry called a safe was a fortified steel file cabinet with a combination dial about the size of my fist with a sturdy lever type handle. Every scientist had a similar safe. Some had two drawers like Heinrick's, others four. If the thief had accessed the safe, he wanted us to think otherwise: the drawers were closed and the cabinet looked unmolested.

I took two steps to the safe and pulled my handkerchief from my back pocket. Using the handkerchief to cover my fingers, I jiggled the handle and yanked. Locked.

"I'll have the contents inventoried and dusted for prints," McHenry said.

Spies preferred photographing documents instead of stealing them. Missing documents were always assumed to be in foreign hands, and steps taken to discredit, invalidate, or obfuscate the secrets within. The killer had made no efforts to hide the fact he was a professional, so why hide the fact he'd stolen documents? Now everything in the safe would be considered compromised. My gut said because he hadn't been interested in the safe's contents.

"Who found the body?" I asked as I scanned the sides of the safe.

"Dr Nichols."

Dr Gladys Anne Nichols, thirty years old—seven years younger than me—had four degrees from Vassar, Wellesley and Cornell. I had reviewed her personnel file a week ago when she arrived, but hadn't met her. I thought she worked dayshift.

"Where's she now?"

"Roma's office."

"I'll have a chat with her. Let me know when the Chicago PD arrives."

"General's orders are he talks to you first."

I jerked my gaze onto McHenry. "Chicago PD hasn't been notified?"

"You have to talk to General Groves first."

The implacable set of McHenry's jaw said he wasn't saying more, but I wasn't in the habit of leaving dead bodies lying around.

"You haven't reported the murder yet?"

"The Army doesn't report to local police."

"This isn't a military installation," I said.

"You were going to talk to Dr Nichols." He turned to the side, indicating I should precede him out of the room.

I stared for a long moment, but knew he wasn't going to budge until I left the crime scene. I strode from the room, McHenry closing the door behind us and taking up guard in front of the door as I kept going. "Damn Army by-the-book-board-up-their-asses attitude," I muttered as I turned the corner in the hallway. I used to like that about the Army when I served. I guess I was young and dependent back then.

A moment later, I halted in front of the closed door where Dr Nichols waited. The name painted on the glass read: Dr Enrico Roma, the alias of the great scientist and Nobel Prize laureate Enrico Fermi. The alias didn't fool anybody but the ignorant. Light shone through the milky glass window. I blew out a breath. The last thing I wanted to do was interrogate a hysterical woman.

I opened the door and stopped dead at the sight of a shapely blonde leaning against Fermi's mahogany desk. I stared as realization sunk in that the Veronica Lake look-alike standing there was the same egghead pictured in her personnel file. The glasses she'd worn were absent and, despite the red-rimmed eyes and drawn expression, the single overhead light warmed the creamy complexion that had looked bland and colorless in the photo.

Thick blond hair slid across her face in a broad wave and flowed down slim shoulders. Suddenly, I understood the reasoning behind the functional bun in the picture. Despite the legs that mesmerized a man all the way down to the high heel straps, the tweed skirt and blazer she wore emphatically stated the bombshell figure was off limits. But the moment a man laid eyes on her luxurious hair all bets were off. My breath caught with bloodlust as I drew in her scent from across the room.

Gray-blue eyes stared from behind the drape of blond hair. Her gaze flicked to my waistband and I realized she'd glimpsed the colt holstered beneath my suit jacket.

"You wear your gun like a gangster," she said.

I startled. Her voice, low and sultry, held a shaky note, but I knew the remark was payment for my staring.

"This incident requires I carry a weapon." My drill sergeant used to berate any reference to the word gun. *Your gun is between your legs, son. Your pistol or rifle is called a weapon.*

She continued to stare, and guilt stabbed at me. She'd discovered a colleague who'd been brutally murdered, and I stood in the doorway gawking at her. I swallowed, feeling like a school kid.

"Dr Nichols, I'm Agent Pierce, head of nightshift security."

Her fingers tightened around a lace handkerchief gripped in her right palm. I didn't want to step closer, but had to. Her pheromones were making my blood, or what was left of it, crave an infusion from her veins. "What happened?"

Her gaze dropped to the hankie and she began working the fabric with both hands. "I was working late and needed Leon to come to the lab. I couldn't get the Geiger counter to calibrate. I knocked. When no one answered, I opened the door and…" Her eyes swung up to meet mine. "So much blood." Her gaze remained locked with my eyes as if demanding a response.

"I'm sorry," I offered. "I thought you were assigned to dayshift."

She swiped at the corners of her eyes with the handkerchief. "I switched shifts yesterday so Leon and I could calibrate the new equipment."

I nodded. The scientists worked a twelve hours on, twelve off schedule seven days a week. We were in a race against Nazi scientists while men died in Europe, North Africa, and the Pacific. "Did you notice anything unusual tonight?" I asked.

"Nothing."

"Hear anything strange on the way to Dr Heinrick's office, pass anyone in the hall?"

She shook her head. "Maybe he's still here."

Something in the way she stared at—through—me, searching for answers and fearing what she might find, threatened to tip me off balance. "The murderer is gone," I replied in a level voice.

"How do you know?"

"A hunch," I said, and meant it.

"Why kill Heinrick?" she said. "Why not Compton or Fermi? But Heinrick…" Her voice trailed off.

"Are you saying Heinrick didn't know anything worth killing for?"

"I suppose we all know *something* worth killing for. Each scientist on this project is top in his or her field. But the project will go on without Heinrick. If we lost Oppenheimer, or Fermi, the project would be delayed, if not brought to a standstill."

"Did you enter Heinrick's office?"

"No, I took one look and ran."

The response, given without hesitation, or guile, made me wonder if this woman ran from anything.

"This was the first office I came to," she said.

Her story made sense, and my instincts said she was telling the truth. I had learned to trust my sixth sense, especially the last eight months. This ability was another one of those things I couldn't explain, like being conscious of the way her pheromones where working on me double-time.

"Are you staying in the dorm?" I asked.

She nodded.

"I'll have someone escort you there."

Desire to go with her shot to the surface with the heat of a volcano. I pictured white skin, full breasts, and blond hair between perfect thighs. I forced my breathing to remain even, and the swelling in my shorts abated. I'd never experienced such sudden, intense lust. If I escorted her back to her room I would drink her blood—and God only knew what I would do to her afterward. My pulse jumped with the thought of her warm blood flowing past my tongue down my throat… and her tight walls closing around me as I entered her.

"I have to complete my measurements before the day shift," she said. I jarred from the erotic thought. "There's not enough equipment to go around," she added.

I nodded. "Of course."

Clipped footsteps sounded almost noiselessly on the linoleum floor of the hallway and I recognized McHenry's walk two seconds before Dr Nichols's eyes shifted over my shoulder.

"Pierce."

I glanced back to see him standing in the open doorway.

"The general wants to talk to you."

A measure of sanity reasserted itself. I had to get away from her, *now*. "Could you escort Dr Nichols back to the lab?"

His expression lightened. "No problem." He stepped aside and motioned toward the door with an open hand. "Dr Nichols."

She cast me a farewell glance and headed toward the door. I tried tearing my eyes from the gentle sway of hips as she walked past, but couldn't, and felt the heat swell to the surface again. I had to find one of the small rodents whose blood I drank to keep my thirst for human blood at bay, or go back to Heinrick and hope the congealed blood in his decaying body would make me forget the craving. Rising desire twisted my insides and I feared even Heinrick's dead blood wouldn't work against the warm, pulsing blood of Dr Nichols.

I waited until their footsteps receded down the hall, then started forward. My gaze caught on Fermi's portable chalkboard on wheels, and I stopped. Equations filled the board that would have looked like Greek to me in my former life. Now, they sparked a story in my mind. Differentials, integrals, and algebra flowed in an almost perfect melody. The first time I saw calculus after becoming infected with this disease, I stared, fascinated. After flipping through a text on advanced mathematics I found in the small but well stocked CP-1 library, I could visualize the differential as rates of change, the integrals as sums, and functions as shapes and movement.

I stared at the puzzle of Fermi's equations, one side of my brain working the numbers, the other side stuck on the murder. Heinrick's eye had been stabbed in a careful, deliberate manner to inflict maximum pain *without* killing. Yet no one had reported the screams, which must have penetrated his office walls. Why? Like the equations on the board, the evidence didn't fit. Except, equations could be fixed. Heinrick would be dead forever.

I stepped up to the chalkboard, picked up a stick of chalk, and tapped down the chalkboard alongside the offending column of calculations. Halfway down, I fixed an exponent and turned a minus sign to a plus, then fixed the equation below, which didn't equal zero as Fermi had written. I circled the answer and connected the derivation on the right hand side of the board to the bottom equation on the left, which now equaled each other. I stood back. Harmony now flowed between the equations. I didn't know what they represented, but they were now correct.

The first time I stood in front of this chalkboard and recognized a mistake, I had walked away. If anyone discovered my abilities, I would be consigned to hell in some biological laboratory I dared not contemplate beyond the knowledge of its existence. Later that night, I found a communiqué on my desk from General Groves reporting ninety-eight men had died, including Rear Admiral Daniel Judson Callaghan and Captain Cassin, when the USS San Francisco sank during the battle of Guadalcanal. Groves had handwritten a single sentence on the Teletype page: *This is why we're doing this*. I had rushed back to write my solution, but found Fermi had erased everything. Since then, I didn't chance leaving Fermi's mistakes uncorrected.

I set the chalk back in the tray and brushed my hands on my trousers. As for my personal problem, even if I found a cure for the need to drink blood, I would still never be the same after this war, no one would. Yet, whatever I was, I would still be alive. Many men wouldn't be.

www.scarsdalepublishing.com